D0770805

Other Books in The Vintage Library
of Contemporary World Literature

The Guardian
of the Word

The Guardian
of the Word

Kouma Lafôlô Kouma

Camara
Laye

Translated from the French
by James Kirkup

AVENTURA

The Vintage Library of Contemporary World Literature

VINTAGE BOOKS   A DIVISION OF RANDOM HOUSE   NEW YORK

In testimony of sincere gratitude to Madame Reine Carducci, grand-daughter of the academician René Grousset; to the signatories of her appeal which enabled me to receive treatment for a serious illness at the Necker hospital in Paris, 1975–1976; and to all my doctors and professors in Paris and in Dakar, I once more express my profound indebtedness.

An Aventura Original, March 1984
English translation copyright © 1980 by
William Collins Sons & Co. Ltd.
All rights reserved under International and
Pan-American Copyright Conventions. Published in
the United States by Random House, Inc., New York.
This translation originally published by Fontana Books,
a division of William Collins Sons & Co. Ltd., London, in 1980.
Originally published in French as *Le Maître de la parole*
(Kouma Lafôlô Kouma) by Librairie Plon SA, Paris, in 1978.
First American Edition

Acknowledgments
The author has consulted:
Les Empires du Mali, Etude d'Histoire et de Sociologie Soudanaise
by Charles Monteil (G. P. Maisonneuve et Larose,
11, rue Victor Cousin, Paris 5ème)
A thesis of history defended in Dakar in June 1974 but not
yet published, kept at the Literature Faculty of Dakar

Library of Congress Cataloging in Publication Data
Laye, Camara.
The guardian of the word—Kouma Lafôlô Kouma.
Translation of: Le Maître de la parole.
1. Mandingo (African people)—Folklore. 2. Mali empire—History.
3. Storytellers—Africa, West. 4. Oral tradition—Africa, West.
5. Mandingo (African people)—Social life and customs.
6. Africa, West—Social life and customs.
I. Title. II. Title: Kouma Lafôlô Kouma.
GR350.32.M33C3413 1984   398.2′0966′2   83-40388
ISBN 0-394-72441-0
Manufactured in the United States of America

CONTENTS

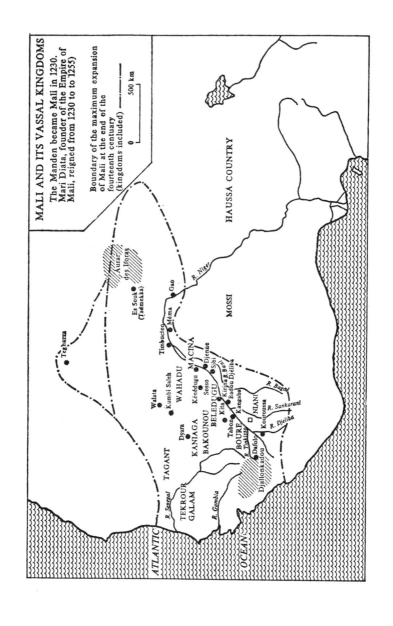

MALI AND ITS VASSAL KINGDOMS

The Manden became Mali in 1230.
Mari Diata, founder of the Empire of
Mali, reigned from 1230 to 1255)

Boundary of the maximum expansion
of Mali at the end of the
fourteenth century
(kingdoms included) ————·—·

0   500 km

ATLANTIC

OCEAN

R. Senegal

TEKROUR
GALAM

R. Gambia

TAGANT

Dyara

KANIAGA

BAKOUNOU

Walata

Kumbi Saleh

WAHADU

Kéndougu

Sosso

MACINA

Djenne

Sibi

BELEDUGU

Kita

Taboni

BOURE

R. Tinkisso

Dafolo

Koutoussa

Diallonkadou

R. Bani

Kirina

Kangaba

Badou Djéliba

NIANI

R. Sankarani

R. Djeliba

R. Bagoé

Timbuctoo

Méma

Méra

Gao

R. Niger

MOSSI

HAUSSA COUNTRY

Es Souk
(Tadmeika)

Aouar
des Iforas

Teghazza

TRANSLATOR'S PREFACE

The Guardian of the Word is a West African *Roots*. However, it is much more authentic and convincing than that overpraised best-seller. Camara Laye really digs deep into his native past in the ancient Empire of Mali, and even further into the almost pre-historic past of his race, using the recorded words of a traditional griot or soothsayer, who is the 'guardian of the word' or con-server of tribal customs, history, legend, poetry and culture. It is largely through the griot's often incantatory words that Camara Laye takes us into the splendid richness of Malinké language and native arts and ceremonials.

The language of the griots is complex and poetic, indeed almost epic in its primitive nobility, exhibiting many of the charac-teristics of primitive story-telling and the folk tale – magic, incantation, repetition, songs and the folk-wisdom of ancient proverbs. The tremendous battle scenes in the latter half of the book could justly be compared with the Achilles and Patroclus episodes in the *Iliad*, and there are some vivid, poetic and often humorous love scenes that recall erotic passages from *The Arabian Nights*.

In addition, we find the religious fervour, the impassioned purity and mystical unity of Islam, married to Animism and the animist practices of the savanna, forest and jungle tribes. The great River Niger, with its many tributaries, provides an ever-moving, ever-present background to this record of a legendary African past in which we also find descriptions of the ordinary daily life of villagers, blacksmiths and hunters.

The second part of the book introduces us to the marvellous boy, the 'Nankama' or Predestined One, born with both legs paralysed but who through magic and faith cures himself of this handicap and eventually becomes Mali's first Emperor. Also, in the person of the cruel, sadistic and evil King of Sosso we may perhaps find resemblances to contemporary African rulers or tyrants like Francisco Macias Nguema, Bokassa and Idi Amin Dada.

Camara Laye has written his book in the hope that it will help

9

both Africans and non-Africans to follow and understand 'the slow and difficult road of African evolution'. I have tried faithfully to reproduce the often hypnotic tone of this elemental yet highly sophisticated story-telling art. However, as the author himself admits, some of the terms, and some of the marvellous poems and chants, are so intensely local as to be almost untranslatable. The beautiful, dignified and poetic Malinké language does not translate well into either French or English, so I have retained the originals of poems and chants: one can easily read them aloud and enjoy them even without understanding the words, but Camara Laye and I have provided literal versions whose inevitable banality cannot, alas, do justice to the magnificent originals.

Camara Laye's first two chapters contain much that is of interest both to the African specialist and to the general reader, who will find in the rest of the book the charm and excitement that distinguish *The African Child* and *The Radiance of the King*: the work can also be regarded as an important development of themes found in *A Dream of Africa* and is certainly a great landmark in the evolution of Camara Laye's writing

When we read *The Guardian of the Word* we realize that the atmosphere of that haunting novel, *The Radiance of the King*, is not based on fantasy, but is an aspect of the real Africa. Camara Laye has always denied that his novel was influenced by Kafka, though it was written at a time in the early fifties when there was a great Kafka boom in the West, particularly in France. *The Radiance of the King* reminds me much more of Dino Buzzati's *Il Deserto dei Tartari*, which incidentally was translated into French in the early fifties, when it won the Prix Renaudot. (A rather unsatisfactory French film was made of the book some years ago, redeemed only by the extraordinary face of Laurent Terzieff: why doesn't someone make a film of *The Radiance of the King*? The obvious choice would be the great Sembene Usman, creator of several very fine African films, the latest of which, *Cedda*, bears many extraordinary points of resemblance to *The Guardian of the Word*.).

It is possible that Camara Laye was influenced by Dino Buzzati's rather Kafka-like tale, but I think it is even more likely that *The Radiance of the King* came simply from the author's vivid personal experience of Africa, as portrayed in *The Guardian of the Word* – though there may also be a childhood memory of Jules Verne's remarkable fantasy, the posthumous novel entitled *La Mission Barsac*. This book is set in Conakry and its hinterland. There is an Esplanade, a strange fortress-like city built in the desert, and a mysterious leader. The name of one of the characters is Camaret! Camara Laye may well have had a special interest in this Jules Verne work because of its associations with Conakry and West Africa. At any rate, when we read *The Guardian of the Word* we realize that so much of Camara Laye's work that seems like fantasy is firmly based on history, legend and solid fact. It is his special genius to be able to combine so convincingly the supernatural and the natural, the life of the spirit and the daily occupations of the people, the instinctive poetry of the native African and the observation and imagination, as well as the scholarship, of a lively Western mind.

Kyoto, Japan
June, 1979   *James Kirkup*

BLACK SOUL

Black soul, African soul,
It is to you I pray this evening, kneeling on my mat;
You whose rich body is fragrant with palm oil,
You whose flexing muscles catch reflections of the radiant sun of
    Africa!
You who as your only garment wear a strip of cotton –
You are beautiful, at ease in your strength and in your dignity;
In the tireless tiller of the soil, carrying his daba, leaning hard on
    his plough, I sing of you.
And you, blacksmith with the rugged hands!
And you, fisherman, back bent with days of craft and patience!
And you, young workers, students, labourers in the fields, the
    future of Africa!
And you, Black Woman, bearing within your breast the spring of
    life!
And you, patriotic politician, emancipator of your people!
All, all of you are my goddess with the hundred faces.
Black soul that the savannahs and the underwoods have permeated
    with a carefree calm,
Black soul sold into slavery, victim of slander and calumny,
Black soul! Mystic black soul!
Awaken, arise, raise yourself up!
Proclaim to the universe the power of your creative genius,
O black soul, African soul!

AFRICA: VOICES FROM
THE DEPTHS

When people live for years in freedom or within some sphere of influence, either in a feudal state or under colonial domination; and when their own lands – even if they become French-speaking, like the country of the colonizer – are nevertheless as different from France in their customs, nature and climate as Africa is from Europe: then it is natural that such people should return to their roots, should investigate their past, and, delving into that past, should enter upon a passionate quest for traces of those beings and those things that have guided their destiny.

First living in freedom, then under colonial oppression, and assimilated almost totally by an alien political system, the peoples of the Upper Niger, despite their subjection, none the less continued, under the influence of their griots, to re-create their past, and to draw sustenance from their traditional civilization.

In fact, that civilization is a very ancient one. Specialists in this field will one day surely inform us, perhaps irrefutably, that there occurred exchanges between the heart of Africa and Carthage, between that heart and ancient Egypt herself – something that has already been demonstrated to have taken place between the peoples of the Upper Niger and animists with a tinge of Islam. Known too with absolute certainty is the fact that this civilization – more rural than urban – experienced, at the time of the Mali Empire, an extraordinary leap forward, and reached its apogee in the fourteenth century. Since then, apart from a few fleeting revivals, it has remained more or less stagnant.

But if the peoples concerned, having each achieved political independence, open themselves up, as indeed they should, to external influences; if they seek each other out and make common ground, we may then witness the awakening of a new civilization, one so vital that within the next few decades the immense territories watered by the Niger will in many ways become unimaginably prosperous.

'The unfortunate thing is that there exists no written infor-

15

mation on how the various kingdoms of West Africa were governed. Mali has no archives; official declarations were made orally. During Mansa Moussa's pilgrimage in 1334, Al Omari's informants told him that the people of Mali almost never wrote down their administrative proceedings. The orders of the king, the proclamations, were transmitted by the human voice, following a centuries-old custom. At this period, the heralds – in this case the griots – formed a veritable governmental ministry. It was they who, working only from memory, were the repositories of customs, traditions and the royal principles of government. Each royal house had its own griot, a specially appointed conservationist of natural traditions. But mainly because of the inroads of the slave traffic, well-structured hierarchies of ancient Africa, in which everyone had his own appointed place, were thrown into confusion.'

From then on, the scale of values changed. Today, we live in a world where the griot has not yet found his appointed place; he finds himself condemned to journey from one capital to another, to make recordings, when formerly he was the representative of the arts of speech and music in the royal households. Because the Black Continent has always been an 'oral' continent, we can well believe that there is a dearth of written documents on the Upper Niger. But the griots, as we shall see further on, are living documents, with the gift of speech.

In these circumstances, how can we fail to be encouraged to lend our support to the task of collecting the traditions of that past, so distant now, and yet still so close to us? For if civilizations, just like men themselves, must also decline and die, should not the present be born of the past, and the future of the present? Should not the wisdom of the Ancients and of their past serve as an example to our rising generations? In a continent where the heat in certain regions reaches 40° in the shade, should our African 'emancipation' consist of the three-piece all-wool suit and the bottle of scotch? Should it not rather have its source in our own deep roots in that distant past, and, at the same time, in the opening-up of our new frontiers to universal values?

In these circumstances, how can one fail to be encouraged to write down the legends of the the peoples concerned, and of the guardians of their traditions, when in fact, through the teaching received in European schools, each African tribal unit is in a position to participate actively in the collection and the diffusion of the Black Continent's true oral tradition, by writing it down in the languages of Europe as well as in the language of the griot?

Therefore it is essential that each generation of our peoples should contribute to the collection and dissemination of these legends, before it is too late; for these legends constitute the very foundations of our history and of our individual traditional civilizations.

If today's Africa is a new continent, because it has only recently seen the birth of national sovereignty; if our continent is to stop playing the part just of an assimilator of civilizations; if this Africa, in order to rehabilitate herself in the eyes of other continents, is to introduce her own more vigorously-rhythmed dance in that universal measure to which each and every civilization lends its own individual steps, it is our oral tradition that can most fittingly release the movements of that dance and the beat of that rhythm.

It is in this tradition that are to be found all the values of the African past, on the three levels of morals, history and socio-politics. Among the Malinké, these values form an ethical unity that comprises native generosity, loyalty, chivalry, respect for a man's word, the practice of Islam, the Cora and the Cola.[1]

---

1 *Cora*: The cora is the African harp with twenty-one to twenty-six strings. It was created in the remote past by the griots of Cabu. Its strains enlivened the entertainments of the nobility in the Empire of Mali. Today, the griots use it to enliven with their rhapsodies the entertainments of anybody who wants it. Thus, through their music, they are enabled, by the re-telling of the lofty deeds of their ancestors, to give to the hearts of hearers the resilient temper of steel.

The Cora repertoire is very rich. The first tune a griot musician learns to play is the song of Kelefa the Warrior, after The Great Kelefa, a most redoubtable Mandingo warrior. There are also the Duga, the Sundiata, the Sumaoro, the Boleoba or 'grand air' played for men of note, and tunes for all the ancient kings of Mali. The Cora is a very harmonious and melodious musical instrument.

Cola: the cola is a fruit tree of the *sterculiaceae* family, native to the West Coast of Africa. Its fruit, called the cola nut, contains stimulant alkaloids. In West Africa the cola nuts play the same role as flowers in Europe.

17

The foundations of our individual traditional civilizations! Yes, but before we go any further, it would be in order first of all to define this concept of civilization. Certain people confuse, perhaps more unconsciously than consciously, mechanization and civilization. And when they are told of the civilizations of Europe and America, and particularly of the achievements of those continents, they only see in those achievements the technical side, the mechanical basis; in other words, the rationalism of Europe or America.

Now civilization is not that. It is something more than machines, and certainly something more than bombs and interplanetary spacecraft. Civilization is more a way of doing things, of living . . . And civilizations existed before the industrial age, before all the technical progress that resulted from it, progress that Africa does not reject – that she impatiently waits to share, rather – but that she considers, and will wisely continue to consider, along with René Grousset and other excellent thinkers, as merely complementary to civilization as such.

For if a man's body has its needs, so does his soul, and after all the soul comes before the body, even though inseparable from it – even though it can be separated from the body only at the moment of death! – even though the body, too, as long as it lives, is not to be disdained. Sometimes one can witness the strangulation of the soul in big cities, its suffocation under the burden of machinery. There, the soul often finds itself so constricted, (oppressed as it is by so much progress of no concern to the soul), that it chooses, in order to escape that oppression, paths and forms that are often very bizarre, more bizarre, certainly, than anything that strikes us as so extraordinary in our old beliefs based on western rationalism. But we know western civilization only very imperfectly, or, as we might express it, only peripherally.

Nevertheless we must make no mistake about that rationalism, (which is infinitely more present in words than in the mind), When we cast our eyes upon France – where I lived a long time, ten years, from 1946 to 1956 – and which I therefore am better, much better acquainted with; when we cast our eyes upon that France, upon what is most authentic in that land, it is not machines we see shining at the summit of her achievements – it

18

is books, it is paintings, it is architecture. And our ears are greeted, not by the roar of machinery, but by the harmonies of the orchestra.

What is most lofty and authentic and profound in France, what makes it a great land inhabited by a great people, is not the extent of her territory nor the density of her population – though they, too, are all part of it – but the noblest and highest ideals that land and that people have given birth to; it is her mind, therefore, the message of her writers, of her researchers, of her professors, of her painters, of her architects, of her musicians, of her moralists; it is her voices calling from the depths hidden in every being. And those voices, and that message, which are the very soul of France, are values far higher, infinitely greater than the values of mere rationalism. It is an actual vibration of the soul, a voice calling insistently from the depths of the soul.

This vibration, this voice of which we have just spoken, is even more insistent, I believe, in the African, for the simple reason that there is no intermediary as yet between him and nature; indeed, it is if not more insistent, certainly more generalized. Moreover, we see at once that the European experiences more vividly the voice from the depths in the presence of a work of some unusual character. We see too that the European is not particularly sensitive to that voice from the depths through a simple contact with beings and things. On this subject we could have a great deal to say, for example, in recalling the attitude of the Romantics to the night; but we shall take that up later. For the moment, let us confine ourselves to stating that the African, for his part, is extremely open to the call of the voice from the depths. He is aware of it in his contact with nature and with beings; he is very sensitive in his responses to a work of art, a mask or a fetish, but not for the same reasons as the European, or not entirely for the same reasons.

The philosopher Karl Jaspers has recently described, most illuminatingly, in a book translated into French, what the European of today feels when confronted with a work of art resonant with this call from the depths, with Van Gogh in particular.

'Van Gogh attracts me,' he writes. 'It seems to me that some secret spring of life is opened to us for a moment, as if the depths hidden in every existence were unveiled right before our eyes.

19

There is in all that a vibration which we cannot long endure, which we soon try to escape from, which appears to relax its intensity for a while in certain masterpieces of Van Gogh, without our being able to submit ourselves to their power, either, for very long; this vibration does not induce us to assimilate this foreign element, but to transmute it into a form more suited to our smaller scale. It is very exciting, it is extremely exciting – but it does not belong to our world.'

Is that also our African stance? Not at all. Confronted with beings and things, we Africans seem to feel that a secret spring of life is opened to us, not for a moment, but constantly, and that (not 'as if') the hidden depths in every existence were unveiled right before our eyes. This is not a vibration which we cannot long endure, which we soon try to escape from, but instead a vibration which we can endure without ever tiring of it, and which we do not seek to escape from – from which, in truth, we are unable to escape.

'This vibration,' Karl Jaspers goes on, 'does not induce us to assimilate this foreign element, but to transmute it into a form more suited to our smaller scale.'

Here again, our reaction is the opposite. We assimilate absolutely this element which we do not consider strange, and we would never dream of transmuting it into a form more suited to our smaller scale.

'It is very exciting,' Karl Jaspers concludes, and we agree with him, 'but it does not belong to our world'; but it most certainly belongs to *our* world.

Is this world peculiar to Africans? Karl Jaspers also tells us that 'the European is obsessed by a desire for unlimited illumination'. But is this absolutely true?

Are we to believe that it is only the African who thinks there are more things in heaven and earth, and in beings, than we can comprehend with our intelligence, than there are things we can explain by the light of reason? Can we believe that the African is the only one who can be on equal terms with the mystery, the only one to beware of belittling it, the only one to recognize it as an irreducible whole, the only one to accept, to demand no more of the mystery than did, after all, the philosophers of ancient Greece? That, we fear, would be putting too cheap a price on man's sense of religion, on his quest for God. No, it does not seem to us that James, or Lautréamont, or Kafka, all very conscious of the divine presence (or that of the Devil), try to escape any more than the African does from this world that is vibrating all the time behind daily reality, this surreal world, this world so much explored, so much unexplored!

And this is where we must ask a very important question: are there works of art totally lacking in the voice from the depths? Perhaps our criticisms are misplaced, perhaps they are too much from an African viewpoint; but it seems to us that the most transparent works, those in which the desire for unlimited illumination is perhaps at its highest point, are also among those most deeply impregnated with the voice calling from the depths. It would take a long time to develop this theme, but, taking a brief example, does one know with all that certainty exactly what the Gioconda is concealing behind her smile? Does one know what sort of a man Hamlet really is? Does one know what is prompting the heart of Bérénice? One sees that this is far from a complete list, these three figures taken from the works of men whose sanity is not in question. Doubtless, in the example of Van Gogh, we are dealing with a man mentally sick . . . But James, Lautréamont, Léonard da Vinci, Bernanos, Kafka – are they mentally sick?

But, perhaps you are wondering, what are you getting at, with all these aesthetic and philosophical considerations?

The answer is Africa, or more precisely the Upper Niger, as it can be seen through oral tradition. The history of this region of the world is set down partly in writing; when we consult the monumental work of Professor Yves Person on Samori, our heart is filled with joy, for we are in complete agreement with him on the subject of the Upper Niger. The history of Samori has been written, and for all time.

The interesting thing about the sayings of Babu Condé is that these sayings are set down in the language of the most competent griot – we were about to say, the most celebrated in Upper Guinea. When all the oral traditions have been collected, when translations have been made of all the manuscripts, some of which are in Europe, others in Africa, when researches have been systematically undertaken, then one day the history of the Black Continent will be written, completely, in all its detailed truth.

'But already, we can state with certainty that in this vast territory more or less stable and relatively centralized states succeeded one another, whose political and social organization, so complex, owes little to the Arab influence, since we find the same political institutions in kingdoms like that of Mossi, which were always protected from exterior influences.

'On the other hand, the Upper Niger had always entertained relations with North Africa. Arab historians and geographers have been able to furnish precise information, either from direct evidence (as in the case of El Békri in the eleventh century, of Ibn Khaldun and Al Omari in the fourteenth century) or from messengers sent by them to these lands, like Ibn Haukal in the tenth century, Ibn Batutah in the fourteenth century and Leon the African, whose true name was Ibn Mohammed el Wazzan es Zayat, at the beginning of the sixteenth century.

'From the sixteenth century onwards, our sources are historica₁ chronicles written in Arabic by learned blacks living along the banks of the Niger, such as Mahmud Kâti, Abdherramane as Sâdi, who was government secretary, a post which required him to travel frequently in the Macina and in the Upper Niger.

'From all these sources we discover aspects of an original civilization. It has often been asked why this civilization did not subsequently enjoy a development similar to that seen in Europe. The reasons for this are the Moroccan invasion and the slave trade which drained Africa of a considerable part of her population . . .'

Our major preoccupation in this study is the version of history made by the griots, and made in the language of the griots, those very griots who truly constitute the soul of ancient Africa. Without them, our traditional values would already be dead; those griots about whom so many foolish things have been written! We hardly know what makes us say such stupid things. Perhaps one can say such things about everybody and anybody, by distorting facts, and with the help of psycho-analysis.

At the present time, when one speaks of griots, one thinks of the instrumentalists, of those music merchants, those choristers or guitarists who wander through the big cities, looking for recording studios. They are certainly griots, but they are music peddlers who willingly deform historical realities; they know only a few scraps of African history, just sufficient for them to carry on their jobs as music peddlers.

The true griots, namely the Bélen-Tigi, or masters or guardians of the word, do not wander round the big cities; they are few, travel very little, remain attached to tradition and to their native soil; one of them is to be found in every province, but those very griots, the authentic ones, are accused of taking forgeries for ready money. And when, concerned with retracing the history of Africa, they people their talk with angels, medicine men, juju priests, guardian spirits – those guardian spirits whom very often they bring to our aid through prayers, sacrifices and incantations; when the griot presents Africa and her mysteries, those mysteries that are real and not at all imaginary – her beliefs, so many things that take a long time to enumerate, yet are still current in Africa, and astonish the European, even though Europe herself also once possessed her own mysteries and beliefs, different from ours;

it then suffices, or should suffice, to recognize this fact in order to accept our own beliefs.

In truth, the griot, one of the important members of that ancient, clearly-defined hierarchical society, is above all – preceding his status as an historian and consequently as the custodian of the historical tradition he teaches – is above all an artist, and, it follows, his chants, his epics and his legends are works of art. Therefore the oral tradition is more of an art than a science. And just as the African sculptor works, the griot does not represent historical reality in a matter-of-fact way; he recounts it using archaic formulas; so the facts are transposed into entertaining legends for the ordinary man, but they have a secret meaning for those who can read between the lines. Because 'for the African all true science is a secret'. It is not ideal beauty that interests the griot, but rather the expressive beauty of his chant of his legend or of his tale. Sometimes even, he transforms them so much that historical truth becomes submerged in the song or the legend. But what we actually hear is an abstraction that does not go to the extreme of covering up history's original traces, an unsystematic abstraction that remains rather exceptional in the sculpture, the painting, the song and the legends of Africans, and that appears rather as the result of an expressionism taken to its limits, uncertain as it is of those limits.

The griot never shows any calculation in his presentations of reality; he lets his heart speak in a natural way, and thus, his transformation leads him into an exaggeration of the facts – or a deformation of the truth – which first of all underlines and accentuates the expression, the spirituality, and then, as a natural sequence, calls up other exaggerations (or deformations of the truth) intended to balance the first and to complete it. He creates thus a system of discourses which entertain the layman (for he is a master of the art of periphrasis) and which instruct the initiated, eager to learn their history. There are always, in the tale, in the chant, in the legend, two truths: a first truth, consciously created and peripheral, intended to amuse the audience; but on the reverse side of the first truth there is a second truth, profound, close to the truth, to reality, but in a different way that the layman finds difficult to detect: that is the historical truth.

We think it is not without interest to linger a while over these

25

exaggerations and deformations. It must straight away be said that they are not a game, that they are not gratuitous, that they answer a need to complete a given spiritual expression.

But perhaps you will object that if they are not gratuitous, if they are not a game, how is it possible to imagine that they can be organized with such mastery in all our African legends? Here we touch upon one of the fundamental aspects of the African soul: the word, the love of palaver and dialogue, the rhythm of talk, that love of speech that can keep the old men a whole month under the palaver tree settling some dispute – that is what really characterizes the African peoples.

We raise the veil slightly on this aspect of the African soul, but we raise it only slightly, for the subject in its entirety would require so many words . . .

Finally, there is something easily forgotten: that the griot's words – we mean the words pronounced by the traditional griot – are words which it is not necessary to be an African to pronounce. It is not a question of continent; they can often be heard pronounced in Europe; in truth, one is always hearing them – in a very attenuated fashion, it is true, but one hears them all the same – despite the advances of technology. For the truth is that whoever speaks of civilization speaks also of its component parts; beings and things, consequently mystery, that mystery which, without the soul, could not exist within us.

Yes, in short, the traditional griot finally comes to that – the ineffable; to that patient and everlasting quest in which all beings – white, yellow, black, red – belong to the ineffable; to that quest which makes us look at all peoples, in their close union with heaven and earth – planet turning dizzily with us, turning on itself, turning round the sun – far beyond the screens of the industrial age, and which binds us, wherever we may be, to the same fate, the same destiny; to what is destiny itself, our mysterious destiny – that of every man, which is to be a voyager upon this earth.

BABU CONDÉ: "BÉLEN-TIGI", OR TRADITIONAL GRIOT

Babu Condé, author of the legend that follows – we are but the modest transcriber and translator – was to traditional African society what the primitive cathedral sculptors and painters were to the European Middle Ages: the idea that he should sign his work – for he is a fine Arabic scholar – never entered his head. He was a man who considered himself a simple story-teller, not an artist, a man who had no desire to serve his own ends, but only the needs of society – to serve the word and the world beyond the word. He was, finally, a man whom no one would have dared to interrupt, once he had begun to give tongue under the palaver tree, unless he wanted to draw down upon his head trials and tribulations induced by Babu's maleficent occult forces! Because for Babu himself, as for all the Malinké, the word of Bélen-Tigi signified only one thing: magic. He often liked to remind his listeners that to talk without saying anything was the mark of three categories of people: the baby learning to walk, a jealous woman, and a madman! But to talk without saying anything is not the mark of a man who wears breeches

Thus it was that, during grand ceremonies, his word would make the thatched roof of a hut shift all on its own! Through the magical power of his word, the gendarme birds perched on the summit of the palaver tree would stop singing. Those that persisted in going on singing would drop dead, as if struck by lightning, at Babu's thrice-repeated invocation! Thereupon, every bird would fall silent; and no one would dare say a thing in the audience; no one dared speak; no one dared do such a thing. Only the Bélen-Tigi, bearing his long baton, went on speaking as he walked up and down. From time to time, he would fix his gaze upon the summit of the palaver tree. What could he see there? We do not know. We do not know exactly. That apparently abstracted gaze did not tell us anything. But upon what or whom was it fixed, if not upon the guardian spirits of the word? Were

27

not they the ones he gazed upon at such times? Was it not their succour and friendship he called upon? Yes, it must surely have been those guardian spirits, who caused him to prophesy, to look into the year ahead, and beyond that into the future.

How old was he on the fifteenth of March 1963, when we paid him a visit? Eighty, ninety years old? We do not really know. He stood tall and frail, his body weakened at the hip by the hernia that afflicts all the old Malinké men. The deep-channelled wrinkles that ravaged his emaciated, bony visage showed that he was old, very old. But we knew – as all the Malinké know! – his reputation as a story-teller. We knew that to him had fallen the honour of giving tongue to the word at the great funeral ceremonies, that it was he who handled disputes at law, for he was the sole repository of oaths; and he would recount the oaths made by the ancients at the time for the division of the earth by Sundiata Kéta[1]. We knew well that his wisdom and knowledge reached to the very boundaries of Malinké existence; to the vast plain of the Malinké people, to its savanna, the most beautiful of all savannas, a savanna park; extended to its great river, to all that inhabits that plain's level distances, the all-powerful Djéliba River and the very sky itself; his wisdom extended to its animals and trees and plants, as his knowledge did to all its men, and to the ancestors as well; to the heavens, and to God also!

We knew he was the Bélen-Tigi, by which we meant he was the scholarly custodian of the history of all the districts of Kouroussa, regions peopled by nearly one hundred thousand souls. Lastly, we knew he was the learned authority on the Africa of yesterday, and of its precisely-structured societies governed by patrilinear laws, and it goes without saying that he inherited his knowledge from his father, to whom it had been passed down by his own father. The forefather of Babu Condé, Frémori Condé, was the griot of Imuraba Kéta, son of Manden-Bory,

1 It was at Ka-ba (Mali, in the clearing of Kuruké Fuga) that Sundiata the Mansa, the Emperor, in the presence of all Malinké peoples, proceeded to the partition of the world. It was in 1230; one by one the conquering kings of Sumaoro received their kingdoms from the hands of Sundiata himself.

founder of the Hamana, Kouroussa (Guinea). Manden-Bory was the brother of Sundiata Kéta. He came from the Manden with his griot. It was from that remote date that the male children of the tribe of the Condé of Fadama had practised, from their earliest boyhood, the art of speech. In order to develop their memories, there were prepared for them sauces containing 'bull's intelligence'[1], which they consumed mixed with a holy water from the Koran.[2] From that time forward it was agreed that the oldest male of the tribe of the Condé of Fadama would become the Bélen-Tigi or Guardian of the Word. So, at the age of eighty or ninety years, Babu Condé had become 'the bag of words'.

Before leaving our village, Kouroussa, on the fifteenth of March 1963, for Fadama, the traditionalist griot's village, situated some fifty kilometres further east, we asked one of our Kouroussa notables what precautions we must take to facilitate our interview with such an ancient, for the collection of oral traditions demands an intimate knowledge of the milieu and the rules of that particular milieu. We had already suffered some discomfiture at Accra (Ghana), and at Ouidah (Dahomey), in 1958, simply because, in making our researches, we had not taken the proper etiquette into account, or because we appeared incorrectly garbed according to current local custom.

This local dignitary advised us to wear on this occasion the Guinean tunic or caftan[3] in order not to look like a government official, which could have unpleasant consequences for us, for then the griot would say little, or nothing at all. He also recommended us to offer our Fadama host ten white colas, the small change of Guinean courtesy, and a sheep, or the price of a sheep.

1 Bull's intelligence: Babu Condé called 'bull's intelligence' a nerve next to the oesophagus. It was extracted after the bull had been slaughtered.

2 The marabout inscribes the appropriate verse of the Koran on tablets that are then washed. The water collected in this way is used to cook the 'bull's intelligence', which is served with couscous to budding orators in order to develop their memories.

3 Caftan: a long over-garment, stitched down both sides, worn by Africans of Guinea, Senegal, Mali, Gambia, Guinea-Bissau and Mauretania.

This advice had a favourable result: we were received and the next day the griot agreed to be interviewed and recorded on tape, something more convenient, naturally, than a notebook.

Thus, during the first three days of a stay which lasted from the sixteenth of March to the sixteenth of April, we learned that the Malinké of the Hamana have four categories of Words. But we shall return to this later.

For the present, we shall confine ourselves to listing them:
- KUMA LAFOLO KUMA, the history of the great Sundiata, the son of the buffalo-panther woman and of the lion, the first Emperor of Mali, or the History of the First Word;
- KUMA KORO, the history of the men before our era, or Ancient Word;
- KUMA KOROTOLA, or Ageing Word, the genealogy of the various tribes of the Upper Niger;
- KUMA or Word, the history of the Almamy Samari Touré (1830–1900), and of the men of our time.

As can be seen, the matter of our research is vast, but the zone of our investigations seems of small extent. As we have stated above, it concerns four categories of Words, therefore, the Upper Niger viewed through oral tradition, and consequently through the griot who, although speaking on oath and deeply conscious of the need not to travesty the truth, is above all an artist who, like all artists, has to give utterance to the voice of his heart.

The Upper Niger as it is described to us by Babu Condé is a cluster of kingdoms inhabited by various Malinké tribes. According to his account, in this Upper Niger region there had at one time been the kingdom of Tabon, situated between Siguiri (Guinea) and Bamako (Mali); it was brought into being under the sun of the Prophet Mahomet[1], that is to say, around the seventh century. Its first king is said to have come from Arabia, like Bilali Ibunrama, the forefather of Sundiata. He was called Abdul Wakas. At first he had stayed for some time in Egypt, then had gradually come down the valley to install himself finally at Tabon. There, because he was versed in Arabic, the Tabonka made him their king. He proceeded to unify that vast territory torn by internal feuds. Later he married the daughter

1 The sun of the Prophet means the period of the Prophet Mahomet.

30

of the Camara 'Dalikimbon'. His cousin, who had followed him a few years later, had been proclaimed king of Sibi. This cousin married into the family of the Camara 'Sininkimbon', that is to say the Camara who were not blacksmiths; it was the Dalikimbon who were the blacksmiths.

The last great king of Tabon was called Waman Camara or Fran Camara surnamed Tabon Wana by the Malinké, which means 'the formidable man of Tabon'.[1] He was the contemparary of Sundiata. Tabon meant 'house of fire' or 'house of the master blacksmiths', or, by extension, 'land of the men who have tamed the fire'.

Babu Condé talked to us about four categories of Words, but here we shall translate only the first: perhaps this legend, studied on its own, will allow us to lift the veil on certain aspects – no, that would be going too far! – on a few elements that are new in the study of the Malinké world and the Upper Niger, that world of the Malinké which has recently been studied by that eminent and Malinké Africanist Professor Yves Person.

Perhaps also it may persuade African peoples to sit at the feet of the Ancients, to draw the wisdom, the knowledge, the history of the Black Continent from its most authentic source, namely, the traditionalist griot. For it is easy to illuminate, as with a searchlight, trained on a half-dark stage, the stagnant obscurities of Africa's socio-political spheres. Or rather, no, that is not so! Actually, the stage on which Africa's stagnant socio-political obscurities are being played is not in semi-darkness at all: it is illumined by broad daylight; that is why we shut our eyes to it and see so little!

This stagnation is caused by the disruption of ancient hierarchies, by our lack of roots in what was most admirable in our ancient traditional social structures. We repeat that generosity, loyalty, respect for a man's word, chivalry, the practice of Islam, the cola, the cora – these were the foundations of Malinké socio-political life. Our stagnation is caused also by our lack of openness towards universal values.

1 Tabon was a kingdom situated between Siguiri (Guinea) and Bamako (Mali). But this kingdom exercised authority over the mountains of the country, which are known today as the Futa-Djalon.

That is why the Black Continent is groping in the dark. It is a continent in quest of a vanishing spirituality, a continent pursued by a too-immediate reality, a continent in search of itself.

In fact, the Bélen-Tigi or Guardian of the Word was a man who had a place of honour in traditional society; he had the sacred mission of guiding the people; he guided them perfectly; we mean that his emotions and their expression were greater than the emotions and their expression of his people; thus it was that he obtained the effect desired. Because if art has to have some influence on life it must be more powerful than daily existence. It is the law of ballistics: when shooting, one must aim above the target, if that target is moving.

Today, are our political leaders really great? Apart from one or two, it is really doubtful whether they are; they turn politics into a bloody massacre. They starve our peoples, exile our tribes, sow death and destruction! Theirs is not a politics for the advancement of the African peoples, but for their regression. They do not serve Africa: they make Africa serve themselves. They are far from being builders, organizers, city administrators, but are rather gaolers who deal with the men, women and children of our peoples as if they were cattle. They are peripheral apparitions over Africa; they are agents of evil who will not quench our peoples' thirst for life and progress; they are the ones who cause non-Africans to laugh at the immaturity of Africa, without doing anything to resolve the fundamental problems of the Black Continent.

Only a few leaders achieve that, in their wisdom, their talent, the fruitful dialogues which they establish with other nations, and through the tolerance they exercise within their own countries. These few African chiefs sweep away prejudices that hurt Africa and cast a clear light upon its secret visage, its secret language, both of which are gradually disappearing into oblivion, by their re-affirmation of the personality, the dignity of the African in the tumult of the present time.

In our eager desire to learn to know Africa better, we have travelled – for almost twenty years, 1958 to 1976 – in the following countries: Guinea, Ghana, Benin, Togo, Nigeria, Liberia, Sierra Leone, Ivory Coast, Senegal, Gambia, Guinea-Bissau,

Mauretania, Mali.

After this introduction, we think it is now the moment to give ear to the word of Babu Condé, the griot Bélen-Tigi or Guardian of the Word of the Hamana, Kouroussa (Guinea). We should require more than one lifetime to translate everything Babu Condé spoke on that occasion! – from the sixteenth of March to the sixteenth of April 1963 . . .

The Bélen-Tigi is speaking here of the Manden, of its kings and of its history; he tells especially of Sundiata, son of the buffalo-panther woman, who became the first Emperor of Mali, and is considered by him to be the greatest of the Malinké. But in fact, Kuma-Lafolo-Kuma is the first story a traditionalist griot tells Malinké who have just become adults; and it encompasses the entire period between Sundiata and the Almami Samori, that is, the period from 1230 to 1830. But the legend we translate here tells of the birth, the difficult childhood and the life of Sundiata. This first working seance with the traditionalist griot has as its theme:

MOKÉ MUSSA AND MOKÉ
DANTUMAN

There were once two hunters, the elder called Moké Mussa, the younger Moké Dantuman[1]. A sudden anger seized them. 'What!' they cried. 'A buffalo can prevent a whole people from living in peace and eating their fill? . . . We'll go and see to this buffalo.'

Again a sudden wave of anger seized them. But it was now an anger directed at the Buffalo of Dô. Why, just now, had they turned it upon the hunters, upon all the hunters unable to bring to its knees the buffalo of Dô? Actually, these two hunters were not lacking magical powers; they were real Simbon masters[2]. They were nothing much to look at, these two young men, with their *sèrèbu*[3] all torn and ragged, they certainly were nothing much to look at! But by dint of roaming the world, visiting all their country's wise men, they must have known a good deal more about the hunting art than all other huntsmen.

So they set off on their mission; the two sons of Damissa Ulambana set off for Dafolo[4]. All through the dry season they

1 Moké: even today, the Malinké like to put their mother's name in front of their own name. This was the custom in the Middle Ages. Thus, the two hunters, Mussa and Dantuman, were known as Moké Mussa and Moké Dantuman, as Moké was their mother's name.
2 Simbon is the hunter's whistle. Simbon is also the title given to a master of the hunting art.
3 Sèrèbu is the hunter's garb. The trousers are as narrow as jodhpurs. The overgarment, wide and long, and the trousers are of a reddish brown, a colour on which their game is not likely to leave clear traces of blood. It is a garment whose colour allows the hunter to camouflage himself more easily. It is generally of cotton, and so of local manufacture. The hunters dye it with tree bark, then they dip it – just as they do the garment of those about to be circumcised – in the waters of a bush pond, where it lies several weeks, until the desired colour is obtained.
4 Dafolo was the capital of the kingdom of Dô. The ruins of Dafolo can be found some hundred kilometres from Farana (Guinea). The kingdom of Dô comprised present-day Sankaran (Kouroussa) and Sankaran on the Farana (Guinea) side. Dô was the native land of Sogolon Condé, mother of Sundiata.

journeyed, or rather the end of the dry season, for the various ever-changing occupations of that season – fishing, harvesting of scanty crops, hunting, and playing the war drums – had considerably reduced its length. Moké Mussa and Moké Dantuman strode on valiantly. The sun burnt down fiercely upon them, and profound silences, silent as the silences of the Kri savanna[1], would suddenly alternate with the hurly-burly of hamlets, bringing a peaceful, an infinitely peaceful atmosphere. The path they were following went twisting among all kinds of plantations. Sometimes, the roaring of a bull, the bleating of a sheep, disturbed by the passage of the two hunters, would warn them that they were approaching primitive, robust palisades guarding enclosures, made of wooden stakes cut in the nearby forest.

According to Babu Condé, the buffalo was the ancestral totem, the 'tana' of the sister of Dô-Samô, king of Dô[2]. The name of this sister of the king was Dô-Kamissa, so Babu told us. The animal had been named 'Dô-Sigi' which means 'the buffalo of Dô'. It had carried out too many depredations as it ravaged the land of Dô to merit such an honourable name!

When his father died, Dô-Samô proceeded to make a division of the old king's possessions. But consciously or unconsciously, and perhaps more consciously than unconsciously, he deprived his sister Dô-Kamissa of that part of the inheritance that was due to her by custom. And why exactly this woman? He had deprived her of her part of the possessions of her dead father simply because she was a woman! At least, that was the reason generally given.

But in medieval Dô, what was the actual position of women? What was a woman in those far-off days if not an object whose duty it was to bring children into the world, and to bring them up; and who did not enjoy the same rights as a man in the distribution of an inheritance? We have no clear explanation of her position, especially since the Malinké of Sangaran have regained their autonomy and rehabilitated woman, raising her up to the same level as man.

1 Kri was a province whose ruins are found now in Mali.
2 Dô-Samô: the king was called Samô Condé. But the princes of the Middle Ages liked to follow their names with those of their kingdoms. So we have Dô-Samô, Dô-Kamissa, etc.

Feeling herself badly treated, Dô-Kamissa shook the dust of Dafolo, capital of Dô, from her feet. She left the place for good, founded her own village some kilometres away, and settled down there. But Dô-Kamissa, who had shaken the dust of the kingdom's capital from her feet, was the sister of the new king Dô-Samô; she was a true princess of the blood, but a woman just like any other, and like any other woman felt overpowered by a sense of frustration. She was in a state of absolute perplexity, and she decided to take her revenge. She told no one about her decision. Although she was a woman, although they had deprived her of her rightful share of material things, she had nevertheless inherited magical powers, the extraordinary supernatural powers of her ancestors. Consequently, she had the ability to transform herself into the buffalo, her ancestral totem!

As soon as she had settled in her own village, she turned herself into a buffalo and began devastating the rice-fields. Her lust for vengeance was so strong that again and again she kept returning to the form of her ancestral totem, scouring the twelve villages of Dô, every day killing one of their inhabitants, and ravaging their fields. The ravening beast would tear to pieces with its sharp horns any hunter who dared approach it. It goes without saying that the death of one inhabitant every day and the buffalo's continual destruction of planted fields and harvests had the effect, the immediate consequence, immediately felt, of a lack of food in the region, arousing the discontent and the anger of the inhabitants of the twelve villages forming the kingdom of Dô.

It was in order to avenge the people of Dô, by killing the buffalo that all other hunters had shown themselves incapable of killing, that the two hunters had set out. But when undertaking any journey of great extent, the Malinké, and hunters in particular, always consulted a wise man or soothsayer. For their part, Moké Mussa and Moké Dantuman had consulted a friend of their father's, the most accomplished soothsayer in Kri. This wise man assured them of complete success in their victory over the buffalo, but on certain conditions:

1. Once they had set out, on the road to Dafolo, they must pay no heed to any calls people might make to them.

2. They should do everything they could to win the good graces of a little old woman they would meet by the river outside

Dafolo: the key to the mystery of the buffalo was in her hands!

3. They must give their word that they would choose as a wife, after their victory over the buffalo, the ugliest of the innumerable girls in the twelve villages of Dô when they were introduced to them by the king of Dô-Samô.

Armed with these precious instructions, the two hunters set out for the land of Dô. Already they had been walking for more than a week. They had been striding along very quickly, as quickly as if the sun were not at its fiercest – in the dry season it is always at its fiercest! – and then, when they had reached the last village before Dafolo, they had unwillingly relaxed their pace, because of the weariness that now overcame them; their foreheads were abundantly bathed in sweat, sweat had soaked their *sèrèbu*, sweat poured down their backs. So then they made a halt: they decided to spend the night in that village. There, before cock-crow, they heard a voice calling to them, a voice which seemed to come from the sky and reached them only faintly, muted as it was by the chatterings of insects and the weeping voices of night birds: 'Moké Mussa, Moké Dantuman, you have laid yourselves down to rest, but you shall not sleep today!'

However, the two young men, obviously remembering the advice of their soothsayer in Kri, did not open the door of their hut; obedient to his recommendations, they made no reply, and lay as if dead. But the voice, piercing the darkness, went on until dawn.

When the cocks had finished crowing for the second time, the young men got up. They hadn't slept a wink all night. At that early hour, there was almost no one in the lanes of the village. In a few enclosures there were women preparing breakfast for the labourers in the fields; and from time to time a man would be seen carrying his *daba*[1] over his shoulder, or his axe. The sun was now risen on a magnificent, harmonious countryside, and on fields far richer than those in Kri. There were fields on either side of the path they were following: but the fields had a neglected look, as if they had been laid waste – fields of rice and fonio, fields of ground-nuts and maize. Then beyond the fields there was a vast orchard – an orchard of orange trees and other luscious fruits, all this indicating that they were approaching Dafolo.

1 Malinké word for hoe.

and a refreshment for the eyes in the early morning sunlight. Far away on the horizon there were two mountains: Konkon Sada and Konkon Gnaulen. A little to the left of these mountains there was a long, dense trail of shrubs, the kind of greenery that surrounds streams.

They hastened their steps; the sun had not yet risen high above their heads, but it was hot; it was hot already. They valiantly climbed those two mountains; they climbed them even before the sun had reached its zenith. They had not been mistaken; when they reached the shrubs they found water, and there was a big tree called a *sandan*[1] at the edge of the stream. Under this giant tree, and in the river, there was already a great crowd, and beyond these shrubs and this river could be seen the first huts of Dafolo – a crowd joyously chattering, composed of women who were washing their clothes by beating them on the black rocks of the river, while others were drawing water in calabashes which they placed on their heads and carried away towards the town. There were no men. They had already left for the fields. A little further down the stream there were girls cackling and jabbering and having great sport splashing each other with water.

Moké Mussa and Moké Dantuman were about to take off their *sèrèbu* or hunting clothes in order to have a bath when suddenly something stopped them. At first it was a kind of hesitation, then a change of mind. No, they could not possibly show themselves naked in front of all these women. They crouched on the bank and made do with drinking the water from the palms of their hands. When they had quenched their thirst, and stood up, their eyes were inevitably drawn to the river shallows, to that joyous throng of women, and feasted their gaze upon them. A little upstream, at some distance from these women, they caught sight of a little old woman who resembled strangely the one the soothsayer at Kri had told them about. With a small white loincloth tied round her hips, resembling curiously the under-loincloth of married women[2], she was standing in the stream, up to

1 The *sandan* is a tree that grows in the savanna, often tall as a tropical citron. *Sandan* is a Malinké word.
2 The under-loincloth is a small loincloth that women tie under the loincloth. Malinké women call it a *pendéli*. They use it to wipe the husband after sexual relations.

her knees in the water, washing her clothes without paying attention to anyone. Her limp breasts, dried-up, dangled. She looked wretched, and indeed she was very wretched.

The two hunters, doubtless remembering their soothsayer's advice, went towards her and greeted her:

'Good morning, Mother[1], do you want any help? That is hard work you're doing!'

But Dô-Kamissa did not appear to have heard. She had by now arranged all her freshly-rinsed clothes in a basin and was looking at it intently. The basin had lost most of its enamel, for it, too, was no longer in its first youth. It had grown black, and one could see only the metal, which was black, as black as the soap in her hand. Then the old woman moved: she took the basin in her skinny fingers, then, dragging it behind her, she came out of the water and began to wring the clothes she had freshly rinsed. Thus, even if she had heard what was said, she had also refrained from answering.

'What are you doing, Mother?' Moké Dantuman, the younger of the two huntsmen asked.

'Can't you see? I'm washing my clothes!' Dô-Kamissa replied.

Big drops of water were falling from an indigo loincloth, in rags, which she was wringing in her hands. When she had finished, she carefully arranged all her clothes in the old basin, which she then hoisted with a burst of energy. This unexpected way of lifting an apparently heavy basin – it was full of wet clothes – gave an impression of great vigour, but obviously it could only be an impression, and certainly a false impression, because everything about the person of Dô-Kamissa gave the inverse impression of extreme old age; nevertheless the first impression persisted along with the second. Then she appeared to be making her way towards the *Massidi Sandan Koro*, not far from the river, as if the cool of its shade had attracted her. As soon as she set foot under the tree, the girls there ran away, leaving the entire place to her. She sat on a stone and began to gaze intently at the water. Whole clumps of grass were passing by, swept along by the current; others remained caught up at the river's edge. They displayed their tiny roots, like tubers calcified by bush fires.

1 Mother: any woman of the same age as your mother is addressed thus.

Then Moké Dantuman realized that Dô-Kamissa's hair was white, her skin wrinkled and horny like a lizard's; but she had arms with muscles bigger than a man's. The impression of vigour came from the way in which the limbs were developed.

Meanwhile, the two huntsmen were still standing on the sandy river bank. They had watched Dô-Kamissa with stupefaction; she had walked towards the *Massidi Sandan Koro*; she was bent by age and hard work. Now that she was walking, one could see how ridiculously short was the kind of loincloth that was her only clothing: a kind of loincloth, yes, for one could not honestly call that rag a piece of clothing; and perhaps it was even going too far to call it a loincloth; it was . . . No, no! They were not going to evoke that wretchedness a second time: just to think of it made their hearts heavy . . .

'We shall share our tasks,' Moké Mussa told his younger brother Moké Dantuman. 'I shall go before you into Dafolo, to announce our arrival to the king, and you will take care of the old woman. But be careful: remember that one never digs a rat's hole with a pestle, for if one does, one runs the risk of blocking the hole completely and never reaching the rat[1]. A rat's hole? That is always dug with a hoe!'

'I know that when the egg falls on the stone, or on the rock, it is the egg that breaks; when the rock falls on the egg, then it is even worse!' said Moké Dantuman[2].

'When your hand is in a mouth full of teeth, you must tickle the person; when he laughs, you can withdraw your hand intact. You should never give him a punch in the jaw at such a moment, for then the mouth will close brutally and the teeth will bite off your hand as if they were sharp chisels,' Moké Mussa ended[3].

The two brothers parted thus, with an exchange of proverbs. All wisdom is contained in proverbs; when young hunters parry proverbs to perfection, it is a sign that they have learnt much from the lessons of their Master Simbon.

1 If you abuse the kindness of a generous person, you run the risk of his refusing you everything.
2 When a young person has unpleasant dealings with an old one, it is always the young one who is wrong.
3 When your life depends entirely on one person, you must be very adaptable and careful, in order not to discourage him.

When Moké Dantuman caught up with the old woman under the *Massidi Sandan Koro*, she was no longer watching the water; Dô-Kamissa was still sitting on the stone; her head in her hands, she was weeping heart-brokenly, bent right over as if trying to hide her face. She was day-dreaming of past years. How many years had she spent in Dafolo, when her father was king, when her father was still alive – years without care, the years of her youth? Since then . . . Ah! those years – where were they now? 'To be a young girl! To be a princess and a young girl of twenty summers!' she said to herself. And she sobbed softly, and was suddenly the young girl, the young princess weeping before the old, disinherited woman she had become. She started to burn as feverishly as a body struggling with a bout of malaria, for the woman she had become no longer existed: that creature was nothing but a little old woman, disinherited, forgotten, racked with hunger. Perhaps she was also mourning her approaching death? Perhaps – because she was a witch, and a witch has the power to take possession of the thoughts of others. She had an even more astonishing gift, really supernatural, the power to read the future . . .

She had bent her head in order to concentrate better. When she raised it, she saw Moké Dantuman bent over her, holding her tenderly by the shoulders. The next moment, she took her hands from her head, and sat up straight, her eyes bathed in tears. He dried them for her, and said . . . what was he saying? Everything and nothing, but it did not matter at all. Dô-Kamissa could understand nothing of what he was saying; the mere sound of a human voice, of a voice that for the first time was speaking tenderly to her, was all she heard, and it was enough; her sobs gradually died away, grew rarer . . . she became calm. The torment that had been dammed up in her for so many years had at last been released. The fever had fallen.

Moké Dantuman took a joint of dried meat out of his *sassa* or game-bag and offered it to her. Dô-Kamissa hesitated for a while. The joint was tasty, but probably she was thinking otherwise. She looked at it, then consulted herself; and again she looked at it then looked into herself a while: she was hungry. It was a real tussle with her conscience. Something to do with the virtue of a disinherited princess in a confrontation with honour; the honour

42

of eating well and eating her fill, of course. She wavered no longer: the meat was held out towards her, she took it and ate it. She even ate it with relish. She had forgotten she was so hungry. Now she could feel her whole body yielding itself to the meat as a distracted fish yields to the open jaws of a crocodile, a famished crocodile. She ate the meat down to the bone, and even licked the bone.

She dropped the bone on the ground; she could lick no more off it and she leaned back against the support of the giant tree. Moké Dantuman sat down beside her.

'I have eaten,' she said. 'I have not eaten so well for many moons! I thank God, and I thank you, young hunter; you are a generous young man. I wonder if you have come here to try your chance with the buffalo? I can tell you that many bold hunters have tried before you, and they all met their deaths in doing so.'

She smiled, uncovering gums in which there were still a few teeth here and there; her smile suddenly stretched from ear to ear, becoming a mocking smile, but not without kindness. It was as if her three or four teeth were tearing the bursts of laughter as they issued from her throat. Her little slanting eyes were sparkling; perhaps they were sparkling more vivaciously than they had done for many moons.

'Why are her eyes sparkling like that?' wondered Moké Dantuman. There was no reason for them to sparkle like that. Or was it really because she had eaten so well? 'People eat well, and even too well, during the feasts of circumcision, after Ramadan, the tabaski festival, or when they have the good fortune to meet someone generous . . . '

But this explanation did not really satisfy him. What Moké Dantuman saw in her eyes was not the little gleam of someone with a full stomach, nor yet the little flame that dances in the eyes of the old. It was like flashes . . . It took him a long time to find the words . . . 'lightning flashes!' he suddenly told himself. But the word was too strong. In Dô-Kamissa's gaze he could detect a disturbing expectancy, an expectancy mingled with hope and impatience; yes, she was impatient to see her ward, Sogolon Condé, for whom she had cared for such a long time, all the time, married to a man of substance before the old woman's imminent demise.

'But I . . . I'm just a hunter . . .' said Moké Dantuman.

He rubbed his head in embarrassment, rubbed it dreamily. He threw a pebble into the bush to see if there was any game. And he began to wonder what would be the outcome of all the kind attentions he had given the old woman. Nothing at all, probably.

'What has that got to do with it?' she countered. 'If you are that hunter – and who would you be if you were not he? – do not deny it, do not try to deny it. You can trust me; your generosity has won me over to your side.'

'Oh!' said Moké Dantuman.

'Yes, it has won me over,' she repeated. 'For years I have been taking revenge upon my brother Dô-Samô, who had deprived me of my fair share of the inheritance after the death of our father. Now, I have had my fill; and besides, the day is drawing nearer – the day of my death!'

'The king conducted himself in a very improper way with his sister,' Moké Dantuman agreed.

'The king! I detest him!' she cried. 'He's a man without a heart. How could a man like that be happy?' she went on. 'But you shall be the conqueror of the buffalo of Dô; I shall grant you that honour, for I am that buffalo! Yes, the buffalo with the tail of gold and the horns of silver.'

'Surely a man like that could not be happy,' he repeated, sententiously. 'So you are the buffalo of Dô?'

'Yes, I am the buffalo of Dô . . .' she said. 'But a man who makes a woman suffer, a man who underestimates the power of a woman, is an errant fool. So to punish that proud king I have killed one hundred and seven hunters, the most celebrated hunters in the land; I have wounded seventy-seven; I killed one person every day in each of the twelve provinces of Dô, year after year! I laid waste the harvests of the king . . .'

Once more she eyed him from head to foot; she was weighing him up, in a more friendly manner than before, as if measuring the effect her words were having on his mind. And surely her words must have had a great effect, because Moké Dantuman, overcome and disconcerted, lowered his head; and she went on:

'King Dô-Samô has offered the hand of the most beautiful girl in the twelve provinces of Dô. When he has brought them all

44

together in Dafolo, and when you are asked to choose your
future wife from among them, you shall turn your attention to
the crowd of women watching – for you will not find her in the
ranks of beautiful young women – and you shall see her seated
on a mirador[1], sitting there as a spectator, at the side of the
festival square. Oh! you shall have no difficulty in recognizing
her, for she is an ugly girl, much more ugly than any of the girls
you have ever encountered so far, more ugly than you could ever
imagine. But you must choose her. This is the price you must pay
to be conqueror of the buffalo of Dô; only on these conditions
shall I submit to you. The girl is called *Sogolon Kedyon*, Sogolon
the Ugly, and *Sogolon Kuduma*, Sogolon the Hunchback. If you
succeed in possessing her, she will be an extraordinary wife; she
is my double; she will have an even more extraordinary son. But
you must swear that she is the one you shall choose.'

Moké Dantuman swore solemnly on Sani and Kontron[2] held in
the hands of the old woman to take Sogolon Condé as his bride,
after his victory over the buffalo.

Then, out of a basket which she must have placed under the
Massidi Sandan Koro before she entered the river, she took the
symbols of her magic: a distaff, a flat stone[3], an egg. Over these
three symbols she whispered, in conformity with tradition, the
formula of malediction, recited in the manner of the ancients.
Thus the buffalo lost the power that had been formerly granted
him, using the same symbols, and reciting the formula of bene-
diction.

'Here, young hunter!' she said suddenly, 'take this distaff,
this flat stone, this egg. On the plain of Urantamba, I am browsing
on king Dô-Samô's harvests. When you get there, before using
your weapons, first aim at me three times with the distaff; my
body will tremble and I shall rush towards you. You shall cast
the distaff behind you, and when I am about to catch you, throw

1 A platform or balcony.
2 Sani and Kontron are the twin divinities of hunters. They are inseparable. When they give themselves to a hunter, he never returns
empty-handed from the chase, for it is Sani and Kontron who are in
command of the bush.
3 Women who are spinners use this flat stone to separate the seeds
from raw cotton.

45

the flat stone behind you; then your last resort is your egg. Do not throw it behind you until I have been chasing you for a long time. The Word has already granted power to these three objects, and there is no doubt that you will be the victor over the buffalo of Dô.'

Filled with joy, he slipped them into his game-bag and that afternoon Moké Danteman said farewell to Dô-Kamissa. He went off towards the town with an escort of some of the women, carrying calabashes on their heads. The sun was beginning to go down over Dafolo. A great rosy flame was swiftly descending, drawing after it the evening mists, and everything became the same rose colour as the flame: the mists and the huts of Dafolo all became rose-coloured. Then the mists thickened, and the town was dark. Suddenly, night fell.

'Well! . . . so the egg did not fall on the rock?' Moké Mussa said with a laugh when he saw his younger brother.

'No! and the rock did not fall on the egg, either,' said Moké Dantuman, bursting out laughing.

'Did you dig the rat's hole well with your hoe?' Moké Mussa asked.

'Yes!' replied Moké Dantuman, smiling, 'And I caught the rat, too. He's in my game-bag.'

'Did you tickle properly the person with the mouth full of teeth so as to be able to pull out your hand?' Moké Mussa went on.

'Yes! I have come back bringing my hand unharmed,' answered Moké Dantuman, laughing louder than ever.

As soon as dawn broke, the two hunters set out for the plain of Urantamba. It was half a day's march away, at the very most, but the journey seemed much longer to them, because they did not know the region of Dô. The younger described to his elder brother the thoughts that had bothered him the day before; he was speaking to him of the uneasiness he had felt in the presence of Dô-Kamissa when he had found her under the *Massidi Sandan Koro*, when suddenly a band of red-haired monkeys appeared before them, crossing their path. The two hunters looked at one another, looked at one another meaningfully, then burst out laughing.

'This family of red-haired monkeys must be very happy,' said

46

Moké Mussa, turning to wink at Moké Dantuman walking behind him.

'That's why they are dancing along. They are pulling faces, as if both showing their pleasure at seeing us, and making fun of us,' remarked Moké Dantuman.

'I don't care what faces they pull!' shouted Moké Mussa. 'I could just die of laughing whenever I see monkeys.'

'Monkeys!' echoed Moké Dantuman. 'Yes, red-haired monkeys are funny enough for sure. But they could be something more than just red-haired monkeys: they could be a sign – a sign that our enterprise will be crowned with success.'

'Oh, yes, I know that!' Moké Mussa retorted. 'Our master taught us that red-haired monkeys, or any antelopes we might see on our way, are always a good sign.'

'On the other hand, seeing wild boars or a weasel in these circumstances – so he told us – is a bad sign, the sign of bad luck and disappointment,' added Moké Dantuman.

They had already been walking some time, the elder, Moké Mussa, going in front of the younger, Moké Dantuman, along a path winding through the bush. If the buffalo had to be faced, thought Moké Dantuman, then it would just have to be faced! Surely it would be better to face it together, in the sort of shoulder-to-shoulder confrontation that bound him heart and soul to his brother, and which was always like a last defence against imminent peril.

Yet however close their shoulder-to-shoulder stance, and however great their confidence in their hunter's training, nevertheless the elder, Moké Mussa, was terribly distressed by this silent march after the recent comforting noises of the town, this march beneath a stupefying sun, far from the busy streets of Dafolo, far too, from the plain of Urantamba towards which they were heading, the plain which all hunters shunned now; and finally he was made terribly uneasy by the unseen presence of the buffalo of Dô, lying in wait for them perhaps among the bushes their path wound through. The way seemed to him so long, and he was not expecting to reach the plain of Urantamba all that quickly. He could not see it in the same way as Moké Dantuman saw it. No, by Allah! Not in that way, not as a victory! He was in no hurry to get there: he was filled with foreboding. Craven-

47

hearted, he was in no hurry to get there. Had not the buffalo of Dô already killed one hundred and seven hunters and wounded seventy-seven master 'simbon', master hunters? His mind was in total disarray; his soul wavered like the flame of a wind-blown torch . . .

The plain of Urantamba was not far away now; at any rate, it did not seem far; it was at the most only five hundred paces away. But to Moké Mussa it seemed much nearer, and the buffalo even nearer; so near, in the plain, that he found himself trembling with fear. Was fear putting Moké Mussa at a disadvantage? Was not fear forcing him into a position inferior to his younger brother's? Perhaps, for now Moké Dantuman had taken the lead in front of his elder brother, and was striding on valiantly. He suddenly giggled, as if trying to persuade his brother to rid his heart of fear. Moké Mussa felt a desperate longing to abandon the expedition, and to return to Dafolo, despite the reassuring words the day before of Dô-Kamissa, despite the red-haired monkeys they had encountered, which were a good sign.

As soon as they sighted the plain of Urantamba, Moké Dantuman suddenly forgot his fatigue and regained courage; he felt his whole being swell with courage. Now it was that reckless courage that was leading him on to confront the buffalo. And because he had regained all his courage, he was no longer the Moké Dantuman of just a short while ago; he had become a real master 'simbon', a real master hunter, striding forwards with vigilant eyes.

'Despite everything Dô-Kamissa told you yesterday,' whispered Moké Mussa, 'I don't feel very confident – I think she deceived you.'

'What do you mean?' Moké Dantuman asked in a low voice.

'What I mean is this,' went on Moké Mussa, his voice still in a whisper. 'This buffalo is an evil spirit, and we cannot attack an evil spirit! And don't forget that we are the only two sons in our family.'[1]

1 Other traditions attribute the killing of the buffalo of Dô to Damissa-Ulani, younger brother of Damissa-Ulamban. Babu says this is not incorrect, for Moké Mussa and Moké Dantuman were sons of Ulamban. Therefore the story is all in the same family.

'I see now how it is!' said Moké Dantuman in a low voice. 'You are afraid. But we've been walking a whole week now . . . we cannot turn back.'

'If so, then I'm going to climb a tree and watch how you do it; I feel so terribly afraid,' whispered Moké Mussa.

'Do as you please . . . I have given my word of honour, and so have you, and we must not go back on our word,' replied Moké Dantuman in the same low voice.

'But don't you see, there's no chance, no chance at all, of your succeeding,' Moké Mussa whispered.

'Of course! But all the same we have to try our luck,' the other retorted with some asperity.

And Moké Mussa quickly scrambled up into a tree, the tallest tree he could find on the borders of the great plain. But his younger brother, Moké Dantuman, went on his way. He walked on, with bated breath, his body bent. Suddenly, he saw the buffalo in the middle of the plain; it was browsing, and its silver horns were gleaming in the hot sun. Moké Dantuman saw that the plain was empty; there was no other creature, apart from the grazing buffalo, its head lowered in the very position in which the young hunter had imagined it, but not in an instinctively threatening position, because for the moment the beast was unaware of the hunter's presence on the plain; it went on grazing peacefully.

Moké Dantuman was immediately tempted to use his bow and arrows, but doubtless remembering the advice of Dô-Kamissa, he pulled the distaff from his game-bag, his *sassa*, and aimed it three times at the buffalo before using his weapon: the arrow sped whistling from the bow. Almost at once, the buffalo lifted its horned head and saw the hunter. It snorted angrily, its whole body trembling, then gave a long bellow, and, golden tail in the air, gave chase in the direction of the fleeing hunter, fleeing across the dry plain. The beast, galloping furiously, was almost upon him; but as he ran, Moké Dantuman swiftly took the distaff from his game-bag and threw it behind him. As if by magic, a forest of bamboos shot up into the air, separating him from the buffalo, which the buffalo had a hard time forcing its way through. But by battering a path with its powerful horns, the buffalo finally managed to get through the forest. Now once more it was in pursuit of the young man, who was screaming with terror and despair.

All this time, Moké Mussa, perched at the top of his tree, gave no sign of life; he could not move. When he and his younger brother had left the town of Dafolo, the sun had been firing its first rays at the darkness, but now, its afternoon light was illuminating the countryside with merciless clarity. In the mind of Moké Mussa also, and in the darkness of his spiritual night, there was a first shaft of radiance, a piercing shaft of enlightenment: when, the evening before, Moké Dantuman had told him that he had not dug the rat's hole with a pestle but with his hoe; when he had told him that he had got away with his hand intact after pulling them out of the mouth full of teeth where he had plunged them, because he had tickled his captor – then all had become clear to Moké Mussa, everything had been violently and cruelly illuminated. Now Moké Mussa finally realized completely what a coward he had been; and he realized clearly that his craven spirit debased him and would debase his offspring. All that terror, all that torment that had been plaguing him until now, that had unaccountably frozen his blood, had suddenly seared his conscience, like some irreparable shame, and was now pounding upon his head like torrential rain. And when, from the top of his tree, he saw Moké Dantuman heroically confront the buffalo in the plain, this shame had grown to enormous proportions, and he was feeling literally annihilated.

And certainly he would have done well, when he reached the plain of Urantamba, to follow the advice of his younger brother; he would have done well to follow Moké Dantuman into the plain instead of hiding himself away at the top of the tree. But in all the regions of the Mandingo there had grown up such a frightening legend about the buffalo of Dô; and now, with the beast's horns being vigorously flourished in the sun that struck sudden lightning from them, there appeared to be so much menace, so much danger, that he could not have brought it upon himself to venture into the plain.

Moké Dantuman, in his confrontation with the buffalo, was on the run, still on the run. Exhausted, he threw the flat stone behind him: it was transformed into an immense labyrinth of

50

stones that the buffalo could not pass through at a gallop, for it was constrained to walk slowly, as slowly as a man would have had to do in similar circumstances. And the young hunter kept on running all the time, so that the buffalo might not catch up with him and kill him with thrusts of its savage horns. When the beast had finally emerged from the labyrinth of stones it started galloping faster than ever, and soon began to gain on the young man. But Moké Dantuman was racing on like a hare: he was keeping up the pace, keeping it up very well despite his weariness, and the horns, looking ever more pointed, seemed to reach out as if wanting to throw him, run him through and dash him against the ground! Moké Dantuman was hurtling along like a meteor. Perhaps in place of legs he had grown hare's feet, yes, four hare's feet had unexpectedly but most certainly sprouted now in place of his legs. He was panting. Probably his chest was rising and falling with the exertion, but his hunting garment kept it from sight. All at once he realized he could no longer keep up that hellish pace. His final resort, the egg, was in his game-bag; he took it out and flung it behind him. At once the egg was transformed into a vast muddy marsh. The beast plunged into it, and its hooves got bogged down in the mud of the vast marsh – or was the beast's magical power draining away? – and it fell heavily into the clinging mire. As it lay there in the muddy depths, it bellowed even more loudly, and even longer. That hoarse bellowing took Moké Dantuman by surprise, though he had been expecting it, awaiting it; but is seemed to go right through him, as if he had not been expecting it, awaiting it. It was like a bellow of distress, and his heart froze within his breast. Valiantly, he took his bow and put the beast out of its misery . . . the buffalo of Dô finally was slain . . .

Moké Dantuman raised to his lips his hunter's whistle, his *simbon*, which was hanging from his *sèrèbu*, his hunter's garment, and began giving long blasts on it. These were victory signals; such was the sudden calm over the plain of Urantamba that the whistle could be heard for many leagues. And the sound of the whistle must have carried really very far, because contrary to Moké Dantuman's expectations, Moké Mussa, having climbed down from his tall tree, appeared almost immediately, and chanted:

51

Eh! Eh! Eh!
I bara ké kosson di, la-diya-dô-kala!
I bara ké Sékun di, 6in-na-kassa!
I bara ké todi di, dji-dô-kossô!
I bara ké Wara-sa di, tâ-tâ-kônô!
I bara ké Méléka di, Nigi-tâ-Mansa!
I bara Ke Sunsun Méléka di, Djina Mansa
Kondali Djina Wolosso!

Which, being translated, means:

Eh! Eh! Eh!
You have turned into a scorpion, the scorpion-pimento!
You have turned into a fly, the poison-fly-of-the-grasses!
You have turned into a toad, the toad-that-defiles-waters!
You have turned into an eagle, the eagle-king-soul-taker!
You have turned into the angel Sunsun, the spirit-king, the
spirit-stupendous!

Moké Dantuman, amazed at the beauty of the voice and the
profundity of Moké Mussa's words, chanted in reply:
Kôrô tum-bâ-ké Djéli di a Dian-ba-té!
(If my brother were a griot, none could resist him!)
The expression Dian-ba-té later became Diabaté. Thus, the
descendants of Moké Dantuman (Dantuman-si) kept the name
Traoré; those of Moké Mussa (Mussa-si) took the name of
Diabaté.
They cut off the golden tail of the buffalo and started on their
way back. As evening began to fall, it got cooler, the air became
lighter and moister; it was a sudden freshness after the stupefying
heat of mid-day, made all the fresher by the dew clinging to the
tall grasses through which their path went winding on. Their
progress was no longer fraught with anxiety; their return to
Dafolo was a triumphal return. Night suddenly fell, but the
moon was full; its milky, ghostly radiance illumined everything,
and tenderly caressed the leaves of trees. Moké Mussa was no
longer afraid that the buffalo, lying in ambush perhaps some-
where among the bushes, might rush out and run him through
with its sharp horns: the mysterious beast now no longer existed

for him and for the people of Dô; but that people did not yet know it. 'Tomorrow! yes, tomorrow the royal tabalas will drum out the good news and the twelve provinces of the land will have a victory celebration,' he thought. The two hunters gaily kept up their easy stride as they returned leisurely to Dafolo. There they would pass a dreamless night . . .

The next morning, they introduced themselves to the king, Dô-Samô, bearing the buffalo's tail, proof positive that they had triumphed over the beast. The king commanded his men to bring back the mutilated body of the buffalo; it was exhibited in the festival square. The next day, the nine royal tabalas of the great land of Dô – each beaten by two energetic young strongmen – took up the tale and broadcast it far and wide; the nearest villages heard it, took it up in their turn and transmitted it to the most distant villages. At the end of the day, the whole country knew that the buffalo had been slain; and every father of a family came to Dafolo, accompanied by a daughter of marriage-able age. The festival square was soon packed with people. As soon as the people were all gathered and the daughters all lined up in the festival square, King Dô-Samô, accompanied by his griot, by Moké Mussa and Moké Dantuman, made his appear-ance. The griot was strutting along proud as a peacock; his bearing had a deliberation which tried to appear noble; but in the eyes of the two young men it was like an irreverent aping of the royal progress.

As they passed by, people turned and gazed at them in ad-miration; many were obviously making remarks, though there was nothing to indicate that such remarks were unfavourable – rather the contrary. At any rate, everybody paid tribute to the intrepid valour of the two hunters. Was it only their intrepid valour that people praised? This was hardly likely, because the two young men – particularly the younger one! – were built like heroic athletes and really had the appearance of genuine master 'simbon'. But what the young girls were commenting on was also, was above all the beauty of the two young men of the Manden, a beauty that suddenly set every woman day-dreaming in the festival square. Others, in ecstasy, shrieked insults at the buffalo that had killed certain of their relatives.

The king and his escort took their places in the centre of the esplanade, in the shade of the mangrove trees. It was the king who was to show the people the great hunter who had rid the land of the dreadful scourge, the buffalo of Dô. After a while, Dô-Samô stood up, towering up to his full height, and his griot and the two young men followed his example. When the four men were on their feet, the musicians stopped playing their instruments, and everyone was silent, motionless. Dô-Samô then addressed his people; he spoke very softly and as if to himself – for speech was a feminine art reserved solely for griots and women. The king, who practised a masculine art, the art of governing a people, could not appropriate that other art, and could not shout at the top of his voice! It was the griot who proclaimed the royal decrees he was allowed to hear, commenting on them and elaborating them.

'Certain kings,' he announced, 'are very generous with all kinds of promises – as generous, abundant and incontinent as a horse's belly. But when it comes to keeping those promises, well – better not count on it. But things are different with us here in Dô. I have promised the hand of the most beautiful girl in my country – just as *Kala-Diansa* gave the arrow as a reward – to the hunter who would rid us of the buffalo. Here, in this square, are all the girls of marriageable age from the twelve provinces of Dô. Moké Dantuman, make your choice! When you have chosen, I shall give you your reward.'

In these words, Dô-Samô was speaking in the name of his people, in the name of his ancestors who founded the powerful kingdom of Dô: Frémori Condé and Féréndan Condé, two brothers from the Manden, from Kri, one of the nine provinces of the Manden, accompanied by their griot Sora Koro. Frémori, a married man, did not have any children. With the consent of his wife Kan Koroma, he married his sister-in-law Wasa Koroma. From this second marriage were born nine sons: Kabafing Kegmi known by the name of Koli-Kaba; Mami-Maghan, Gbérè-Sadi, Fan-Sai, Sila-Kidi, Fran-Solomudu, Fran-Djogo[1], Gnara Daba and Danfa-Missa. The descendants of the first eight sons shared the power in the land of Dô. Danfa-Missa, a great sorcerer, who had fallen out with his brothers, left them to settle

1 Maramani Kaba, ancestor of the Manika Mori, settled at Kankan when Fran-Djogo was king of Dô.

54

in the Manden, where he created a town bearing his name: Damissa.

When Moké Dantuman stood up, he had no sooner approached the lines of young girls than the griots who had come to greet his arrival and sing his victory began to cover him with flatteries: 'You are a true king!' they chanted. 'Dô-Samô is the king of the cities, but you are truly *Konko-Mansa*, the king of the bush. In all the lands of the black peoples, you are the first hunter, you are the most illustrious!' The griots, playing their eight-stringed hunters' guitars, thundered their praises; the rhythm was marked by a faint beating of drums, and the melody was released harmoniously through the picking of the strings of many guitars. Excited as if they had been Moké Dantuman, the hunter himself, they were as exalted as if the *Dô-Sigi*, the buffalo of Dô, had been slain by their own weapons. And when Moké Dantuman came right beside the young girls, the griots could no longer restrain themselves from intoning in chorus the *Konko-Mansa*, the king of the bush, the great chant which is sung only for the most illustrious hunter, and which is danced to only by him.

At the first notes of the *Konko-Mansa*, Moké Dantuman uttered a cry in which there resounded equal parts of triumph and pride: triumph over the dreaded buffalo, and pride at being crowned king of the hunters of Dô. Brandishing in his right hand his great bow, the hunter's weapon, and in his left hand the buffalo's golden tail, symbol of his victory, he danced the triumphal dance. Children perched like grasshoppers on the branches of the trees sat gazing in awe at the spectacle. No sooner had he finished than the crowd gave a roar of acclamation.

All the young girls of Dô were now seized by a desire to find favour in the eyes of the hero of the moment, to be admired and chosen by him. And of course they were lent an additional adornment in the sun, shining forth with rays of the utmost brilliance – as it does indeed in the land of Dô – that made their golden ornaments sparkle. The ebony black and sombre bronze of their naked flesh lent their jewellery mysterious fires. Moké Dantuman began passing them in review, and made several inspections of the ranks of young girls.

But, he wondered, were these really young girls? He greeted each one as if she were the fairy of Dô. And people must have been asking themselves how he was going to make his choice. It could fairly be said that he found them all seductive, for there was something so attractive, so provocative, in their eyes, in their smiles, but above all in their breasts, that he soon found himself unable to tear himself away from the ranks of young girls.

All the same, he was suddenly brought to his senses when, at the end of the esplanade or festival square he saw a hawk hovering above the crowd, gliding to and fro as if enjoying the festive scene; then without warning the hawk made a vertical plunge – it seemed to be seizing some prey. But what could there be for it to capture? For many moons, indeed, for many years, from time immemorial no mother hen and her brood of chicks would ever have ventured on the festive square – but the hawk plummeted three times in succession!

To the crowd, this was simply a game played by a bird of prey; to Moké Dantuman, too, it was simply a bird of prey; but above all he saw in it a sign – a sign seen only once every ten years, his master had told him! – a sign that in that spot over which the hawk had suddenly dived three times, or not far from it, there must be some extraordinary young girl. He moved in that direction. The women there were massed in great crowds, and seemed to have come there simply to give pleasure to the eye. He strode through them slowly and majestically; his bearing was that of a a true master 'simbon', and it was impossible to guess what was in his mind. Perhaps the young girls whose ranks he had several times inspected guessed his purpose? One could not be certain; but as soon as he left them, their eyes and their lips no longer smiled invitingly.

Just then, Sogolon Condé saw Moké Dantuman walking towards where she was seated on the mirador, in the midst of the great crowd of women. For the past week, in fact, she had known what would happen after the buffalo of Dô had been slain – her aunt Dô-Kamissa had told her about it before her death at the very moment when the hunter of the Manden overcame the beast – so she had been expecting this moment, the moment when she among all of the young girls of Dô would be chosen by the hero of the day. Now that this moment was drawing near, she hardly knew whether she was awake or dreaming. Yet Moké Dantuman seemed no longer to have eyes for the girls lined up

56

in the middle of the square, lined up for him alone. He was gazing straight before him. Sogolon was seated on the mirador, draped in a cotton veil of immaculate whiteness to hide her humpback.

'Alas! Young hunter, no other girl in this square is as ugly as I,' she thought. 'Is it me you are going to choose, hunter? I do not have a beautiful body. On the contrary, the hump on my back makes me completely deformed and gives me a horrible appearance! Not to mention my staring eyes! . . .' And she covered her head with her white veil. 'No! he will not choose me,' she told herself. 'As soon as he sees me close up, my ugliness will strike him in all its horror, then he will certainly not choose me!'

Unless it was in her stars? 'Your extraordinary star, your own, already mentioned by Dô-Kamissa and whose influence is confirmed here this very day by the three swoops of the bird of prey,' – this is what the young hunter's slow, deliberate stride towards her seemed to be saying. Suddenly she felt deeply troubled and absolutely desolate. She wished she could vanish from the face of the earth! Even though the reliabliity of the verbal promise made between Dô-Kamissa and Moké Dantuman under the *Massidi Sandan Koro* induced Sogolon to remain seated on the mirador, all she wanted to do was to run away . . .

But the young man kept on striding straight towards her; all of a sudden, he broke through the assembled mass of women; he beheld Sogolon seated on the mirador – it was constructed of branches stripped of their leaves and supported on forked timbers, and it seemed to be floating on the tumultuous waves of jabbering women massed there in a vast mob. He nimbly ascended the ladder leading up to the platform, and took Sogolon by the hand; then they both proceeded towards the centre of the square. Thereupon the crowd, far from hailing the pair with rapture – as would have been the case if the prettiest girl in Dô had been chosen – barely gave Moké Dantuman and Sogolon a single glance. And that glance was of the utmost indifference, the most sombre, the blindest of glances. But then Moké Dantuman indicated Sogolon with his finger.

'Oh King Dô-Samô,' he said, 'I have the honour of presenting to you the girl I have chosen among all the young girls of Dô. It is she whom I wish to marry.'

'I've stumbled on a madman,' thought Dô-Samô. 'He doesn't

know his own mind!' At that, he could not help bursting out laughing at such a paradoxical choice. The whole mob uttered peals of laughter, screaming with laughter in a particularly insulting manner. At that moment, Moké Dantuman must have wished that Dô-Kamissa was at his side to encourage him and comfort him in his choice, and to silence the mocking laughter of the great mob, now seized with a frenzy of scorn. Alas! she had given up the ghost at the same time as her ancestral totem.

His heart suddenly froze. 'They're mad . . . really mad!' Moké Dantuman muttered under his breath. Did he have to continue suffering this spectacle of the crowd whose jeering laughter was directed at Sogolon and himself, and, through him, at his elder brother Moké Mussa? He felt as if his heart were about to burst. Suddenly he turned his back on Dô-Samô, and, accompanied by Sogolon and Moké Mussa, he strode out of the square. Once he was out of earshot of the howling mob, he shook himself, slapped his hunter's costume with the back of his hand, as if to brush off the dust, or as if literally giving the brush-off to so much ill-feeling. Then the three of them made their departure as quickly as possible, as if escaping from people afflicted with a mental aberration. Sogolon, feeling slighted, was softly weeping.

Yet for one brief moment, Sogolon the ugly girl – monstrously ugly, with her pop eyes and the hump that deformed her back, giving her the look of a zebu – had known happiness: that moment when, on the mirador, Moké Dantuman had chosen her, out of all the beautiful young girls on earth! It is the sort of moment girls know only once in their lives, indescribable, more resplendent than the sun at noon.

Thanks to the gentle attentions of the two young men she gradually calmed down; as the trio left the festival square, a great silence should surely have fallen, but in fact, the square became even noisier than it had been a moment earlier. All those insulting peals of laughter, each time accompanied by the phrase 'Only someone of the Traoré tribe would behave so!' which the mob had heaped upon the trio's heads because of the strange choice of a girl, now took on, in their hearts, a considerably intensified resonance. Those peals of laughter flamed like a bush fire. The three companions heard them crackling like a prairie conflagration. They could hear each tongue of flame crackling as

58

it leapt up the tall grasses and along the green leaves of the trees; and they seemed to hear everything mixed up in a multiple and furiously resonant crackling.

It was the younger of the two hunters who led the way when they shook the dust of the land of Dô from their feet and set off for the Manden, their country of origin. They advanced in single file, between two walls of tall grasses. Sogolon was in the middle, and Moké Mussa, the elder, brought up the rear as he followed behind her. The two young men, out of consideration for the young lady, Sogolon, shortened their stride, so that instead of taking two weeks to reach the Manden, they took a good month.

But they hardly noticed the length of the journey, for it was made pleasant by the presence of a woman and by chatter about this and that, about all kinds of things, about all and nothing.

'Tell me,' Moké Dantuman suddenly cried, 'is it the custom among the people of Dafolo to be so nasty towards strangers? In our land, the Manden, the stranger is sacred, he is a king!'

'I should have credited Dô-Samô with more intelligence,' said Moké Mussa.

'But why do you say these awful things about the people of my country?' Sogolon demanded indignantly. 'It is discourteous even to speak badly of termites when one finds oneself sitting on a termitary! I am not going to keep following you if it is only to hear you vilifying the people of Dafolo and King Dô-Samô. The king is the king: he was ridiculous and not at all generous in his behaviour, but it is certainly not for me to judge or condemn my father. And anyhow, the crowd in the festival square at Dafolo was not unsympathetic, but only became so after you had made your choice; they were expecting you to choose the prettiest girl in Dô, and instead you chose the ugliest. Apart from the three of us, no one knows the reason why you did so; it affects me much more than you, and that is why I was weeping so at the start of our journey.'

'Don't worry, Sogolon, we understand everything; we were saying those things only to tease you,' said Moké Mussa.

'We have no intention of slandering the people of Dafolo, and certainly not the king; but we cannot understand why they greeted our choice with such mocking laughter,' said Moké Dantuman.

'Don't start getting worked up again,' Moké Mussa told him. 'You are just antagonizing Sogolon with your repeated questions; you are like a child; and you antagonize me, too, because, in spite of myself, I have to listen to both of you. Now everything is well and truly settled. Dô-Kamissa is in her tomb, where she rests in peace because we have not betrayed our word – the man who does not keep his word is lower than the beasts – we chose Sogolon, and she is adorable. Don't you think so?'

'Time will tell,' Moké Dantuman replied.

Sogolon undid her scarf and rearranged it on her head.

'But first of all, if you agree, we shall spend the night in the next village. It is not wise to travel at night in the company of a young girl; she cannot defend herself against wild animals as we can, and night will soon fall,' said Moké Mussa.

'Yes,' she said.

And she gave a sigh.

'You seem suddenly very tired; at the next halt you shall lie down and rest, if you wish,' said Moké Dantuman.

Once more she undid her scarf and then re-wound it round her head.

'Very well,' she answered.

'When we reach the village, we shall have a good meal,' said Moké Mussa. 'If we can't get a good meal, at least we shall have a big one. In that way, quantity will make up for quality. In our country, we eat well, because we order the women to prepare our favourite dishes.'

'But you are not in the Manden. We're not at home yet, you know . . .'

Their path made a turn to the right. In fact, it was a wretchedly narrow path and surely it was more like a sheep track than a path suitable for walking. But it was a byway, the sort of byway that generally leads to a village.

'This path is not as good as the one we were on just now; it is narrow, stony and overgrown with grass,' murmered Sogolon.

She was thinking of the broad, clean paths that linked Dafolo with its farming hamlets.

'It certainly isn't!' the two hunters agreed. 'But don't you hear anything?'

Sogolon listened. Then she seemed to hear voices, coming from not far away. But how could she tell whether these voices were coming from a nearby village, or whether they were the voices of shepherds? The voices were mingled with the louder bellowings of cattle returning to their enclosure.

'I cannot be quite sure,' Sogolon answered. 'I can't make out where the sounds are coming from.'

'There's one sure way. Lift your head and look further on,' they told her.

Sogolon gazed admiringly at the thatched roofs of huts in the distance.

'After coming this far,' said Sogolon, 'I think the first thing to do is to take a bath, to refresh my blood. I feel half dead. Ah! we stayed too long in Dafolo, where our presence is now undesirable, and where I was so deeply insulted.'

Now night was about to fall. After having walked so far, they had at last reached a village. Here they were lodged in two huts; the young girl occupied one, the two brothers the other.

'Sogolon!' Moké Mussa suddenly said, 'Give us a drink of water before you go to the bath.'

She went to a corner of the hut where there was fresh, cool water in a water-jar standing on some gravel. She came back with a goblet filled to the brim; she handed it to Moké Mussa, who took it at once and raised it to his lips. While he felt the cool freshness of the water trickling down his throat, he was looking from under his lids to observe what gesture the young girl would make after handing him the goblet. 'This is the most favourable moment, the unique and very brief instant in which one can grasp something of a woman's nature!' his master had told him. 'Once this brief moment has passed, she retires into herself and once more becomes very complex – deeper than the river and vaster than the sky itself.' When the two hunters had finished drinking, Sogolon took her leave of them and withdrew.

'Did you see that?' Moké Mussa asked, when he had recovered from his astonishment.

'Did you see that?' Moké Mussa asked. 'That young girl will be a faithful wife and mother. Didn't you notice that after she gave you the goblet to drink from, she immediately placed both hands on her hips, arms akimbo? It's the best sign or omen you could have. And now you should go and lie with her.'

61

There was a pause.

'But what's stopping you from going and lying with your wife in her hut? You were the one who was victorious over the buffalo, not I,' said Moké Mussa.

'You are the elder,' replied Moké Dantuman. 'It is fitting that you should take a woman before me, your younger brother.'

'Well, then,' said Moké Mussa, 'it is not fitting for me, nor is it fitting for you to flaunt a custom established by our ancestors.'

He waited a while, for he wanted to be sure that she had already gone to bed, and he wished to be quite sure that none of their host's women would be coming to visit her. 'No one will be coming to see her now!' he thought, and he slipped into her hut. Sogolon, naked, was reclining on her bed; that night it was fairly cool. Moké Mussa's heart was beating hard, very hard, beating so hard it seemed it would burst, for the attitude that Sogolon had taken up as she lay there made him forget completely her humpback and her staring eyes. It was the attitude that makes every girl on earth look irresistible!

And moreover, what he was about to perform was something perfectly lawful. Had not his younger brother, Moké Dantuman, waived his rights in favour of his elder brother? Was he not obeying ancestral custom in accepting? So, greatly daring, he took off his hunter's garment and lay down beside her; she was already sleeping.

But then Sogolon, feeling a certain warmth that was not the warmth of her own body, and feeling a strange hand exploring her, instinctively called upon her double. At once, every hair on her body became very, very long and spiky, like the sharp quills of a porcupine, which prevented anyone from approaching her or stroking her even, much less exploring her secret parts.

Of course, Moké Mussa for his part was not without his own double; he was a great sorcerer, and so he in his turn called upon his double. But it was much less powerful than Sogolon's double, so he did not succeed in overcoming it, and consequently did not succeed in possessing the young girl. Thus, the two doubles waged a bitter war all night long; but in the end it was Sogolon's that triumphed.

At dawn, half dead with weariness, and feeling unstrung by his unsatisfied desire, Moké Mussa rejoined Moké Dantuman in their hut.

'Nothing! I'm telling you! Nothing! I couldn't do anything,' he cried angrily. 'You were the one who triumphed over the buffalo, you – eagle-with-live-charcoal-in-his-beak – and so it is up to you to make her your wife.'

Then, puffed up with valour and pride, puffed up too by his many sorcerer's talents, Moké Dantuman replied without a moment's hesitation:

'I shall go and lie with her tonight!'

At break of day, the three continued their journey towards the Manden. As on the day before, they proceeded at a leisurely pace, and by nightfall they reached a village where they were again lodged in two huts; as on the previous night, one hut was for Sogolon, the other for the two brothers.

Moké Dantuman said: 'Sogolon! I shall come and visit you in your hut tonight, as your lawful husband. You followed me of your own free will, and with the consent of your aunt Dô-Kamissa. So under the circumstances, I hope that we shall both behave in a reasonable way.'

'Reasonable – both of us?' she asked, meditatively, giving Moké Dantuman a long look.

'Don't you think that would be best for both of us?' he said.

'I don't know!'

Later that night, Moké Dantuman took leave of Moké Mussa. 'I am going to visit Sogolon in her hut, Sogolon whom I have chosen from among all the young girls of Dô,' he thought. 'Perhaps she does not know the nature of the agreement made between the late Dô-Kamissa and myself? She could not have been aware of all that was involved in the agreement, for she was not present under the *Massidi Sandan Koro*. But the essential point in that agreement was that she is henceforward bound to be my lawful wife; if she pretends to know nothing about it, I shall bring it to her notice. I shall tell her that she no longer belongs to herself, that we belong to one another for ever, and that, as my lawful wife, it is her bounden duty not to avoid her conjugal obligations!'

Moké Dantuman rushed off. When he tried to make his way

into Sogolon's hut, the interior, though it was lit by an oil lamp, suddenly went dark, became black, very black, became more black than a moonless night; and, with one leg across the threshold of the hut, and the other still outside, he was struck motionless, as if frozen solid on his own two feet. At once he was overcome by sleep; he immediately fell asleep in that attitude, and was snoring until daybreak! When he awoke, he rejoined Moké Mussa in their hut. He explained at great length his misadventure with the young girl.

'Does she imagine things can go on this way?' he said.

'That girl's head is full of spells, or at any rate fuller of spells than ours are, and so things can go on like this for an eternity,' replied Moké Mussa.

'I failed miserably with her, just as you did,' said Moké Dantuman.

'Sogolon is not for us,' Moké Mussa bitterly agreed.

'So the wisest thing is not to try anything else, and just proceed quietly on our journey. Before we get back to the Manden we must come to some sort of decision about her,' Moké Dantuman answered wretchedly.

Yet the week before, Moké Dantuman had been over the moon with joy. In choosing Sogolon from among all the young girls of Dô, he really thought he had won a great victory. Already he had been dreaming of the extraordinary son that would be the fruit of their union, and who, after his death and beyond the grave, would perpetuate his name! But what a defeat he had suffered! And how much better it would have been for him if he had never chosen this girl! How much better it would have been if he had not respected the agreement between the late Dô-Kamissa and himself! Then he might have married the prettiest girl in Dô, and by now, probably, the marriage would have been consummated!

Sogolon the ugly girl would have gone on living at Dafolo among people who would boo her day after day – he didn't care. Every day she might feel more and more insulted – he wouldn't comfort her! People could cast him the dirtiest looks, laugh at him in the most insulting manner – but he would remain utterly indifferent.

BILALI JBUNAMA AND HIS DESCENDANTS

Farako Maghan Kégni, or Farako Maghan the Beautiful, whose real name was Maghan Kön Fatta, was the king of the Manden at the time when Dô-Samô was on the throne of Dô. He belonged to a less powerful dynasty – whose ancestral totem was the lion – but one which was very old, certainly older then the dynasty of Dô. The Manden-ka[1] came from the Levant. They settled with the Bambaran people. The first ancestor of the kings of the Manden was Bilali Ibn Ka Mâma, whose name the Malinké pronounced Bilali Ibunâma. When he reached Mecca, the Arabs usually called him Bilali Kabs, or Bilali the Slave[2].

Originally from Chad, he was held in captivity at Yaundé (the Cameroons) by Kalifa, then king of that country. Nevertheless, he was a very devout man who kept his faith in one unique and all-powerful God; as he was not a free man, however, he was unable to practise the faith he believed in.

When the idolatrous King Kalifa had constructed a hut for his fetishes, he naturally had thought of using a slave to guard them. When he had bought Bilali, it had quite simply been in order to install him in front of this hut at the centre of a courtyard enclosed by barbed wire to discourage intruders.

Why did he not give some other task to this slave, who had an unshakeable faith in the one God, instead of putting him in front of the idol hut? Bilali had no choice; a slave certainly would have no choice in the matter. He was just a chattel of his master,

1 The Manden-ka: locative derivative: someone born in the Manden.
2 Bilali was not an Ethiopian, as certain historians claim, but from Chad. In the seventh century, Arabs who knew very little about the African continent thought all blacks came from Ethiopia, just as Europeans, before the dawn of Independence, thought all blacks were Senegalese. But according to all the griots of the Manden, Bilali Ibn Ka Mâma or Bilali grandson of Mâma was from Chad.
Bilali comes from Bilal. Bilali means 'my Bilal'. Bilali belongs to the ethnic group dwelling round Lake Fitri, in the prefecture of Balka, Republic of Chad.

and, as such, inevitably had to submit at all times to the latter's whims.

Bilali was well aware of the barbed wire – in daylight, under the violent illumination of the sun, one could hardly not be aware of it – but until then he had not realized that though it had been placed there to prevent any intruder from entering the fetish hut, it was also there to stop him from escaping.

One day however, when one of the king's attendants had caught him at his devotions, praying in the manner of the monotheists, he had denounced Bilali to Kalifa, who decreed an exemplary punishment to be carried out upon him the next day. To avoid the royal wrath, Bilali realized, the only solution was escape. He sat watching closely and patiently the barbed wire fence separating the fetish hut he guarded from the other huts of the town. When he saw that there was no one outside and that he could get over the fence, which was not very high, it no longer seemed to present a serious obstacle to him, for he was of athletic build and a good jumper. He was sure his feet would not be caught by the top of the barbed-wire fence. So he decided to try his luck; he took a good run, then – jumped!

Now he was wandering in the streets of the town. Was he hoping to find a caravan leaving for Chad, that he might attach himself to without being noticed? Perhaps. Perhaps, too, he was not hoping to find anything; perhaps he was just happy to be wandering, enjoying the newly-discovered air of freedom, parading through the streets with that sense of ease and liberty whose inestimable value – like good health – makes it so precious to a man who has lost it, or is about to lose it. But Liberty is the daughter of Health! A slave was not a free man, and this escapade could not be of long duration. Bilali was spotted and betrayed to Kalifa; he was recaptured by brutal young guards, bound, and dragged back to his master.

Now, he was stretched naked on the burning ground, his face towards the fiery sun; they had put a big, heavy stone on his chest. Wretched and pitiful slave though he was, he had never before been so cruelly treated! It was . . . but how could one describe what it was? It was sadistic, to humiliate a human being like Bilali in this way!

'What is all-powerful?' howled Kalifa, 'Me and my fetishes,

or your one God to whom you pray all day long?'

'It is my one God who is all-powerful,' Bilali groaned between clenched teeth. 'I believe in Him alone and in his representatives òn earth; I do not believe in your idols.'

'Put a heavier stone on top of the first!' Kalifa commanded. 'Then perhaps he'll come to realize which is the more powerful, his one God or me!'

'Saviour! Saviour!' Bilali moaned.

But despite the slave's repeated pleas, Kalifa did not relent. On the contrary, he became more threatening, and in the end wanted to give full vent to his anger by killing the slave.

Before the load on Bilali's chest was increased, the Archangel Gabriel, sent by the Lord to succour one of his best servants, came down from the heavens in less time than it takes to tell! Gabriel made the two heavy stones feel lighter than kapok.

On that very day, Bubakar Sidiki, faithful companion of the prophet Mahammadu (may God's peace and mercy fall for ever upon him and his companions) was on a mission to Yaundé and heard of this monotheist slave's courageous stand; he decided to buy Bilali, so at once went and saw the king.

'What are you offering for him?' asked Kalifa.

'I'm offering you gold!' he replied.

'I do not accept gold!' said Kalifa. 'Do you expect to sell salt to the sea? I alone am the maker of gold!'

So Bubakar Sidiki returned quickly to the caravan encampment hoping to find there some valuable object that would appeal to Kalifa. While he was absent, Bilali could not tell if he would be able to rescue him from his difficult situation; he thought of his rescuer as a shield. He realized now that this shield was trying to come between Kalifa and himself; yet he was afraid that his rescuer might not return. But Bubakar Sidiki soon came back and appeared before the king carrying a fine white jellaba.

'Will you surrender your slave to me for this white jellaba?' he asked.

When he displayed the jellaba, all those present gave admiring cries: 'How magnificent it is! It is truly a vestment fit for a king!'

This enthusiastic clamour persuaded the king to accept.

'Yes! Now I can accept your offer. I'm perfectly satisfied,' he announced.

He tore the jellaba from the hands of Bubakar Sidiki and ordered the slave to be released.

As soon as his ankles and wrists had been untied, Bilali gazed for a moment in disgust at the two huge stones placed on his naked chest; then, with an immense effort, he tossed them angrily far from him. It was really the first time, in his life as a slave at everyone's beck and call, that he had been so badly treated – and perhaps it was now the last time, too!

'Bilali!' called Bubakar Sidiki.

He got up slowly and painfully, his eyes still blinded by the piercing rays of the hot sun, staggering like a drunken man; then, fearfully, went towards his new master.

'Now,' proclaimed the latter, 'now you are liberated. In me you now have a new master who is certainly more humane. But now, too, a new contract begins. Bilali, I hope that you will not cause me to regret my step, and that you will prove yourself worthy of the new task entrusted to you, which is to serve faithfully him to whom I destine you: the prophet of Islam.'

'Certainly I shall prove myself worthy of your confidence in me, master,' he replied. 'To be able to serve the prophet Mahammadu is all I ever wished for; the Lord has heard my prayers; I am overwhelmed.'

'Come, now, and follow me. It is time for the ship to sail,' said his rescuer.

They spent months on the sailing vessel. During that time, Bilali was able to give free rein to his thoughts: 'I am safe in their hands, and glad to be no longer the guardian of Kalifa's fetish hut,' he told himself. 'If I could cover my skin with ashes, I would be white like the Arabs, and then no one would ever see the difference between them and me,' he thought.

But what has the colour of one's skin to do with faith? 'Man is just like a sword, whose sheath represents the pigmentation of his skin; but the sharp edge of the steel blade symbolizes moral values that count much more!' he thought.

Yes, henceforward he would live at Mecca, would bow down five times a day to the Kaaba, along with all the other believers of that land, all united in the same act of humility, all united by the recitation of the same verses of the Koran. The same faith in the one and all-powerful God would bring them together day after day, each and every one of them living in the hope, the identical hope, of being utterly merged with God. Was it not that flame, that flame of hope illuminating the soul of every believer – much more than the pigmentation of the skin – that made all the faithful brothers in God? It was only and unchallengingly that faith in the One, in the Being so close in his inaccessibility, so inaccessible in his proximity, which should – much more than any other consideration – knit the faithful one to another, making them all one, as the limbs are all one with the body.

His deepest self, he realized, was the sum of two innermost beings. The first, completely identified with life as he knew it, fashioned according to his existence as a slave at the beck and call of everyone, and having an imperious need to repose itself in the faith of the Supreme Being in order to survive, was at war with the second, a personage of some complexity and vaguely racist, who dreamed of being the equal of the Arabs by covering his body with ashes to whiten his skin. But the first carried the day.

Bubakar Sidiki, whose return was impatiently awaited, and above all Bilali Ibn Ka Mâma, whose arrival was not expected, created a sensation; so much so that nearly all the inhabitants of the outer suburbs of Mecca had come to meet the travellers, even before these reached the mosque where the prophet of Islam was conducting prayers. At the moment when they finally entered the place of worship, the salaam was already completed. Bubakar Sidiki, followed by Bilali, advancing towards his friend, gave solemn salutations to the crowd of the faithful who had joyously risen to their feet to greet him; then, turning to the prophet of Islam and giving him the ceremonial embrace, he announced:

'I am bringing you an unusual servant; he believes, as we do, in the one all-powerful God!'

Then he gave a detailed account of the slave's bitter, painful experiences. From that day forward, Bilali Kabs or Bilali the Slave, as the people of Mecca usually preferred to call him, faithfully served the prophet Mahammadu for years. Then one day, crouching beneath the date palm at a respectful distance from his master, and lost in thought, the latter said:

'Bilali! Come here and clean up this mess round my prayer rug. A hen has been round here; oh, how dirty it is!'

Bilali smiled; for the first time in years, he let out a loud laugh;

this laugh sounded particularly lacking in respect. What could
have made him laugh so much? He was thinking of his past life,
and of his native land, Chad, far beyond the sea, thousands of
miles away. He was filled with nostalgia as he day-dreamed about
it; he considered his position as slave, his pitiful state; then he
thought of Kalifa in the Cameroons, who had had him bound to
the hot earth and exposed him to the full fury of the burning sun,
in humiliating conditions. And he began thinking of those of his
compatriots in captivity as he was, who had been uprooted from
the soil of the ancestors and transported against their will all over
the world, to every corner of the world. But he was thinking of his
present condition above all, and feeling that he had been especially favoured by chance. Was he not living at Mecca, and was
he not in the service of the prophet of the faithful? However, one
unfortunate phrase had struck him, and had suddenly recalled
to him his sad state of eternal slavery. But he cleaned the ground
round the prayer rug.

'Bilali!' the prophet said, 'Explain your laughter; were you
laughing at the hen, of what she had done next to my prayer rug,
or were you laughing at me?'

'No, master!' he replied. 'I was laughing at myself. Did you not
say the hen was dirty? But is she not far superior to the slave who
feels dirty in his soul because he is not free?'

'You are right,' said the prophet, his heart touched by these
words. 'From this moment on, I grant you your freedom. From
this day forward I shall ask all my companions no longer to
address you as Bilali Kabs, or Bilali the Slave, but to call you by
your true name, Bilali Ibn Ka Mâma. So now you are free to
marry, as we are, in the same societies, and I shall personally pray
to the Lord to grant your descendants all prosperity, and eternal
rest for yourself.'

'My eternal gratitude to you for freeing me, but I shall continue to serve you with devotion, in the true faith.'

Bilali Ibn Ka Mâma married and had several sons, but the one
who came to the Manden was called Latal Kalabi. Latal Kalabi
was the first king of the Manden; he had as his son Damel
Kalabi, who had as his son Lahilatul Kalabi, who in his turn, had
two sons: Kalabi Bomba (Kalabi the Tall) and Kalabi Doman
(Kalabi the Short). It was the elder son, Kalabi Bomba, who took

power, his younger brother preferring to devote his life to commerce. It was also Kalabi Bomba who first introduced into the customs the ceremony of Konden Diarra[1] for young boys.

Kalabi Bomba had as his son Mamadi Kani, the royal master hunter, who introduced, for his part, the *sèrèbu* or garment of the hunter, into the customs; finally, he also introduced the hunter's whistle, the *simbon*, and created and organized a confraternity of men of the bush. He made many conquests. Mamadi Kani had four sons: Kani Simbon, Kanignogo Simbon, Kabala Simbon and Simbon Bamari Tagnogokelen, all of whom were initiated by their father into the art of the hunt. However, it was his youngest son, Simbon Bamari Tagnogokelen, who took power. He had as his son NBali Néné whose son was Mansa Bélé. It was Mansa Bélé who introduced the dance of the *Coba* into the circumcision rites[2].

Mansa Bélé had five sons: Missa, Barry, Namandian, Kono Koro Semba and Bélébakön, but it was the third son, Namandian, who took over the reins of government. Missa separated from his father and settled in a village which was named after this separation: Faramaya[3]. Barry settled at Timbo, known today as Futa-Djalon[4].

However, it was the son of the fifth son, Bélébakön, who came to power; the son of Bélébakön was Maghan Kön Fatta or

1 *Konden Diarra*: see *The African Child*. Additional information: Babu Condé, the famous traditionalist of the Hamana, claims that the ceremony of 'Konden Diarra' was introduced into the customs by Kalabi Bomba, the fourth king of the Manden, nearly one thousand two hundred years ago. Its aim is to initiate Malinké children by teaching them to overcome fear. Though this ceremony has the character of a game, and is largely a mystification, it is also a test and a means of toughening a boy's spirit, a rite that is a prelude to manhood.
2 *Coba*: see the ceremony of circumcision in *The African Child*.
3 Faramaya is a village founded by Missa, the eldest son of Mansa Bélé. Years later, when Mansa Dankaran Tuman fled Sumaoro and settled in this village, it became known as Kissidugu. Ever since, the village has kept two names: Faramaya-Kissi. Faramaya means 'separation'.
4 The second son of Mansa Bélé, who was called Barry, settled in Timbo, present-day Futa-Djalon. The Barry, descendants of the kings of the Manden, came from the Upper Niger, and were not descended from foreigners, as Sékou Touré claims.

Farako Maghan Kégni or Maghan the Beautiful; he was naturally beautiful and was a good king beloved of his people. He especially liked to spend every afternoon seated under the bombax tree that towered over his palace of clay and the royal capital, Niani, as if the shade of this great tree were calling to him. He certainly did not go there to hold audiences, but rather to take a rest from his kingly duties. He would sit there, surrounded by his griot Dua, his eight-year-old son Dankaran Tuman – whose mother, Fatumata Bérété, sister of a great marabout, had just given birth to her second child, princess Nâna Triban – and by all his personal court attendants. His counsellor, confidant and spokesman, the griot Dua, who was always present, would never have dreamed of leaving the service of the king.

Moreover, this griot, just like his master Maghan Kön Fatta, was of an ancient lineage that had loyally served the kings of the Manden.

The first griot of the kings of the Manden also came from the Levant. He was called Sorakata Kuyaté.

Sorakata Kuyaté had a son Mundalfa who had a son named Faruku. Faruku had a son Farkan who had a son named Kukuba who had a son named Batamba whose son was Niéni-Niéni. Niéni-Niéni had a son Kambassia who had a son Haryni whose son was Dikisso. Dikisso had a son Dantuman who had a son Kaléani whose son was Gnankuman. Gnankuman had a son Dua, known to the Manden-Ka as Gnankuman-Dua[1]. He was the griot of our hero Maghan Kön Fatta called Farako Maghan Kégni or Maghan the Beautiful.

Gnankuman-Dua had a son Balla Fassali Kuyaté, the griot of Sogolon-Diata, the son of the buffalo-panther woman Sogolon and the lion man Maghan Kön Fatta, first Emperor of Mali.

Balla Fassali Kuyaté had three sons: Missa, Missa-Maghan and Batru-Mori[2] whose descendants were dispersed all over the Empire of Mali. Even today, one still finds numerous griots all over West Africa.

1 The name Dua is preceded by that of his father. Qjnan-Kuman-Dua was then usually called Gnankuman-Dua.
2 The same applies to Batru-Mori whose mother was Batru. The griot was then called Batru-Mori also.

Well, one afternoon, Farako Maghan Kégni, seated under the great bombax tree of Niani, not far from the palace, and in the happy company of his associates, saw coming towards him a man wearing the short jacket and tight trousers of a hunter. His garments, all shining with cowrie shells, showed him to be a past master in the art of the hunt. Wearing an ochre-coloured skull cap on his grey tresses[1], he bore accoutrements that clearly accentuated the lines of his black face lit by lively eyes. Of medium height, he appeared slender and alert; he moved to within one pace of the king, whom he recognized from accounts of his legendary beauty; then, bowing, he said: 'I salute you, king of the Manden; I salute your entourage; I was born in Dô. My king is called Dô-Samô-Condé. The hunt has brought me from my land to your walls. On the way, I saw an antelope, to which I gave chase. Thanks to Sani and Kontron and the blessings of my master, my arrows found their mark; I cut it up, and the carcass lies not far from your palace. Here is your share!' He took out of his game-bag an antelope thigh which he tendered to Gnankuman-Dua, who, thanking him, said: 'The king and his entourage, touched, profoundly touched by your courtesy in respecting our customs so scrupulously, wish me to let you know that though you have left your home you may consider yourself back at home again here in the court at Niani!'

Continuing his speech, he went on: 'My master, our good king, and all of us are always well disposed towards people with good manners.' Maghan Kégni approved this speech with a lowering of his eyelids; then, speaking in a friendly and informal way, he addressed the hunter thus: 'You who come from Dô, the most gifted land in divination; you to whom Sani and Kontron, those dread divinities of the chase, have revealed themselves – will you not give us the benefit of your knowledge? In your game-bag are there not

> Sunsun Méléka
> Gna dimin Soro
> Djina Mansa Kondoli?'

1 The hunters of Dô, today as in the past, have their hair plaited like women.

The angel Sunsun;
Medicaments for the eyes
From the guardian spirit king Kondoli?

The hunters of Dô have mastered the art of divination. If the
stranger would be so kind, we shall learn much from him.'

For a moment, the stranger seemed to hesitate. Then he sat on
the mat beside the griot Dua, and took twelve shells out of his
game-bag.

'I shall consult the cowries,' he said. 'I could not very well
consult them if they stayed in my game-bag.'

Before beginning the operation, he lifted the cowries to his
mouth, murmuring incantatory words, then with a nervous
gesture cast them before him on the mat. Then he bent his head
and, with his left hand, shuffled them, muttering incomprehensible words. What could he be saying in such a low voice?
Was his whispering voice not interpreting the position of each
shell, and was he not waiting until he was absolutely sure of the
answer before pronouncing it? That must surely have been what
it was, for soon he raised his eyes; he fixed the king with his gaze,
and said:

'Oh! king of the Manden! The Universe is a total mystery! The
place where the powerful River Djeliba has its source is so small,
one can just step over it! Kingdoms, too, are like rivers; some of
them remain small streams, others grow into mighty rivers! But
in the end the River Djeliba swallows them all up! . . .'

He paused for a moment as if to draw breath, then went on:

'The dread guardian spirit of a powerful kingdom is about to
emigrate into your own kingdom in the person of a young girl.
I see this girl coming towards your capital Niani, escorted by two
young men. But how ugly she is! She has staring eyes and in
addition she is hump-backed!'

For quite a while he kept his eyes turned towards the entrance
to the town. He fell silent. The entire company, including the
king, looked towards the entrance gate. No one said a word. The
silence was no longer interrupted, as it had been a while ago, by
the shuffling of the cowrie shells. The griot was gazing so intently at the hunter that he forgot to go on playing his three-
stringed guitar. Silence, stillness, and a kind of anxiety hovered

over everything. Then, furtively, the hunter lowered his eyes to the cowries, and began to shuffle them again.

'Hunter, your language is obscure,' said the griot Dua. 'Make it as clear to us as the savannas of the Manden!'

After having pondered a long time over the cowries spread before him on the mat, the hunter raised his head and addressed the king thus:

'Today, your spirit is haunted by three thoughts. You are afraid of being invaded and killed by a powerful king. You want to be the father of an extraordinary son.'

A feeling he could not fathom had kept the king from listening too attentively to the hunter's words. But now, these new revelations that corresponded so exactly to the thoughts buried in his innermost being made him leap from his seat and go and sit on the mat next to the soothsayer. The king was filled with anxiety and had no wish to hear any other voice but that of the stranger.

The hunter dreamily stroked his great head with the plaited tresses, which he had unloosened. Then he suddenly began speaking again:

'By Allah, the young girl who will come, escorted by two young men – you must marry her! She will bring into the world a son who shall extend his power over all the lands of the savanna . . . He shall extend as far as 'the salt water' the kingdom you have inherited from your ancestors. He shall make the name of the Manden immortal for ever. This son and his descendants shall exert a hegemony of many centuries over these lands.'

In this case, as in most of the savanna lands, religious beliefs and divinatory practices – today as in the past – are so intimately linked and mingled that the soothsayer did not realize that in using the word 'Allah' he was employing a non-animist vocabulary.

'Did you tell me this in order to . . . ?' said the king. And he left his phrase uncompleted.

'In order to give you pleasure?' the soothsayer completed the question.

'Well, anyhow . . .' the king said.

But he did not finish his sentence, because he was suddenly convinced that in any case all that the soothsayer had told him would come true sooner or later. The latter went on immediately:

'As soon as you have sacrificed a red bull calf, and let its blood sink into the soil of the Manden, that young girl will come all unexpectedly, and take you by surprise.'

The king frowned, for this news was so marvellous, he could not be really certain that the prophesied arrival of the young girl whose offspring were to immortalize the name of his kingdom and its king would ever take place. And he could not be absolutely certain whether the soothsayer was just talking to give him pleasure or not.

'I shall never weary of waiting for her,' the king said.

'I am only a passing stranger, Mansa, and I must return at once to the land of Dô. Farewell!'

'Farewell! And our thanks go with you!' said the king.

The stranger started back along the path, bare-foot, as he had come, his quiver hanging from his left shoulder.

As for the king, was it the search for his country's fame and the triumph of his personal ambitions that made him cherish the undying hope of being the father of a great king despite his distrust of the soothsaying hunter? Perhaps. Perhaps he was also hoping to arm himself in advance against an eventual bloody invasion of his fragile kingdom, and perhaps his inflexible obstinacy was bracing his fanatical determination to marry at all costs this phantom girl the soothsaying hunter had just told him about? There was no doubt about it, because as soon as the stranger departed, the king had sacrificed a red bull calf, and afterwards made sure that its blood had sunk deep into the soil of the Manden.

THE BUFFALO-PANTHER WOMAN

Many moons had passed since the famous lightning visit of the soothsaying hunter of Dô to Maghan Kön Fatta. Prince Dankaran Tuman had grown; he was now ten years old.

Then one day, as usual, the king and his attendants had been relaxing in the shade from break of day – and the day was so long! It was only the giant bombax tree next to the palace that cast a satisfactory shadow. This was certainly the coolest spot in the town. In the dry season – and it was the dry season now – it was terribly hot; the heat itself had a kind of tangible presence; it felt solid, and almost unbearable. There was no protection against this baking heat except the giant bombax tree whose foliage was so dense that the sun, bombarding nature with all its jets of fire from morning to night, was never able to penetrate it. All the other trees of the savanna, at this season of the year, had such scraggy foliage that it could only be compared with the scant leafage of baobabs in the desert regions. That is why the majority of the inhabitants of Niani simply used to go and spend their afternoons beside the Sankarani.

Maghan Kön and his companions, for their part, contented themselves with the shade of the giant bombax tree; they never went on the bank of sand in the river; besides, no one would have understood or even accepted the presence of the sovereign and his followers among the common people on the banks of the river. The royal office in the Manden entailed formal requirements that Maghan Kön Fatta could not waive without incurring the disapproval of the Council of Ancients, even though personally he would have liked, just as everyone else did, to relax on the sandbanks. But the king's movements were strictly regulated, as they had been since time immemorial, and the ceremonial governing them was unalterably fixed. Custom did not allow him to present himself to his people except on the occasion of great festivals.

Well, wasn't this an ideal form of distraction, and one ready to hand? At any rate, neither the population nor the king need wonder what was the best way to spend the stifling afternoons of

Niani, where, as the rainy season had not yet begun, work in the fields was at a standstill. And so people looked upon this period as a holiday time.

Fatumata Bérété, come to charm her husband's idle hours and to listen to Gnankuman-Dua's three-stringed guitar, was also seated in the shade of the bombax tree, facing her king. She appeared to have regained her beauty, with that slenderness of the Malinké woman who, during her 'change days'[1], was allowed to take only a court-bouillon flavoured with a few herbs, with the intention both of keeping her figure and of assuring the freshness and purity of her breath.

She had long, thick, woolly black hair. Whenever the griot accelerated the guitar's rhythm as he sang the king's praises to the heavens, she would be seized by movements that swung her hair now over her broad forehead, now over her temples, as if the harmattan that whips the leaves of trees were now whipping Fatumata Bérété's loosely-plaited tresses. These movements had no relation to her little head – which she kept motionless all the time – but were provoked only by the ecstasies into which the griot's praise-singing plunged her.

This little head was set on a gazelle-like neck; when her hair was shaken in this manner, drowning her face, she resembled the water fairy, familiar to all in the lands of the savanna, called 'Mamie Watta'.

The king, whose reputation for beauty was equalled only by her own, adored her, and was constantly showering her with presents whenever he returned from hunting.

It was the first time the young wife had come to sit before her old husband. Was it the cool shade of the great bombax tree that had drawn her there? Perhaps. But also she had come to sit there perhaps for no special reason, just for pleasure, perhaps; and perhaps it was to remind the king, by her presence before him, that the moment had come to wean princess Nana Triban, now two years old .

1 Change wife: among polygamists, every wife has the right to co-habit with her husband for two days. During these two days she is called the change wife, and it is her duty to prepare the meals. The two days themselves are known as change days, when each wife takes it in turn to live with the husband.

The brother of Fatumata, Tomano Mandian Bérété, one of the five royal marabouts, had given his sister in marriage to Maghan Kön Fatta, the better to attach himself to the throne. Now, in the shadow of the bombax tree, the married pair, having gazed at one another a long time, were smiling. But what sort of smile was it? It was the smile of true love: the love that is crystallized in the crucible of the years, that disregards those interminable disputes inseparable from life in common, and that was obedient to no laws but those of the heart and mutual attraction. The two loved one another deeply. The griot, who alone knew the secret of entering into their most intimate thoughts, was fully aware of the nature of this great love. He gazed at them with envious eyes as, plucking the strings of his guitar like a man possessed, he recalled the great exploits of their ancestors.

Then the royal couple stopped smiling and concentrated their attention on what the griot was singing. Was it his chants they were listening to? Perhaps. Perhaps, too, they were just meditating on the meaning of the chants; and perhaps it was the very ecstasy of his adulation that intoxicated them, and at the same time made them fall silent, as if abstracted.

Yet Maghan Kön Fatta had never coveted power; he had been named king without his wishing it; it was simply that as a successor to the late Namandian the Council of the Ancients had considered him to be the most fitting representative of the royal family of the Manden. At present, was he being drawn insensibly along the slippery path of sensual pleasure by Fatumata Bérété and her thirst for sensation? Perhaps. Perhaps too he was simply fulfilling one of the duties of his royal function; perhaps he was not listening to the griot at all; perhaps his mind was elsewhere.

The queens of the Manden had long since ceased to exercise any political right; yet their influence was still considerable in the private lives of their royal husbands. Thus they acted indirectly upon the king, and, through him, on public life.

Meanwhile, three strangers – two famous hunters and a tall young girl with a hump back – weary with hours of walking, were listlessly making their way towards Niani. They were moving in single file, and already they were within sight of the gates of the town. As soon as she saw the pyramidal thatched roofs of the huts, Sogolon Condé, placed between the hunters and as it were framed by their youthful bodies, suddenly came to a halt. She carefully re-adjusted her loincloth and draped herself in her white veil, then, discreetly, she took out of her travelling bag a fine toothpick. Rejoining her companions, and keeping pace with them, she began a leisurely but studied toilet, paying especial attention to her teeth, her radiant smile. 'In this town I am about to enter, no one knows what I have been through, not the name of Sogolon the Hunchback, which does me so much discredit!' she was thinking.

The three travellers were now following a path that skirted the enclosure for the bulls; because it was so broad and clean, it could lead only to the royal palace.

All at once Maghan Kön Fatta and his companions interrupted their conversation. The griot had stopped playing his three-stringed guitar, and had stopped chanting. Their attention, their entire attention, had been captured by three strangers who were entering the palace grounds, and who were now advancing towards the giant bombax tree. When they had come within two paces of the king, they bowed to him in salutation. On the orders of his elder brother, Moké Dantuman began to speak.

'*Mansa!*'[1] he said, 'we are come from the far-off land of Dô. My brother is called Moké Mussa and I am called Moké Dantuman. We were born in Kri and belong to the Traoré tribe. Our firm resolve to overcome the buffalo that long had terrorized the inhabitants of the land of Dô had led us to that country to try our luck. The young person accompanying us is called Sogolon Condé; she is one of the daughters of Dô-Samô, king of Dô. As she is a princess, we deemed her worthy of becoming your wife.'

The great chagrin Sogolon had known on leaving the land of her birth had changed to an overwhelming joy.

Was it the sympathetic and delicate way Moké Dantuman had presented her to the king that made Sogolon's heart overflow with happiness? Perhaps. Perhaps it was just that she had a naturally smiling face, perhaps she was smiling for the pure joy of smiling, and perhaps it was this offer of her in marriage to the king by her travelling companion that made her radiant with happiness.

---

1 *Mansa* means King; here it means 'Sire'.

The king, overwhelmed, lowered his head. Had the soothsaying hunter's prediction crossed his mind again? Perhaps he was just pondering the matter before giving his final decision, and perhaps lowering his head was the king's way of indicating his agreement.

Fatumata Bérété, always discreet and considerate, had withdrawn as soon as she saw the strangers under the bombax tree; in the Manden, a woman's place during the daytime was at the hearth; she ordered a servant to serve the king's guests with fresh, cold water.

'Sit down and drink,' Gnankuman-Dua told them.

They sat down on the mat beside the griót and passed the goblet from hand to hand. Their foreheads were bathed in great drops of sweat which they wiped off with the backs of their hands. But though Sogolon, draped in her veil, and with lowered head, was able to conceal her staring eyes, the hump on her back stood out clearly.

The griot, sensing how acutely embarrassed his king must be, went on talking.

'As you are from Kri,' he said, 'you belong to us. So naturally you will be the guests of the king! . . . Now tell us what adventure it was that led to this young girl's having to accompany you.'

Moké Dantuman, the younger of the two hunters, but by far the more perspicacious, valorous and audacious, approached the king, kneeled before him, then, fixing his eyes upon the sovereign, began to speak again:

'Like every hunter, we had heard about the mysterious buffalo running wild in the land of Dô and laying waste the rice fields,' he said. 'It appeared that all our fellow hunters in the land of Dô had been wiped out by the beast.'

Moké Dantuman related their meeting with Dô-Kamissa at the *Massidi Sandan Koro*. He told of the marriage agreement with her double, Sogolon, in return for the secret which Dô-Kamissa alone could reveal, and which allowed them to hunt the animal successfully. Finally he recounted their triumph in Dafolo and their return to Niani in the company of Sogolon Condé . . .

Without waiting for the king's reply, he returned to his place, either because he felt he had told everything, or because he was weary of his kneeling position after so long a journey. In any case, to have prolonged the period spent kneeling in front of the king would have been considered discourteous.

As for Moké Mussa, he remained in his place, silent and as it were detached from the proceedings Was he remembering all the discomfiture he had suffered at young Sogolon's hands since their departure from Dafolo? Perhaps. Perhaps, too, he was simply thinking of the way the women of Dô had booed them in the festival square; or perhaps his unexpected return to the land of his ancestors had made him dumb and silent.

The fact is that all those days his brother and he had passed in the far-off land of Dô had really been days of deep anxiety, days during which they had seen not a soul they knew. Also, the country of the Manden was to their eyes not just one country, it was the whole world! It was now, above all, the country where they were among their own people again, the familiar country of the savannas they were luxuriating in, those plains so plentiful during the rainy season, but so barren and drought-stricken during the long dry season.

The griot, who knew exactly how to interpret every one of his master's movements, had as it were insinuated himself into the king's thoughts; so he guessed that the latter had accepted the offer, and replied for him thus:

'You two hunters are the guests of the king,' he said, looking at Moké Mussa and Moké Dantuman. 'You shall stay with us here in Niani until the marriage of Sogolon Condé with our sovereign is celebrated. After the ceremonies you may return home if you so desire.'

From that day onwards the two young men's relationship with the court was one of the greatest cordiality.

When the marriage date had been fixed, Maghan Kön Fatta invited the other kings of the savanna to attend. They, like himself, all had a more or less powerful ancestral totem.

The sovereigns whose names now follow had replied to the invitation:

Maka-taga-Djigi-Dumbuya[1], the eagle man, founding king of Nora-Soba.

1 Maka-taga-Djigi-Dumbuya was the father of Fakali Kumba and Fakali Daba. He returned from Mecca bringing with him the greatest fetishes and instruments for tilling and ploughing to the Manden.

Fula-Mansa-Dian, the lion man, founding king of Uassulu. His descendants are the Sidibé, Diakité and Sangaré.

Sadi Sooro, Camara 'dalikimbon'[1], the serpent man, king of Tabon.

Moké Mussa and Moké Dantuman, the panther men, representing Dô-Samô-Condé, the buffalo-panther man, king of Dô, today called Sankaran.

Sirakuman Konaté, the tiger man, king of Toron.

Dansô Tuman, Camara 'sinikimbon'[2], king of Sibi.

Séni Gnakan Traoré, the monkey man, king of Magnakadu Kankran.

For a long time, in all the lands of the savanna, there was talk of nothing but the marriage ceremonies of Maghan Kön Fatta with Sogolon.

In the Manden itself, each of the nine provinces, each tribe, had sent its representatives.

In Niani itself there were already present the five marabouts, not native-born, but invited by Maghan Kön Fatta who had entrusted them with the Islamization of his people, and who wanted their help, from an occult point of view, in his conquests. They were:

> Tomono Mandian Bérété
> Saidu Koman
> Sengben Mara Cissé
> Sadi Maghan Diané
> Siriman Kanda Touré

Gnankuman-Dua Kuyaté, whose ancestral totem was the hawk, represented the griot castes at Sogolon's marriage ceremonies. All the peoples had sent large delegations to take part in them, so that the birthright of the child born to Maghan Kön Fatta and Sogolon would be recognized by all.

---

1 The Camara Dalikimbon were the blacksmith princes Camara of Tabon.
2 The Camara Sinikimbon were the non-blacksmith princes Camara of Sibi.

One notable absentee was Sumaoro Kanté. Everyone was fully aware of the baneful existence of the blacksmith 'Diarasso'[1] of Sosso, a tidal wave of new-found but already devastating dynamism; and those who were most keenly aware of its power were Sadi Sooro Camara, king of Tabon, and Dô-Samô Condé, whose authority Diarasso had begun to undermine.

Sumaoro's repeated incursions into the kingdoms bordering on Sosso had as their unacknowledged aim the radical transformation of the savanna lands, leading finally, step by step, to their total subjection to his rule.

The engagement and marriage ceremonies were organized, as they had always been, according to custom and an inalterable etiquette.

At dawn on the day before the marriage, Moké Mussa and Moké Dantuman, representing the parents of the young bride-to-be, gathered together on the sandbanks of the River Sankarani all those of the same age as herself. As soon as the sun rose, the young girls eagerly threw themselves into the water, and, to the beat of the tom-tom, they played for some time, singing and splashing each other in fun. What were these frolickings? They were the final revels enjoyed by Sogolon and the girls of her own age, the same kind of revels that would have been organized for her on the eve of her wedding if she had become engaged in the land of Dô.

From time to time the joyful revellers would climb out on the sandbanks and form a circle round the drummer; there they would sing louder than ever, clapping their hands to the rhythm. After a while, one of the girls would leave the circle and start dancing, followed one by one by her companions.

Sogolon and her companions spent the whole day at the river, sometimes bathing, sometimes singing and dancing on the sandbanks, sometimes banding together to pound the worn linen of the old and needy.

Such was the custom in all the lands of the savanna. As for the reason for this custom, why the day before the marriage the young bride-to-be was supposed to associate only with her own age group, one can only say that it was simply the custom. It was

1 Diarasso: the Kanté were the blacksmith princes of Sosso, who had mastered the element of fire.

also the custom for the companions of her own age to gather in the house of her parents (in this case represented by Moké Mussa and Moké Dantuman) and spend a large part of the night there with her.

It may be assumed that the young girls' frolickings in the River Sankarani and the celebrations organized that night at the home of the fiancée's parents served as the one occasion or opportunity her age group had to leave a final happy memory in the heart of their departing sister, a memory she would be able to fall back upon in moments of anguish during her future life as the mother of a family. She would be able to remember that occasion and for a brief interlude return to the happy days of girlhood. This aesthetic emotion was accompanied by another, more heart-felt: the assurance that her membership of her age group would endure beyond all considerations of time and place.

On leaving her girlhood behind, she would retain the bitter-sweet nostalgia of things forever gone, which would afford her constant solace.

When night fell, the girls of Sogolon's age gathered at Moké Mussa and Moké Dantuman's hut for a gargantuan banquet of many dishes. They set to with a will, but naturally there was no question of their being able to do justice to all the bowls of millet and meat that had been assembled for the feast. It was not that the young girls and the numerous female griots they had invited went at it half-heartedly: each member of the group had lent a hand in preparing this banquet, and so they fell upon the food with avidity, with the appetite of young lionesses – nevertheless, they could not polish off the whole of such a mighty meal.

But did Sogolon rejoice at such abundance? She may have rejoiced at the sight, but with some secret reservations. Was it because she dreaded this marriage? Perhaps. Perhaps, too, she was not looking forward to tomorrow's ceremonies and to what would happen when they were over. Perhaps she was longing for the honeymoon, and perhaps the burden of having to take leave of her loving friends the next day was already making her feel sad?

She was forcing herself to smile, but it was a feeble sort of smile. The oldest of the female griots – called Tuntun Manian – in an attempt to alleviate the sadness in which Sogolon felt herself suddenly plunged, began intoning a chant in honour of Sogolon's future husband. Almost at once the assembled guests took up the refrain of this chant:

> Aba agna lo nnédo,
> Agna ni Maraka kalé lé la lo nné do,
> Aba bolo la nné kan,
> A bolo ni koinin gnuma lé la la nné kan
> > > Coba yé!

> Aba sén la nné kan
> A sén ni sambara gbé lé la la nné kan!
> > > Coba yé

> Aba kun lanné kan
> A kun ni Fula gbé lé la la nné kan!
> > > Coba yé

> *When he looks at me,*
> *His eyes painted with the Sarakollé pastel crayon*
> > > *Looking at me,*

> *When he lays his hand upon me,*
> *His hand with its fine rings is laid upon me,*
> > > *How great an event!*

> *When he lays his head upon me,*
> *His head with its white skull-cap is laid upon me,*
> > > *How great an event!*

This went on late into the night, then Tuntun Manian launched herself into a second chant which was taken up almost at once by the assembled guests:

> Sogolon Condé nin kéra di,
> Sogolon Condé nin kéra di?
> Ifa la lu ba wo tori ko,
> Sébéressé[1], ka be ni a tuma,
> Ina la bomba wo tora yé,
> Sébéressé, ko be ni a tuma

1 *Sébéressé*: onomatopoeic Malinké word, performing a musical function in the poem.

Sogolon Condé, what event,
Sogolon Condé what event?
The great abode of your father stands when you have
  gone,
Sébéressé, all things have their hour,
The great hut of your mother stands back home,
Sébéressé, all things have their hour.

This chanting went on until the first plaintive notes of the cock were heard. Sogolon's companions were softly weeping.

She watched them weeping, and the weeping clutched at her heart. She thought: 'Must I leave all these companions on the morrow?' Her own eyes brimming with tears, she turned an imploring gaze upon these young girls attending the pre-nuptial feast, and gathered all around her now, as she kneeled at the centre of their circle.

The next day was a Wednesday; it had been appointed the day for the wedding ceremonies because the Wednesday is considered the day of good fortune. Attention had also been paid to the first quarter of the moon, because in former times nothing important was undertaken during that period. There were many metaphysical reasons for this, besides the obvious physiological ones.

So early on the morning of this day Sogolon had been conducted to the female griot Tuntun Manian who, the night before, had directed the choral chants of the wedding eve and who was also the best hairdresser in Niani. Sogolon's future sisters-in-law joined her there; according to custom, they made fun of her. But Tuntun Manian on the contrary did everything she could to reassure the bride-to-be.

'Tonight you must rub my back because you are now my wife,' one of them mocked her.

'No,' said another, 'we shall divide her into three parts: one part will belong to the king, the second part to you, and the third part will be my own share.'

'Anyhow, my little lamb, your freedom is at an end,' said the third one.

'Now then! Now then! Don't worry your little head, and don't listen to the teasing of your naughty sisters-in-law,' the griot said. 'All girls must sooner or later leave their parents to go and live with a husband. Whatever is wrong with that? Nothing bad will befall you, either. Now that you are going to become a woman, and, as I fondly hope, a happy mother, you must have all your courage. Banish sadness from you. A bride, if she wishes to be loved, must be joyous.'

That day, Sogolon had many duties to perform. After her hair had been formally arranged, the old women took her at once to the bathing place for the ritual bath. They undressed her, then splashed her again and again with cold water, then warm water, all the time murmuring in her ears the words her mother and her grandmother had heard before her. The words the old women murmured as they splashed the body of Sogolon were important for her future as a married woman. They were:

'Oh, Sogolon Condé, know that everything in life has two sides! When a child is born, if it is not a boy, it is a girl; in this life, the opposite of youth is old age; the opposite of wealth is poverty; the opposite of good health is sickness. The other side of life is death!

'Sogolon Condé, know that in the act of marriage God the King the All-Powerful was pleased to make us different from the animals; but in that act there are beautiful days like today, and there are inevitably other days, the bad days; your dignity as a woman makes it imperative that you accept either kind with a smile ... Your honour also requires you to offer your heart and your body only to your husband, and you are to submit them to him absolutely. If you drink honey water with your husband, then too it is natural that you should gladly drink to the lees with him the bitter cup of the bastard mahogany, for your devotion and submission to the laws of marriage are the one certain guarantee of your children's success in life. Have no uneasiness, for custom will protect with the utmost strictness your conjugal rights; God also will watch over them, for he is great, the one Supreme Being. And he favours neither husband nor wife nor child; he favours only one who treads the path of truth. For God is without equal; the Truth alone approaches him in greatness!'

After the ritual bath, the old women stayed a long while with Sogolon telling her their own experiences as wives, experiences intended to illuminate the long path that lay before her as a mother. Then they accompanied her to the hut of her adoptive parents, Moké Mussa and Moké Dantuman, where Sogolon rejoined the companions of her own age who were there already, waiting for her. Naturally, as she was now the 'change wife', the old women had limited the young bride-to-be to a very light diet, with the purpose of breaking down her resistance should she be tempted to resist in the arms of her husband.

As for Maghan Kön Fatta, he was following the opposite kind of regimen, in order to build up his strength.

Before going to meet the one who was to be her sister-wife, Fatumata Bérété paid her formal visit to her husband who sat among his guests of honour, under the palaver tree, not far from the palace. The kings had taken their seats in the chairs of state; the five marabouts, Gnankuman-Dua and the delegations from the various Manden tribes were seated on the ground, on a long mat.

She had decked herself out in all her finery; she was standing in front of the king, turning her back to him, not to tempt him, but to show him her displeasure; and her large eyes were red and bathed in tears, perhaps more tearful than they had ever been during her last ten years as queen of the Manden and mother of a family.

'But why is the face of Fatumata Bérété so sad?' Maghan Kön Fatta wondered. 'There is no call for my wife to be so sad; in marrying Sogolon I have simply been obeying the custom!' he thought. 'Or could she be feeling jealous? A wife never accepts it with good grace when another woman enters her husband's life, even though the Muslim religion allows it!'

However, this explanation did not satisfy him at all. What Maghan Kön Fatta was seeing was not her eyes bathed in tears: it was a refusal (he was a long time seeking the right word) a 'categorical' refusal was the term he suddenly hit upon. But this word was not sufficiently expressive: in the very stance Fatumata Bérété took up there smouldered a savage jealousy, like that of a tigress suddenly become wildly jealous, a jealousy mingled with ferocity; yes, it was a kind of barely-concealed revolt against the king who now, despite their great love for one another, had betrayed her.

The king stood up, took Fatumata by the arm and drew her

some distance away from the guests.

'Don't touch me!' she cried. 'You aren't my husband any more!'

But she did not repulse him: she was weeping, clinging desperately to the king's chest, sobbing:

'So after all, you prefer that ugly Sogolon to me, don't you? Tell me you don't like her better than me!'

'Woman! Woman! You shall always live in my heart. Do not be sad, and do not cry: all I want is to establish solid links between the mighty land of Dô and the Manden; to do that, I have to marry Sogolon. To make up for it, go and take ten milk cows from my herd, they are for you! But I beg you, do not disturb the ceremony this evening.'

'No, I shall not disturb it,' she said bitterly, wiping her tears away with the back of her hand.

So in the end she just gave in; she laid her head on her husband's shoulder and went on weeping noisily. The king too was wiping his tears away, saying . . . what was he saying? Everything and nothing, but whatever he was saying was of no importance; nor can we be sure, either, that Fatumata Bérété understood a word of what he was saying; she heard only the sound of her husband's reassuring voice, and that was enough for her; gradually her sobbing died away and as it diminished she grew calm again.

Having regained her calm, she left the king; having regained her calm, she returned to the group of women and girls. But now she knew that this evening Sogolon would come to the palace, that nothing could stop her arrival. Perhaps she had known this all along, since the day when two young hunters, accompanied by a tall young hump-backed girl, had entered the presence of Maghan Kön Fatta and his entourage in the shade of the giant bombax tree. Yes, indeed, she must have seen the griot Dua bringing the ten cola nuts that were to consecrate the engagement – the engagement that was to lead to the ceremonies of marriage now about to take place.

She had cast every kind of evil spell, assisted by all the old crones and witches of Niani, to prevent this marriage. And all through her struggles, all the time she had discreetly visited every night the sorcerers and marabouts of the town, she had had to watch the wheels slowly turning: first one wheel, then another, and then yet another, until other wheels, many more wheels, more perhaps than anyone could see, began their inscrutable turning. And what could have been done to stop those wheels-within-wheels? One could only watch them turning, watching the wheels of destiny turning, turning. It was the destiny of Maghan Kön Fatta that he should wed Sogolon Condé, the ugly daughter from the far-off land of. Dô! And now, Fatumata Bérété started a revolt – but only a feeble revolt – against the young girl who had come to trouble the peace of her marriage. 'Just let her enter the king's dwelling, that Sogolon Condé! My spells will certainly strike her down more easily in the palace,' she told herself.

At dusk, the procession began to line up in front of the house of Moké Mussa and Moké Dantuman. Suddenly a great clamour of tom-toms throbbed on the evening air. Sogolon, escorted by old women, emerged from the hut, while the female griot Tuntun Manian intoned the chant of departure and the girls joined in. The nuptial procession moved off towards the palace of Maghan Kön Fatta. The bride-to-be was perched on a horse, which one of her age group was leading by the bridle. Soon there was a river of lifted hands and heads covered with iridescent scarves slowly flowing down the main street of Niani, the hands clapping rhythmically, the heads singing the chant of the bride's departure:

> Ilé Ba Wa tunkan na,
> Ina té tunkan na, Ifa te tunkan na,
> Hé Hé Hé Ha, ndoni an bè sogoma dé;
> tunkan ma Lambé lon!

When you leave for another land,
Your mother is not in that other land,
You father is not in that other land,
Hé Hé Hé Ha younger sister may we meet on the morrow;
The land you are going to knows nothing of rank and status.

The great crowd that had gathered on the processional route divided and lined up on either side of the road. The river of clapping hands and singing heads continued to flow between two rows of admiring men, women and children howling with delight.

The two rows formed by the crowd to let the river pass were dense, compact. The men standing at the back must have seen little more than Sogolon, all in white, perched on her horse. But the children, naturally, joined in the spreading wake of the procession that they helped to swell. It was always so: the men were never able to see more than the bride on her horse. But that was enough for them; the bride-to-be's departure was a women's affair. Men! No, men had no say in the matter.

The female griot, Tuntun Manian, went on singing in her noble voice, and the procession tirelessly responded, echoing her chant.

Sogolon was not without qualms about her passage from the life of a young pubescent girl to that of a married woman. If the truth be told, she was very anxious. Of course the marriage ceremonies were familiar to her, because since her earliest childhood she had watched young brides-to-be departing for the conjugal hut; but there was a whole important area of a married woman's life that remained unknown to her, apart from what happens on the first night spent with a man, which all the young girls knew was pretty stormy. And as the procession approached Maghan Kön Fatta's palace, Sogolon's thoughts kept returning to that first night now awaiting her. But the choruses of her young companions sustained her, the tom-toms sustained her.

When the procession had reached the centre of the town, it paused for a while and there was silence. The tom-toms were silent, then the procession started again, repeating the new chant that Tuntun Manian had begun singing:

> Itama kognan Nkodo Mussoni
> i tama Kognan ikana bila gbangban dô.

> *Tread softly, my little big sister!*
> *Tread softly, and you won't get covered with dust!*

Now the river of hands and heads was flowing in darkness, for night had fallen; but on that night it was fairly light: the torches lit by the women, and which they held high above the crowd, illuminated the principal street, supplementing the pallid radiance of the rising moon.

The human river's meandering flow was now approaching the palace of king Maghan Kön Fatta, who was sitting there surrounded by his guests of honour. He was talking to them in a loud voice, gesticulating vigorously; he seemed to be addressing them as a group, but it was as if he no longer knew quite what to say to them: the progress of the nuptial procession, which was now within view, must have been fully occupying his thoughts. Could he have been asking news of his guests' families, or could he be engaged in some political discussion? Perhaps . . . But he had no more time to continue those palavers: the noise of the procession would have drowned his voice. So he sat dreamily stroking his beard and eyeing the bride-to-be as she passed by on her horse, as if borne along by the river, the tumultuous river of chanting and hand-clapping young girls. The light in his eyes grew livelier; he suddenly had a vision of the naked body of Sogolon and he thought of the way their two bodies would embrace – the youthful body of Sogolon, so seductive, and his own, now old: a sombre, fiery current ran through his loins; he choked on his own spit, and was ashamed of his drooling.

But in a little while, would he still feel ashamed, in the marriage chamber? There was no way of saying; he sighed, and stopped stroking his beard.

A large crowd of men and children had rushed to the palace to await the arrival of the nuptial cortège. The whole town was rejoicing; only the very old did not take part in the dance and the celebrations. But not being able to leave their huts did not deprive them of participation in that night's rejoicings. From their homes, they could hear the rippling beat of the tom-toms and the chanting of the young girls.

But when the procession suddenly stopped a hundred paces from the palace, the fever that was making them chant, the fever that had seized the tom-tom players ceased abruptly, because Sogolon's youthful companions, for a joke, had laid hold of the horse, holding it back as if to prevent it from advancing, as if to detain among them just a little longer their betrothed sister. But Sogolon, still perched on her horse, was forcefully seized and lifted down by the king's cousins – sons of Kono Koro Semba and Namandian – who ran off with her sitting astride their shoulders. The bride-to-be's companions followed close behind,

93

and all of them entered the marriage chamber.

Maghan Kön Fatta, sitting some way apart with his assistants and his guests of honour, watched this part of the procession entering his palace and could hardly contain his impatience. But he would wait until later, much later, before joining Sogolon.

Fatumata Bérété, trying to conceal as best she might her jealous rage, pretended to be nice to the one whom she had no desire to see entering her husband's bedchamber, by helping her into the king's bed. A sister-in-law of the king entered the nuptial chamber and placed the symbolic calabash of honey under the bed; when she had done so, she joined in the dance with her sisters, intoning the chant of welcome to the family of the bride-to-be:

> Ke ba yé kolon kodo bu lé di,
> é Fu . . . u . . . u, é Fa . . . a . . . a!

> Man is but millet dough in the old mixing-bowl,
> é Fu. . . u . . . u, é Fa . . . a . . . a!
> Gone with the wind . . . Gone with the wind!

Perhaps this chant recalled those words whispered in her ear during the ritual bath? Perhaps, too, they were a warning against any deceptive promises made her by her husband during the honeymoon, and which might not be kept; and perhaps it was simply the custom for the sisters-in-law of the bride-to-be to sing this chant.

It should merely be noted that after her attendants had introduced her into the nuptial chamber, it was the custom for the sisters-in-law to start a dance and to sing this satirical song.

Later on, in the middle of the night, Maghan Kön Fatta took leave of his companions and entered the palace whose courtyard now was silent, for his sisters-in-law had stopped their chanting and dancing; he felt sure he would find Sogolon all alone in the bridal chamber. But when he quietly peeped into his dwelling he saw a host of young girls noisily surrounding his bride; almost at once his impatience had fled; such a crowd! Why did they not leave? 'Will my bride be surrounded much longer by such a turbulent throng?' he wondered. And silently, not wanting anyone to see him and recognize him, he made his way back and spent a long time walking up and down one of the sleeping streets of his town; then he went back to his dwelling. There, finding Sogolon stretched naked on the wedding couch, under the mosquito net, and now completely free of her companions, he lay down beside her, very close beside her . . .

Just as she had practised her spells on Moké Mussa, she now exercised them on the king himself. The sovereign Manden-Ka time after time vainly invoked his double, who did not succeed in overpowering the bride's double. 'Why won't you submit to me?' he asked her. But almost at the same moment he reproached himself for having asked her such a question: how could Sogolon have answered such a question?

At dawn, the air had begun to get warm again – during the night it had been cool – and already he was feeling ill at ease, but not on account of the heat. He seemed to feel that the departing night was carrying off all his chances of success in possessing Sogolon, whose categorical refusal to submit to him had completely annihilated his manhood.

Was the bride wanting to show the king the power of her own double by refusing to submit to him? Perhaps. Perhaps, too, she was resisting simply out of feminine caprice on this first bridal night, or perhaps the absence of an actual member of her Dô family at the marriage ceremonies had annoyed her?

When the cock had finished crowing for the third time, the griot Gnankuman-Dua presented himself at the palace. He peeped through the front door of the royal dwelling, and caught sight of the sovereign Manden-Ka stretched out on the nuptial couch; without further delay, the griot began to intone praises upon praises;

> Trublu Kabala Simbon,[1]
> Dion Sina Dugu Sina, Manden Koliba Sina
> Dombon na Maghan, Kababo Maghan,
> Sosso Simbon Salaba, Sama Sogho Simbon Salaba,
> Diu rulen Ko Senkan na wonti koli

1 Malinké incantation composed of untranslatable nominalizations, intended to rouse the king to ecstasy.

Samo Dayara, Bakary Dayana,
Kri Danfa, Danfa ani Fuén Kuru,
Fatumata Dandan Brissa,
Ni imi idan na kali iti idan na ko Lon!
Trublu Kabala Simbon.

He who resembles the man, resembles the village, resembles Manden
  Koliba,
Dombon na Maghan, uprooter of rocks!
Sosso Simbon Sabala, Simbon Sabala, the elephant hunter!
Diu rulen Ko Senkan Wonti Koli!
Samo Dayara Bakary Dayara!
Kri Danfa, Danfa ani Fuén Kuru
Fatumata Dandan Brissa
He who feels and knows no limits!

The king lay watching the griot on his threshold with a care-worn expression on his face.

Such excessive praises were surely more likely to embarrass than to encourage him. Had he really been successful during the night? Absolutely not. Despite his invocation of his dread ancestral totem, he had been roundly defeated: defeated by a young bride, for Sogolon's double had shown itself to be even more redoubtable than his own. Maghan Kön Fatta would have liked to ask the griot to be quiet, but that would have been contrary to custom. So he pretended to be listening to his praises for some time, before wearily replying:

'I appreciate your praises, griot,' he said, 'but nothing, absolutely nothing I could do was of any avail. Is this young girl I married at such great expense a human being or a monster? I can't make her out. During the night, I invoked my double: he did not succeed in overpowering her! Her hair sticks out like the prickles of the porcupine whenever one tries to embrace her.'

As Maghan Kön Fatta spoke, the deep distress into which his young bride's resistance had plunged him appeared clearly in his face and could be heard in his shaking voice. Meanwhile, the old women who had come to the palace to get the loincloth of ravished virginity, which was to be displayed to the public, and the calabash of honey, were driven away by Gnankuman-Dua.

The king, stretched out on his bed, lay all day shut in his room, though with the doors ajar. Suddenly he was overcome with melancholy forebodings. 'Is Sogolon really strong enough to resist my advances?' He raised his eyes and gazed at the woodwork of the roof, as if trying to count its bamboos, then lowered his eyes again. 'Though she is hump-backed, and only a young girl, she certainly possesses a most extraordinary power, and an ancestral totem that could never be tamed. But was such untamed behaviour fitting in the circumstances? A young bride refusing to offer her body to the one she had chosen? No, it did not make sense,' he murmured to himself. And began to feel even more abysmally depressed than he had during the night.

When his thoughts turned to his guests of honour, and to the terrible shame he must feel if they learned the sad news, he felt all the more abysmally depressed, even more than at the moment when Sogolon turned her body into the body of a porcupine all bristling with spikes, making it impossible to embrace her. Even more than at the moment when his own double, the lion – the sovereign beast of the savanna – had not succeeded in conquering Sogolon and her spells. Melancholy thoughts occupied his mind again – his defeat at the hands of Sogolon had wounded his male pride and the bitter memory of that defeat still haunted him: this abject state lasted until the daytime's fiery sun, and the warmth that accompanied it, no longer filled the sky.

The king did not leave his palace until it was night, to make a discreet visit to his guests, then returned late, very late, though not to go at once to bed. Instead, he took down from its hook on the wall his game-bag containing the smooth stones which, even to this day, are the favourite divinatory instruments of the Malinké hunters.

Before beginning, Maghan Kön Fatta, a great sorcerer, because he was also a master in the arts of the chase, sat down on a mat spread on the earth of his bedchamber, then poured out in front of him the contents of the bag, which held thirty stones.[1] Sogolon, stretched on the bed in front of him, had fallen asleep long ago.

1 The stones were revealed to Mamadi Kani, king of the Manden, by the gods of the hunters: Sani and Kontron. He passed on the secret to his descendants. Sand, Arab in origin, came to the Manden barely two centuries ago.

Then he divided the stones into three heaps, the first of which, carefully placed to one side, was the heap of spare stones. After that, he took the second and the third in either hand, and, tapping on the ground the back of his right hand, making it bounce as if on elastic, he softly whispered:

Dankun bèrè!
Foloon kun bèrè!
Ko dogoni kalabo ba!
Ika-son-la-son-tan-na!
Ikana-son-na-ma-no-koloon-bila!
Nné ni Sogolon né gnon na,
Nbe fe a sii nkön a son nin tè!
Saraka me nin ndèmè woro!
Ni woro lé, woro yé bo,
Ni sissè lé wodi, sissè yé bo!
Aba – Gbèlèya-kè, Sogolon-di-kè-nnè . . . Mussa di fé
Maro-maro wo yé doon . . . Kumadissè-ni-diaransé Danté!

Stone of the crossroads!
Stone of the catchwater ditch!
Revealer of hidden things!
Find no guilt in the innocent!
Never lose track of someone at fault!
Sogolon and I are at cross purposes!
I long to take her in my arms, but she refuses!
Tell me what sacrifice will help me!
If it is the cola, let the stone say so!
If it is the chicken, let the stone say so!
Whatever happens, Sogolon shall be my wife,
If Maro-maro puts himself between Kumadissè and Diaransé!

Then he turned to the stones in his left hand, the back of which he tapped on the ground just as he had done with his right hand, making it bounce gently:

Féu! Féu! Féu!
Dakun Bèrè!
Foloon kun bèrè!

Ko dogonï kalabɔ ba!
Ika-son-la-son-Tanna!
Ikana-son-na-ma-no-koloon-bila
Nné ni Sogolon né gnon na!
Nbe fe a sii nkön a son ne tè!
Ni a tè nabin féu;
Kadilan Bolo kolon yé bo fondo la!

No! No! No!
Stone of the crossroads!
Stone of the catchwater ditch!
Revealer of hidden things!
Find no guilt in the innocent!
Never lose track of someone at fault!
Sogolon and I are at cross purposes!
I long to take her in my arms, but she refuses!
If what I desire is quite impossible,
May Kadilan, empty-handed, leave the crossroads!

Finally, Maghan Kön Fatta collected all the stones in both hands, and placing them two by two or one by one according to repeated draws, obtained a certain number of figures that the Manden-Ka called 'Bèrè-dén' or 'the Children of the Stones'. In the hexagon of stones thus obtained, were born five children:
  – *Diaransé*, who was a woman, and was composed of four stones.
  – *Kumadissè*, who was a man, and was composed of three stones.
  – *Maro-maro*, who was neither man nor woman: it expressed neutrality and was composed of two stones.
  – *Kadilan* who was a woman, and was composed of five stones.
  – *Séou* who was a woman, and was composed of four stones.
But perhaps we should note that it was not only the number of stones, but also their geometrical disposition that decided the sex or gender of each stone.
The stones chosen by the king, of an elliptical form, having a diameter of about one centimetre, had been selected from those on the banks of the River Sankarani. Before using them, he had ritually steeped them in a decoction of bastard mahogany bark,

so as to ensure the exactitude of the predictions.

After having pondered a long time on the stones which, when they were laid out, had made a sound of rustling shells, a sound that had wakened Sogolon with a start, Maghan Kön Fatta observed that 'Maro-maro', neutrality, had got placed between 'Kumadissè' the man and 'Diaransè' the woman. At once he understood that in order to bring Sogolon from her neutral position it was necessary to frighten her.

All at once, he jumped up from the ground and leaped for the sabre hanging on the wall. Brandishing it wildly, he turned towards the young bride whom he seized by the hair and dragged violently against him.

'Sogolon! Sogolon!' he cried bitterly. 'I shall have no scruples; there is a time for everything, and this is the time neither for scruples nor for joking. I'm going to tell you once and for all what is in my mind. I'm going to slit your throat like a chicken if you continue casting your spells, because you want to humiliate me and that is something I shall never accept! I shall slay you if you persist in your refusal to submit to me, and if I do so no one can say anything against me.'

He had raised the sabre on high as if to slash off Sogolon's head, and he was shouting at the top of his voice. In order to frighten the bride to the point of paroxysm, it was essential for him to shout loudly, in a threatening tone of voice.

'No! No!' she moaned, terrified. 'Don't kill me! I'm yours alone! From now on I'm yours alone!'

He gazed at Sogolon a moment then began shouting louder than ever. For a moment he may have thought that his young bride was going to continue pleading with him. But her girl's fresh face, already streaming with tears, and her imploring eyes disconcerted him; nevertheless he mastered his feelings and went on howling:

'You ungrateful bitch! That's all you are!' he shrieked, furiously; 'The way you entered my dwelling yesterday, at night, was the act of an ungrateful woman, and the way you behaved in my bed was the act of an ungrateful woman. Now tell me, what is the Condé's ancestral totem, that you should be so invincible?'

'The buffalo and the panther!' she replied wretchedly.

'Now listen to me, Sogolon,' he went on.

100

Once more he had begun addressing her brutally, but then he no longer seemed to know what it was he had been wanting to tell her, and he paused. Sogolon's announcement of two such redoubtable ancestral totems had provoked him and probably nonplussed him. Had he been going to tell her that the Condé tribe should content itself with an ancestral totem like those of all the other tribes? Perhaps. But he had no time to say anything: Sogolon's plaintive screams were already ringing through their wedding-hut, as if she had already taken the blade on her neck.

'What's the matter with you?' asked Maghan Kön Fatta. 'Why are you screaming?'

But she could not reply. She was seized by a paralysing terror, the terror of dying, of dying young: she was uttering screams like the bellowings of a slaughtered heifer. Maghan Kön Fatta felt at the end of his patience. He wanted to plug his ears. He did not want to hear any more. He wanted to shut his eyes, so as no longer to see ugly Sogolon bellowing like a heifer; he had the impression that he was seeing before his very eyes an actual heifer, a heifer that the herdsman had left in the corral, while her other companions had been let out to pasture: a distracted heifer, hungry and bellowing with despair.

He clutched her more tightly to him, still holding her by the hair, and nervously whirled his sabre above her head. Then he started shouting at her again:

'So is this all the thanks you give me for what I spent on our marriage? Is this all the reward I get? But get this into your head – you no longer belong to yourself, and don't pretend you do! From now on you belong only to me, because you agreed to it! You agreed to this marriage and I paid out a large dowry for you, as custom demands. Moreover, all the invited guests gave you sumptuous presents. What more do you want?'

She did not reply. She held her hands in front of her, paralysed with fear, as if she wanted to stop the sabre's menacing whirl, as if she wanted to thrust the blade of the sabre away from her. Soon, the force with which he was dragging her by the hair made her scalp tingle as if it were on fire; but she managed to escape that grip of steel that held her prisoner and run and hide in a corner of the room, her youthful face bathed in tears. The king, inconsolable, ran after her and caught her. With his left hand he ripped

101

off her young bride's loincloth and tore her white veil!. . .

'Mansa! Mansa!' she cried pitifully. 'Put down your sabre and from now on I shall be yours, all yours, I swear.'

Without daring to resist, she had allowed herself to be stripped naked, she had agreed, out of fear of being beheaded, to cast no more spells, at any rate not in her husband's bed. There was nothing she would not have consented to.

But what faith could the king put in all these concessions? 'She said: "Mansa! Mansa! Put down your sabre and from now on I shall be yours, all yours, I swear." But will she keep those promises?' He was utterly perplexed.

'Your two travelling companions both agreed that you had behaved like a mighty sorceress towards them,' he hinted. 'It was only after they had failed with you that they handed you over to me. I want the truth! I shall not lower my sabre until you have let me know your intentions'.

'But I've already told you!' cried Sogolon. 'I've told you that from now on I shall be yours, all yours!'

And she raised her hand to lend more weight to this solemn declaration; then, drained of all hope, let it fall again. At the end of her tether, she flung herself trembling on the bed and lay there in the absolute abandonment of her young body. She looked very beautiful like that, despite her hump; the almost demented terror that held her in its grip caused her to retain her human form: she had not thought of turning herself into a porcupine, for she was scared out of her wits by the threatening stance of Maghan Kön Fatta, who suddenly was seized with pity. The king's old heart was moved. He could no longer lift his sabre and whirl it above Sogolon's head. He could no longer shout at her . . .

Now, seeing she had become accessible to male embrace, he went close beside her, very close beside her. He placed the sabre above the bed, as a sort or warning to the young bride, just in case she should be tempted to start casting her spells again or to fight off his advances.

Then, as if spellbound by that feminine nakedness, he hurriedly took off his boubou and his royal pantaloons that he negligently cast on the ground. He did not lose one moment, not even the time necessary for those preliminary tendernesses destined to induce in one's partner the desirable psychological conditions:

Maghan Kön Fatta swooped upon the young virgin like an eagle upon its prey. His massive woolly chest ground the swollen, firm and sensitive breasts of Sogolon the virgin bride. The young girl felt as if her head – already throbbing after such brutal treatment – was now about to burst. But almost like irresistible forces of nature the two naked bodies twined about one another and clung, while she shut her eyes, her face twisting so convulsively she had to cover it with her hands. 'What kind of man is this Maghan Kön Fatta, hurling himself upon me like this, like a wild beast?' she agonized. She was sobbing. The two hearts in their breasts suddenly started to beat as if about to burst, and she felt a kind of searing sensation; she uttered a high, sharp cry, then went on sobbing. What were these convulsions, this cry, these sobs? It was Sogolon Condé's first experience with a man . . .

At that moment, the young bride would have liked to escape, but she could never have released herself from the violent embrace of the king, who, panting, sweating great drops of sweat, held her prisoner in the vice-like grip of his arms. A moment later, when they arose from their nuptial couch, she was already a woman, and, without realizing it, she had conceived that very night. As dawn was breaking at the first cock-crow, and when the cocks began crowing for the second time in the poultry pens, the old female griots of Niani returned once more on their quest at the palace of Maghan Kön Fatta. Sogolon, already awake, had withdrawn to the hut of Kanko, the half-sister of the king, for, among the Mandenka, the most highly-esteemed feminine virtues were indubitably modesty and conjugal fidelity, but also, and above all, filial piety towards all relatives and spouse.

Entering the marriage chamber, the great woman griot, Tuntun Manian, addressed the king in sharp tones:

'My companions and I have come, as we did yesterday, Mansa, to carry out the final act demanded by custom in marriage ceremonies.'

But they did not await the king's reply before seizing the blood-stained loincloth covering the bed, and taking away the calabash· of honey placed beneath the nuptial couch the day that Sogolon entered the dwelling of Maghan Kön Fatta – either because they considered it their natural right to do so, or because they felt that there was absolutely no time to be lost. Indeed, custom decreed that they should rouse the entire sleeping town with their proclamations. So, attacked by this fever, a fever to exhibit virginity's blood-stained loincloth, they could not dally awaiting the king's reply.

As soon as they had taken leave of the king, their sisterhood divided into two groups which took up positions in the palace courtyard, one facing the other.

The first group, in proud possession of the loincloth, displayed it as they began a frenzied dance, clapping their hands and ceremoniously intoning the traditional chant which was usually sung in these circumstances:

Hé ba fani né ni!

Hey! Here is the loincloth of virginity!

But custom also had it that the chant intoned by the first group should be counterpointed by that chanted by the second group, which teasingly sang:

Hé ba fani té
Kai Kurussi kunduné nara
Nu ma ba fani yé!

Hey! This is not the loincloth of virginity,
Now that we all wear short pants
We no longer see the loincloth of virginity!

Was this teasing an indication of a decline in morals in the Manden? Perhaps. But perhaps also these two chants were simply advising a scrupulous attention be paid to these morals, and perhaps after all they were just part of a simple ceremony.

When the women griots considered they had received sufficient gifts from the king and the members of his family, they regrouped and formed a single file. Their eldest, Tuntun Manian, carried on her head the calabash of honey, and took her place at the head of the line. Because of her great reputation, she alone had the privilege of intoning the chants in all the ceremonies. So, drawing her small body to its full height, she gave voice, loudly,

104

as if giving a signal, to the second chant of virginity, a chant which had to be carried to the dwelling of the bride's parents, in this case, to their representatives, Moké Mussa and Moké Dantuman:

> *Ai nbin wo, so mo Lu, bada yé n'kun wo,*
> *Li buda!*

Come all ye village people, on my head I carry a calabash, The calabash of honey!

Then the little line of women set out, walking behind Tuntun Manian, taking up the chant their eldest sister had just intoned. Almost at once they entered the principal street of the township, along which they walked chanting and clapping their hands: it was the same street that the nuptial procession had taken two days before. The young girls, who at that early hour were generally still abed, suddenly were roused from slumber and pricked up their ears as the women griots passed before their huts. From their chanting, which they had heard many times before, they realized that a companion of their maiden games had been found on 'the road of God'[1]. They got up, hastily dressed, then almost frantically – as if Sogolon's good conduct had been reflected on each one of them – ran out to take their places in the line.

The freshness of the dawn air lent their bodies a delightful energy, an energy the growing line utilized to the full, as it strode joyfully along, all singing at the tops of their voices. The singers' bare feet trampled the earth and drew from it an ashen-grey dust, very fine, almost impalpable. As the line progressed, more and more girls joined it, following in the footsteps of the steadily-moving old women griots. In the end it formed an impressive cortège, serpenting solemnly towards the other end of the township, with Tuntun Manian in the lead, the symbolic calabash of honey balanced securely on top of her head.

At that early hour, the streets of Niani were asleep and deserted, but as soon as the serpent-file arrived there, the main street was suddenly overflowing with movement and noise. The snake swayed from side to side, swayed inexorably and irrepressibly,

1 Had been found to be a virgin.

eager to reach the dwelling of Sogolon's guardians.

Once arrived there, the single file moved round it several times, chanting all the more vigorously, and clapping hands with all the more fervour. Suddenly, the two hunters emerged from their hut to receive from the hands of Tuntun Manian and her younger sister the calabash of honey and the loincloth of virginity. Then they addressed themselves to the impressive cortège, which they received with all the eagerness and cordiality which is reserved for the welcoming of such a notable delegation.

Finally, the two guardians would wait until the sun rose in the heavens, when Maghan Kön Fatta would have his griot bring them the cow traditionally destined to recompense Sogolon's mother and reward her for her daughter's good behaviour. The sun soon rose over Niani. A rosy fire rose rapidly into the celestial vault and drove before it the last vestiges of mist. And suddenly, everything became of the same rosy tint as the fire and the mist and the brothers' hut, from which the impressive cortège now took its departure. The mist vanished, and then the capital of the Manden sprang to life. From all the huts, in all the streets, people could be heard greeting one another, with a pang of regret: 'Ambé Sogoma'[1].

Indeed it was a morning and a day devoted entirely to farewells, for, after the ceremonious handing-over of the loincloth of virginity and the calabash of honey to Moké Mussa and Moké Dantuman, the marriage celebrations of Sogolon were at an end. And all the guests of Maghan Kön Fatta – first of all the kings of neighbouring lands, and, after them, the delegations from the villages of the Manden – would depart from Niani before the sun had attained its zenith.

1 Ambé Sogoma means: farewell.

THE BOY 'NANKAMA'

As soon as the linens of virginity had been handed to Sogolon's guardians, the young bride entered the most agreeable – not to say the most memorable – period of her life as a grown woman: the honeymoon. In those days, it lasted three months in the Manden. And in order to guard Sogolon from any untoward encounter with Fatumata Bérété, who was still suffering the pangs of jealousy, Maghan Kön Fatta had entrusted his bride to the care of Kanko, his young sister.

Indeed, in polygamous families, it was not unusual to have conflicts between the wives on one hand, and, on the other hand, between the children born of different mothers. Such rivalry, often very heated, would then become a political crisis.

Therefore, Sogolon only rarely ventured into town: most of the time she remained cloistered in the rear courtyard of the palace in the company of this young woman who had become her actual protector, and whom she willingly obeyed. For though her marriage had brought her into the family circle of Maghan Kön Fatta, Sogolon certainly did not belong to it completely. For one thing, she continued to use her own name, 'Condé', and for another, she was still under cultural obligations to her family in Dô: but the ethics of the Mandenka family compelled her to respect each member of her adopted family.

In addition to the protection of his young sister Kanko, the king had requested Sumusso Konkoba and Kéndakala Gnuma Damba, the two most powerful sorceresses in Niani, to use their discretionary powers in keeping watch over Sogolon against evil spells, and to provide medical attention during her pregnancy, for, besides their magical powers, these two old women also possessed a deep instinctual knowledge of the pharmacopoeia of the savanna lands; they had an intimate acquaintance with all the important floral and herbal properties, and knew well how to turn them to good advantage.

The king would often enjoy paying visits to Sogolon and Kanko. On such occasions he would sit gazing upon his young bride, or rather upon the woman who lay behind their first con-

tact, during that memorable night when the ghostly glimmer of
the young moon only barely illumined the mango trees of Niani.
He would sit there, bringing back to mind the manner in which
he had possessed Sogolon! The young bride, terror-stricken, had
bellowed like a heifer: 'No, I never saw anything like it, and I
don't think I'd want to see such a thing again!' he murmured to
himself. And suddenly he was overcome with deep shame. 'Will
Sogolon ever forget my ignominious conduct?' he wondered.
'Won't she keep brooding over it, keep smouldering the fires of
the hatred I must have started in her on our first encounter?' he
asked himself.

'Certainly she must feel only disgust for me now; and perhaps
that disgust is as bitter to her heart as a *kobi*[1] toothpick is to the
mouth of one who wishes to bring a sparkle to his smile. But
perhaps if I give in to all her caprices from now on I may be able
to regain her confidence, even before the honeymoon is over.'

And with the intention of pleasing his young bride, Maghan
Kön Fatta began by giving in marriage a nubile girl to each of the
young hunters, the first companions of Sogolon. This arrange-
ment worked to the advantage of both the king and the two
brothers, Moké Mussa and Moké Dantuman.

Again in the hope of pleasing her, he would shower her with
presents each time he came back from hunting. He paid her every
attention. And so, feeling abandoned, Fatumata decided to put
an end to the woman who had taken her place as the king's
favourite. She called upon the aid of sorceresses to attain her ends.
Was this because she had not realized the exceptional power of
Sogolon's ancestral totems? Perhaps. Perhaps, too, she had
vaguely heard something about those powers: perhaps in her
state of unrelenting jealousy she had lost her head, and did not
realize that if Sogolon had taken on the form of her doubles she
could have terrorized all the lands of the savanna. Perhaps she
simply did not know that Dô-Kamissa, by taking on the form of
only one of the two doubles of the 'Condé' had terrorized her
brother Dô-Samô and sowed death and destruction in his kingdom? Perhaps, in the end, Fatumata Bérété was unaware that
her project, workable only in her own imagination, was ob-

1 The *kobi* is a tree bitter as quinine. The tree also produces kobi butter.

viously unfeasible, because based upon a monumental error: a confused ignorance of Sogolon's supernatural powers. Moreover, for some time now, seeking to guard her, during the night the owls had been hooting on the roof of the young woman of Dô. But perhaps Fatumata Bérété's mind was clouded by her desire to regain her place as the king's favourite.

Before the period of the honeymoon had ended, Sogolon's pregnancy became perceptible, not only in its symptoms – vomitings, irrational fancies and appetites – but also in the young woman's physical transformation. Maghan Kön Fatta was convinced that the seed planted in the fertile womb of his bride would grow strong and full of sap, thanks to the careful supervision of Sumusso Konkoba and Kéndakala Gnuma Damba.

Finally, the period of the honeymoon was ending for Sogolon; during the three months it had lasted, the king had done everything he could to make his young wife forget, through countless attentions, the rough passage of their wedding night. Now, in conformity with the customs flourishing in the Manden, the two women began taking turns with their husband. And because there was no child being suckled, they each had the right to lie with him for two nights out of four.

It was Fatumata who took the first turn: and it was for her – as the 'change wife' – to prepare the meals. She spent her days preparing succulent dishes, strongly spiced, so as to keep up Maghan Kön Fatta's male vigour.

When day was done and night had long since fallen, she had only a few steps to take and she was with her husband: she would tread lightly in order not to awaken Dankaran Tuman and Nana Triban who occupied the other couches in the chamber.

Now, she was seated on the bed, beside her husband; already two years and three months had passed since she last saw this bed: two long years during which her suckling of Nana Triban had kept her from her conjugal obligations, and three interminable honeymoon months during which Sogolon had separated her from the man she loved so much! The undue length of that continence had been a sore test for her nerves, and had left her somewhat light-headed. Her whole being seemed in revolt. But despite her nervous irritation and her distracted mind, she had made herself beautiful: her hair was freshly plaited, and from her body and her clothes came the heady scent of *ussulan*[1] which filled the conjugal abode with its fragrance.

Unable to wait any longer, she suddenly stood up, undressed, and hung her garments on the rack nailed to the wall. When she sat down again she was wearing round her loins only her little white loincloth. Then she lay down on the bed. Had her long day's work tired her out? Perhaps. Perhaps too the waves of desire rippling over her body only served to increase her mental distraction, or perhaps they were simply preparing her to receive her husband's caresses.

Her eyes, because they were entirely fixed upon the king, appeared more disturbing and more provocative than they had ever been: they seemed to be imploring Maghan Kön Fatta, humbly imploring him. All at once she clasped him to her, as if inviting him to lie closer, much closer. But her husband's obedient responses seemed to surprise her: at first she offered him calculated refusals, then deliberate evasions.

But perhaps these refusals and evasions did not mean anything: perhaps they were only feminine caprices. And because in the couple's past all resistance had been absent, the memory of past joys mixed with the present trickery disturbed the soul of the old king and tormented it like the flame of a torch. He was as if struck dumb.

At first he heard repeated *Nté*[2] spurting from Fatumata's mouth, seeming to burst from her lips with the sound of a fresh corn-cob grilling on burning charcoal. Then she started fulminating against Sogolon, making her the victim of her tyrannous jealousy: she gave herself up frenziedly to the pleasure of describing her co-wife's ugliness, which she shamelessly contrasted with her own beauty, a comparisson that moreover seemed to act upon her like some effervescent stimulus. She obviously did not know that her powers of persuasion over the old king's heart had vanished, that his heart had become as if encased in a hard shell that only interests of state could pierce – the interests of state that had decided him to wed the young girl from Dô. He was no

1 *Ussulan*: ingredient made from leaves and roots and having a deodorizing effect.
2 *Nté* means: no.

longer subject to Fatumata's will: he would not give in to her. He had married Sogolon because all the wise men had spoken so highly of her, and now that she was expecting a child, there was no question of repudiating her, for one cannot abandon a field once one has cleared it – all the more so if that field had already been sown!

'But is a beautiful young girl necessarily the one with a beautiful body? Is she not rather the one with a tender heart, who spreads joy, generosity and peace around her in her daily work?' he found himself thinking.

Now his advances were becoming more explicit: Fatumata was casting off veil after veil of the refusals she had seemed intent on preserving, and her right hand, almost imperceptibly sliding down her body, encountered her husband's, whose gestures she imitated exactly. Then as her body, convulsed by the fires of passion, clung to the body of Maghan Kön Fatta as if to solder herself to him, her jealous woman's subconscious made her cry: *Nté* to the vehemence of his mouth, so refusing with her voice what she as the madly amorous woman she had become had already granted him completely. Later, much later, the king began muttering something in a low voice, and went on muttering. What was he saying? Everything and nothing at all. But it was not important. As for Fatumata Dérété, from the depths of her throat and chest she was now grunting *Hon! . . . Hon!*[1] in long-drawn-out cries like the howlings of the hyena in the plain. Was it in order to deliver themselves up completely that she was howling and he was muttering? Perhaps. Perhaps, too, it was simply that they were clinging hard to the tree of their pleasure, perhaps the ascent to the summit radiant with sun and with their joy was already reaching its climax, all surrounded by countless leaves and branches: and perhaps they were encouraging one another to further efforts.

All that muttering and howling ecstasy continued for a while, then suddenly stopped. It ended, as it had begun, in silence, because the pair had come down from the tree of their pleasure and now found themselves at its foot; and although their hearts were still beating as if to burst, the one melting into the other had

1 *Hon* means: yes.

as it were extinguished each other.

The rest of the night passed in this sweet state. Fatumata, at the thought that henceforward she would spend two nights out of four beside her husband, was radiantly happy. But in the morning when she went back to her hut, she knew full well that the king would never repudiate Sogolon, and that she, Fatumata, would never succeed in persuading him to do so. She understood, too, that her sorceresses could never lay a finger on the young woman of Dô, that the multiple spells and all the evil enchantments they had cast upon her had met with invincible hard rock. She finally realized that nothing in the arts of witchcraft could so much as touch Sogolon, for naturally she had been just a virgin appalled by the male shank, certainly not like a woman, mother of ten children . . .

As she went back into her hut, she said, in a very low voice, as if talking to herself: 'All right! Let him be born, the child of Sogolon! Her child will be much more vulnerable than she; and as surely as the serpent twists on the ground and as the feet trample the ground, so surely shall the two meet.'

There was now a long period during which the two wives took it in turn to lie with Maghan Kön Fatta two nights out of four. Winter had passed and the warm season had come, and the heat, in all the lands of the savanna, had reached its greatest intensity! They were in the middle of the dry season, probably at the end of January, for this season that lasts six months in the Manden begins in November and ends in April, whereas the winter season, of the same length, begins in May and ends in October.

One day, in the land of the fiery sun, the king and his courtiers, in order to escape from the barely endurable heat, had chosen to go and sit beneath the giant bombax tree, where they were to settle a political case. They were perspiring heavily, and kept wiping away the big drops of sweat from their foreheads with the backs of their hands.

Suddenly two cyclones, one coming from the east, the other from the west, met over the town of Niani. They tangled and formed an enormous whirlwind that lifted the roofs off the huts and decapitated the mango trees. Were they the local spirits of Dô and the Manden joining forces? Perhaps. Perhaps, too, that unleashing of fury was nothing other than the nuptial procession

112

of the buffalo-panther of Dô and the lion of the Manden, and now, perhaps, they were consummating their marriage.

Gradually the cyclones, transformed into a whirlwind, became violent gusts that whipped around the courtiers and compelled them to seek refuge among the buttressing roots of the giant bombax. Suddenly the sun was covered with great clouds, while other clouds, like water vapours, rose from the earth and rose into the sky like immense tree trunks in a virgin forest. They gradually spread out until finally the city was plunged into total darkness. Of course, these clouds would have been greeted with joy if, after having shut out the sun, they had brought a little coolness. But the air, which had become stagnant, condensed the heat instead of alleviating it.

When their eyes had grown accustomed to these clouds which were black as coal dust, black as soot, the king and his courtiers noticed that the bombax above their heads was less visible, that it could now be made out only very vaguely, and that it had become nothing more than an enormous grey mass lost in the shadows of the sky. As for the huts, they seemed to be sunk in night . . .

The heavens, as if enraged, thundered frighteningly! They suddenly winked their great eye and a blinding flash rent asunder the clouds from east to west. Was this the sign of some sympathetic acknowledgement of an exceptional event? Perhaps. Perhaps, too the eye of heaven blinked because its breast was heaving painfully, and perhaps it was the prelude to its tears.

Suddenly it poured down tears whose fine droplets, like the drizzle of the month of August, fell down straight and thick. The inhabitants of Niani had retreated in terror to their huts. Alone, Maghan Kön Fatta, garbed all in silver rain, was striding backwards and forwards under the bombax tree. And for a long time he observed the lugubrious aspect of the universe.

'What an adventure!' he cried. 'Never, during the dry season, has there been so much wind and clouds and thunder-threats; there has never been such a blinding lightning flash, not to mention this strange rain that is now ceaselessly falling. Could this be the end of the world?' he cried again.

The waters of heaven continued to fall for a long time, then, suddenly, they stopped as abruptly as they had begun. And as if by enchantment, a brilliant sun immediately appeared, apparently in mid-course.

Then a serving woman, coming from the kitchen, came forward cautiously into the middle of the courtyard of Maghan Kön Fatta's palace, armed with a pestle and mortar. She silently placed the mortar on the ground and was motionless a moment; then, raising her arm very high, she let the pestle fall into the empty mortar with three resounding blows, after which she cried:

'Sogolon Condé has given birth to a fine big boy!'

Perhaps this unusual manner of announcing a birth had been ordered by Sogolon herself? Perhaps. Perhaps, too, this was the custom of the women of Dô. And because three blows of the pestle had sounded in the empty mortar, because the serving woman had then cried aloud the announcement of the birth of the royal child, to this day certain villages in the Manden continue to announce births in the manner of Sogolon's servant.

The king, on hearing the announcement of the birth of his son, was also motionless for a moment, as if stupefied. His courtiers, as soon as the sun had reappeared, had grouped themselves around him again. Gnankuman-Dua, comprehending his sovereign's deep emotion, began to intone, in his high tenor voice, these praises:

> '*Trublu Kabala Simbon!*
> *Dion Sina, Dugu Sina, Manden Koliba Sina!*
> *Dombon na Maghan, Kababo Maghan!*
> *Sosso Simbon Salaba, Simbon Semba Salaba!*
> *Diurulen Ko, Senkan na Wonti Koli!*
> *Samo Dayara, Bakary Dayara!*
> *Kri Danfa, Danfa ani fuén Kuru!*
> *Fatumata Dandanbrissa!*
> *Ni imi idan na Kali iti idan na kolan.*'[1]

Then he added:

'Be not afraid, my beautiful king, neither let your heart be troubled: rather, let us be joyful. Truth itself has burst forth

---

1 A Malinké incantation composed of untranslatable nominal expressions, intended to exalt the king.

before the eyes of all the world, and that truth has enlightened the minds in particular of those who were disposed to doubt the extraordinary destiny of the boy whose birth Sogolon's servant has just announced. The heavens, yea in the very midst of the dry season, by their darkening, their loud cries, their downpourings of tears, could not have given more eloquent witness to their compassion during the painful travail of your wife. Now that the *Nankama*[1] is come among us, as soon as the clouds, the thunder-threats, the lightning and the rain have vanished, behold, the heavens smile upon us with all their teeth, and a brilliant sun appears. Yes, indeed, it as as if the heavens wished to demonstrate, in their own way, their welcome to the 'Nankama', him the whole world will one day know and speak of! But this did not happen during the reign of any other king of the Manden: this came about only beneath the sun of Maghan Kön Fatta and his faithful griot Gnankuman-Dua. O, my beautiful king, let us be joyful!'

But despite everything the king remained silent and as if at a loss. So then the griot approached the tabala on either side of which two slaves were already standing, each armed with a great mallet: at Dua's command they began to beat it with alternating blows. Soon the blows became more rapid and more imperious, sending echoes flying as they announced the good news with drum-beats that seemed to spring from the very entrails of the earth and spread far and wide in the sky above Niani!

When the drum-beats had ceased, Dua ran to the king's side; smiling, and with an air of satisfaction, he addressed his master thus:

'Without any doubt, this newborn child, when he has grown to his full stature, shall become the most illustrious king of our country, and he shall reign long!'

'Why do you suddenly tell me that?' the king asked.

'For us griots, you know, the first drum-beats of the tabala on the birth of a prince or the coronation of a king have a certain unmistakable resonance. The length of a reign and the power of a future king can be perceived in those first drum-beats. The

1 *Nankama* is he who has come to fulfil a heavenly mission. He is the predestined one.

more deeply-rooted in the earth their sound appears to be, and the more widely they spread their ripples in the sky, the longer the reign, the more powerful the king!'

'And what if the opposite should be the case?' demanded the king in an inquisitorial tone.

'Did you yourself not notice, Mansa, that at the birth of Dankaran Tuman, ten years ago, when the drum-beats of the tabala did not spring from deep enough in the earth, I then concluded that he would be a mediocre king, and his reign of short duration? Those drum-beats merely spread out in the sky!'

The king, whom Dua's enthusiastic voice had released from his trance of emotion, nodded his head and, escorted by his courtiers, he proceeded to his palace. After going into his chamber to change his garments, and coming out all smiles, he realized that his residence had been surrounded by griots chanting his praises. The great doors of the vestibule – where the sovereign generally held family reunions and received his familiars – went on opening and shutting. Sumusso Konkoba and Kéndakala Gnuma Damba, who had arrived to congratulate the young mother, made their way towards Sogolon's hut: one of them entered and sat down by the door while the other, in the rear courtyard, chatted noisily with Kanko about this and that. The light in the eyes of the newborn child gazing at her became brighter. Struck by this, she called her sister, who came and joined her. She, too, got the impression that the newborn child was gazing only at her, whereas in reality his enigmatic gaze was fixed upon both of them at the same time.

But perhaps this little one's gaze expressed too much, perhaps he was already a sorcerer? And because he had looked at them and smiled, revealing gums with a complete set of teeth as in a child of two years, the two sorceresses were troubled in their minds, and took their leave of Sogolon as soon as they decently could. And the vestibule doors again started swinging. As they left the palace of Maghan Kön Fatta there was a sort of stupor in their eyes. Was it because they had just seen a newborn baby with a mouth full of teeth? Perhaps: perhaps it was on account of his enigmatic gaze? Perhaps, too, it was because of the serene manner in which Sogolon, escaping their vigilance, had faced, all alone, the supreme test of childbirth, and perhaps it was because

116

of the sign of great compassion given by the vast heavens at the moment of the young woman of Dô's painful travail. In fact, they were now convinced that Sogolon was more versed in the great art of sorcery than they were.

Sumusso Konkoba and Kéndakala Gnuma Damba hesitated a moment when they ran into Fatumata Bérété, for they felt unwilling to give her their impressions of her co-wife's child. But Fatumata, eager to hear the facts, cast the first pebble into the bush to see if there was any game.

'I am going at once to see Sogolon's baby,' she said.

And she smiled. Her smile turned into a nasty laugh, a laugh both unfriendly and mocking.

'You are going to see Sogolon's baby?' Sumusso Konkoba asked.

'That's what I intend to do.'

'Extraordinary! That new baby is extraordinary! You can trust what I say,' said Sumusso Konkoba. 'We are old and we are two of the best-known personages in Niani, celebrated all over the Manden, and consequently we have seen hundreds of newborn children. But we have never yet seen one like Sogolon's, born with a mouth already full of teeth,' she concluded.

'And what is even more astonishing,' Kéndakala Gnuma Damba added, 'wherever you put yourself in his mother's hut, that baby seems to be looking only at you!'

Fatumata laughed. Kéndakala Gnuma Damba also laughed. The pair of them went on laughing as if these revelations were something less than extraordinary.

'Ha-ha!' Fatumata laughed, sneering sceptically.

Then she started laughing louder then ever. At one moment, it seemed as if Sumusso Konkoba was going to give her a piece of her mind. But she withered Fatumata Bérété with a single glance.

Yet perhaps the latter's laughter meant nothing, perhaps her lips were always splitting wide open for no reason at all and because they could utter nothing of any value, and because she showed all her teeth senselessly in order to gain the sorceresses to her cause and to mock all those of Sogolon's clan: everyone had to interpret the laughter of Fatumata Bérété in his own way, either to his own advantage or not.

117

'A baby with a mouth full of teeth?' she asked, suddenly serious.

'Yes! Like a two-year-old child!' Sumusso Konkoba replied vehemently.

'And with a look that remained fixed on everyone at the same time!' added Kéndakaba Gnuma Damba, shortly, as if to put an end to the interrogation.

No, Sogolon's hut was no place for Fatumata Bérété – still torn by a boundless jealousy – she would never dare enter it for she would arouse her co-wife's feelings against her, Sumusso Konkoba thought bitterly And yet, Sogolon would have tolerated, though against her will, Fatumata's intrusions. Ever since coming from the land of Dô, she had kept to the rear courtyard of the palace, where she was often spied upon by her co-wife, who would cast sometimes mocking, sometimes wicked looks in her direction. Only a year ago, the latter had been categorically opposed to her marriage to the king. And was she likely to forget all that now? No, she would never forget, and no co-wife, finding herself in the same situation, would ever forget!

Fatumata Bérété hesitated, then decided to risk it. She took her leave of Sumusso Konkoba and Kéndakala Gnuma Damba; fearfully, creeping furtively with cat-like steps, she made her way, her heart beating strangely, into the hut where Sogolon lay. She felt a deep emotion when she perceived, lying beside his mother, the long-awaited baby, happy and full of milk, and wide awake. Fatumata's evil grimace returned for a second, as if the mere sight of the child caused her spirit atrocious torment. But almost at once she controlled her freelings and pretended to take an interest in her co-wife, whom she congratulated. The latter, who was not deceived, and who in her heart of hearts was convinced that Fatumata, in her hysterical jealousy, was capable of strangling her, if only the occasion presented itself, replied in an indifferent tone of voice. A moment later Fatumata left Sogolon's hut. She felt that the newborn baby was exactly as the two old sorceresses had described him.

All through the afternoon, the doors in the vestibule were swinging. From where he was seated, the king, surrounded by his courtiers, could hear a continuous murmur coming from women who were visiting the mother and the newborn child in little groups. He could hear, near the outer gate, beyond the wall that encircled the palace, the rumbling of tom-toms. He could see the members of his family distributing in his name cloth and grain to the female griots. All Niani was celebrating. But Maghan Kön Fatta could also hear, under the murmurings of women and the rumbling of tom-toms, the cacklings of a hen being killed to make soup for the young mother.

Thus was born to Sogolon Condé, the boy who was to become – because he had inherited two totems from his mother and one from his father – the greatest of the kings of the savanna, and, by his exploits, the first Emperor of the Empire of Mali. It would seem, after numerous verifications, that the event took place on a Monday, at mid-day, in the third month of the dry season – that is, in January, in the year 1202.

The child was given his name on the following Monday, the eighth day after his birth. The ceremonies followed an order established long ago in Niani. And the baptism, because it was a royal one, had an exceptional quality. Delegations of neighbouring peoples and representatives of all the tribes of the Manden were present on that day, at the palace of Maghan Kön Fatta: they had formed a great circle.

The court marabouts had ordered that there should be the sacrifice of a white ram, but one whose eyes, mouth, hooves and sex were covered with patches of black hair. Was this in order that the child's destiny should not fall under maleficent influences? Perhaps. Perhaps, too, they were seeking simply, by this sacrifice, to draw down the clemency of heaven upon the Manden, and perhaps this type of ram was the customary sacrificial beast for the baptism of a prince.

Since daybreak, Tuntun Manian and her sisters had been joyfully pounding the millet that was to be baked for the baptismal bread of Sogolon's child: one year ago, they had led her wedding procession through the town.

On the veranda of her hut, the young mother, whom her serving women were trying to beguile, seemed detached from everything, even from her child, who was making his first appearance outside the hut where he was born for this baptismal

119

day. Kanko, the king's young sister, was busy shaving the baby's stray hairs (*Si diongu*).

The young mother, languorously stretched on piles of soft cushions, was watching with an indifferent face the large, dense crowd that had taken her husband's palace by storm. She seemed sad and anxious, and her face was bathed in tears. But perhaps those tears did not mean anything, perhaps Sogolon was bewailing the absence of her family in Dô, perhaps she was shedding tears of sheer emotion. And because she should have been in a seventh heaven of happiness, and because, on the contrary, everything filled her with gloom; because she had neither the strength nor the desire to look after her child, the women keeping her company assumed she was suffering from that apathy which for a while seizes all mothers about one week after giving birth to a child.

Finally, the king left his dwelling, accompanied by notables among whom one noted the presence of Dankaran Tuman, the griot Gnankuman-Dua and the latter's son, Balla Fassali Kuyaté, who was also being shown to the crowd for the first time. Maghan Kön Fatta majestically entered the courtyard and took his seat upon the platform erected for the occasion. The two adolescents, Dankaran Tuman and Balla Fassali, sat on either hand. The enthusiastic crowd hailed its king: '*Wassa Wassa Ayé!*' they howled in unison, then fell silent. Suddenly the tom-toms and the drums too were silent. And because the silence had become so oppressive, so impressive too, at that moment one could have heard a pin drop.

The griot, spokesman for the king, in ceremonial robes, gazed all around him, then, as if satisfied by the presence at the palace of such a huge crowd, he moved to the centre, right to the very centre of the great circle and began to speak:

Minka an na din Mansa bara bi,
Wolé Manden Mansa la dén ḳun li di
Manden kuma don tôlé an bolo ko kuma-lafolo-kuma
An nu dyéli lu yé wolé folo fo la an bali lu yé
Wo kuma lafolo kuma wo, dén min na boto bi
Ala ma ala ké woli yé an démin
Ka siyaman kafo wola!

Ndén ké min lôni nkéré fé, Balla Fassali Kuyaté.
A san tan né bi, wolé kéto ala dyéli di
A ba bara min ké ata mansaya té lé dô,
Wolé fanan yé wo fôla dunya nyé!
Mansa dan bali lé ka dén baraka madi Maghan kégni ma.
San Méléka lu yé n'séré di!
Missilimin ké-man ni a musso-mân,
Wolu Fanan yé n'séré di!
Mômô té sé ka maniji làdan,
Ka wokè Mô di, Fo Mansa dan bali kélén!
Aka wo ji wolé la dan, ka woké dyélidi,
Ka wo ladan ikô, ka woké sobo kundunédi!
Wo sobo sissèden nikélén ba ata,
Sissè bè di ibi la ano fè!
Wo sobo kundunè wo, woka woo
Konondo lé soden:
Wo kélén na bara ni do ta kè kélén di!
Issimu Ho . . . Ho . . . Ho! . . . Saïba Ho . . . Ho . . . Ho!
A tôlé Naré Maghan Diata iko, afa maghan kégni!
A tôlé Maghan iko, afa maghan kégni!
A tôlé Sogolon Diata ka ana togo la akan
A la ma akè – ra sii mâdi!
  diama Ko amina
Ala ma akèra mô kindé di!
  diama Ko amina
Ala ma akèra Mansa Gnumadi!
  diama Ko amina.

Lo, that which hath gathered us together round the king today
It is the baptism of the son of Manden Mansa[1].
Now the history of the Manden is that which we name Kumo-
  lafólo-kuma!
We the griots, it is we who chant it for those who know us not.

1 *Manden* is a word composed of: *Man* signifying manatee and *den*,
child, so *Manden* means child of the manatee. There lived in a certain
pool a manatee that the hunters were chasing one night: he allowed
himself to be killed, but before that asked for his child to be spared.
The first king, Latal Kalabi, settled in that place and called the land
Manden.

This first word – the child we are baptizing today,
May God grant that his work
May serve to help us make our history greater!
My son who stands here at my side, Balla Fassali Kuyaté
Is ten years old today – he it is who will become this child's griot!
The great works he shall perform during his reign.
Shall be chanted to the world by Balla Fassali.
It is the Uncreated that did give us Maghan the Beautiful, child
    of power,
The Angels above bear witness to me!
All Mussulmans, both men and women,
Also bear witness to me!
None can fashion sperm
To make of it a human being, but the Uncreated!
He it was who fashioned water to make of it our blood,
He too it was who fashioned it to make us flesh!
If a chick take this piece of flesh,
All chickens will follow in its train!
This scrap of flesh has nine holes!
Not one can play the part of another.
None can fashion such a masterpiece, but the Uncreated!
He comes from the Uncreated even before his father was created:
His name is Mari[1] – Diata[2], the very name of his great-great-
    grandfather Mansa-Bélé!
His name is Naré Maghan Diata, the very name of his father,
    Maghan the Beautiful!
His name is Sogolon-Diata, Diata son of Sogolon!
May God accord him long life!
    (the crowd replies: amina!)
May God give him good health!
    (the crowd replies: amina!)
May God make him a good Mansa!
    (the crowd replies: amina!)

At once the female griots shouted the child's name.
    Kanko, who had come to listen to Gnankuman-Dua, with-
drew from the crowd and rushed to the veranda to whisper in

1 Mari means: Emir.   2 Diata means: lion.

the newborn baby's ear his many names: Mari-Diata, Naré Maghan Diata, Sogolon-Diata, so that he might remember them. The tom-toms and drums again began to thunder, while under the bombax tree, the marabouts, as a climax to the festivities, distributed to the population the flesh of sheep and bulls which were sacrificed at the very moment when the griot Dua pronounced the child's multiple names.

THE CHILDHOOD AND
AWAKENING OF THE 'NANKAMA'

Mari-Diata, Naré Maghan-Diata,

. . .

Sogolon-Diata – that was the last name, the one remembered
by everybody: so Sogolon-Diata gradually became, in the rapid
speech of the Manden-Ka, Sondiata or Sundiata.

With his tormented and taciturn air, looking rather like an
idiot, the son of Sogolon had a particularly long and difficult
childhood. By the time he was five years old, he still could not
stand upright: his legs seemed as if paralysed, and indeed they
were really paralysed. And probably it was this infirmity that
always made him drag himself along the ground like a crocodile
crawling on a sandbank.

At that age, all children, in whatever country they live, are the
pride and joy of their parents. Well, things were quite different
for Diata. But perhaps his infirmity was only temporary, perhaps
it could be cured by healers. And because Sogolon had in the
past been initiated by Dô-Kamissa in the use of medicinal plants,
because she had regularly and vigorously massaged her son's
body, as much to give strength to his limbs as to preserve him
from evil spirits, the second wife of Maghan Kön Fatta, in the
depths of despair, often sat in front of her hut weeping sadly,
silently.

Some time later, a second pregnancy fortunately supervened to
brighten Sogolon's morose existence. Then she had become a
little calmer, or at least seemed to accept, from then on, though
not with total resignation, the unexpected destiny that had been
inflicted upon her son.

The second child she gave birth to was a girl who bore the name
of her sister-in-law Kanko. And probably the royal couple chose
this name in order to express their gratitude to that member of the
family who had so graciously welcomed Sogolon. But if the young
woman of Dô seemed resigned to the fate of her son, her husband
was certainly not. 'I've been wronged! The genius child that
Diata should have been is definitely no more than a cripple, a

124

cripple and a monster!' The king's expectations had been utterly deceived. So he wanted to hear nothing more of this son, and still less of the past he had lived with his mother. And as if to efface the memory of that past, he married Namagbè Camara, a girl of legendary beauty, from the royal house of Sibi. It was at this period, when Maghan Kön Fatta married his third wife, that Nagnalen N'Fali Camara of Sibi, and the *Somono*[1] Sumba Traoré founded the city of Kaba.

Namagbè Camara had a son called Nan Bukari: the wise men predicted that this boy would become the right hand of a great king!

Lacking the 'predestined one' the king had so often dreamed of in marrying Sogolon, the sovereign of the Manden-Ka placed all his hopes on this fresh offspring and granted his favours to his mother. However, this new favourite did not live long: she died some time after her marriage and the education of Nan Bukari was entrusted to Sogolon who was clearly a gentler mother than Fatumata Bérété.

The son of Namagbè Camara had a normal development. As for Sundiata, the years went by and he could still not stand on his legs that were forever weary of being dragged along the ground: his mother would watch him with mournful eyes, and would constantly offer gifts to all the divinities of Dô, in the hope that they would bless her son with a normal existence.

The first wife of the king was by no means displeased by Diata's infirmity. She was even more delighted by the disgrace of Sogolon, whom her husband had preferred to her for so long. So it seemed to her the right moment to stir up the women of Niani to come and mock Diata at the royal palace. But perhaps the fallen woman Fatumata Bérété had now become should have taken thought before doing such a thing. Her new situation should rather have encouraged her to seek friendly co-existence with Sogolon, whose fate from now on was no better than her own. And besides, were they not both wives of the king? Did they not, despite their disgrace, take it in turn to share the sovereign's couch two nights out of four? Moreover, did they not both now feel the same resentment against the king? Would it not have been

1 *Somono*: fisherman.

better, in these circumstances, to join forces, to unite in deceiving the king? The hatred both women nourished for the king never weakened. Fatumata, for her part, regularly roused groups of women to come to the royal palace – the sort of women who generally could not be depended upon for loyalty in friendship – to make fun of Diata. It was as if, fishing in a pond, one should have disregarded the fish one had in one's hands in favour of all those swimming round one's feet: all the fish would swim away and one would be left empty-handed.

The young woman of Dô would have liked her son to hide his infirmity in the rear courtyard of the royal residence, in order to escape, when he dragged himself all over the place, the bitter mockeries of Fatumata and her cronies. But she had not reckoned with Diata's character, and it was too much to ask of him. Consciously or unconsciously, and perhaps more consciously than unconsciously, Diata liked to drag himself all round the royal palace. One day, he was crawling in front of Fatumata's hut: when she saw him, she cried:

'Hey! Look here! Will you just look at this boy for whom all the wise men – all liars! – predicted such an extraordinary destiny! They even said he would be the greatest king of the Manden. Well, just look at him there,' she shouted, as if inviting them all to join in her sniggering – and she was soon laughing her head off! 'Just look at him dragging himself along in the dust! We've already seen a one-armed king, and a one-eyed king, but never before a king who couldn't use his legs!'

The entire circle of her intimates burst out laughing, Fatumata more loudly than anyone. All those women were doubled up with laughter, but when Diata, who felt a strong desire to fight back at them, turned his gaze upon them, they stopped laughing at him and hurried inside the hut.

Sogolon's son could not manage, despite his many efforts, to stand on his legs. Could it be true that the wise men's predictions had been empty wind? This is what the members of the royal family often asked themselves.

Naré Maghan Kön Fatta finally decided to have one last seance or consultation with the blacksmith of the Nunfaïriba caste. Nunfaïriba was a celebrated soothsayer, well known throughout the Manden, but he was blind.

126

One day the king, accompanied by his griot, paid him a visit in his vestibule. Was it because he wanted to clear his mind once and for all about this son whose infirmity was making him desperate? Perhaps. Perhaps, too, he was simply hoping the blacksmith would find a remedy to cure the paralysed legs, and perhaps his unexpected arrival at Nunfaïriba's had been advised by his griot.

The blacksmith's divinatory instruments were two flat stones. He had second sight only when he had rubbed them together. So, quite casually, he picked them up and rubbed them vigorously one against the other, as if he had been grinding corn, then laid them at his feet and began to speak.

'What could be more exhausting,' he began meditatively, 'than the incubation of three guardian spirits in one child's body? Your son, Mansa, inherits from his mother the buffalo and the panther of Dô, and from yourself the lion of the Manden.'

'That is hard to believe now,' the king retorted. 'I heard so much about the exceptional destiny of this child! And he is nothing but a cripple! Guardian spirits or no guardian spirits, tell me, blacksmith, whether Diata will one day be able to walk like everyone else, or whether the Manden must be prepared to see him dragging his body along the ground all his life!'

Nunfaïriba took up the flat stones again: again he rubbed them one against the other, then said:

'Sogolon's child will walk! At present, people strongly doubt such a thing. However, all that was predicted of your son by the other soothsayers is absolutely correct! But if the three guardian spirits have a certain power, their development in the body of a very young boy is not as rapid as you would wish. In the present case, the lower members of the person in question are not yet able to assimilate the guardian spirits!'

'Speak frankly, Nunfaïriba,' Gnankuman-Dua interjected. 'The king is in great distress! Will Diata walk or not?'

'He shall walk like everyone else: have no fears about that!' he replied.

'But when?' the king inquired, impatiently.

'Soon, the three guardian spirits within him will be completely developed, and he himself will be able to assimilate them perfectly. Then he shall walk! Within a short time, he shall walk like everyone else!' Nunfaïriba ended, artfully.

Naré Maghan Kön Fatta, followed by his griot, returned to the royal residence. This final consultation and the confidence Niakuman-Dua had in Diata's destiny had restored his confidence, and, to Fatumata Bérété's great displeasure, Sogolon was taken back into favour. Thereupon one last child was born, a boy. He was baptized Dia Mori, and was known as Mandé Bori.

However, the gossips of Niani, aroused by the king's first wife, continued to disparage Diata and his infirmity. And Sogolon, who had now regained the favour of her husband, felt an oppressive sense of guilt in his company. She again began making her son take the medicinal plants she gathered in the nearby forest. But in the meantime, the king and his griot, who had become very old, died, one after the other, without having known the joy of seeing Diata walk.

After the sovereign's death, custom had it that the eldest son should succeed him. So Dankaran Tuman became king. And Fatumata, in consequence, became all-powerful – was it not her son reigning henceforward! – new laws, and very strict ones, began to be observed in the royal palace, where doubtless the presence of Sogolon would have been found undesirable if Kanko, the young sister of the late Naré Maghan Kön Fatta, had not watched over her, and with all the force of her royal authority. All the same, she did not succeed in silencing the slanders concerning Diata's infirmity that Fatumata, through her cronies, continued to spread in the city of Niani.

However, it so happened that one day the woman of Dô, who no longer lived in luxury but had to make do with the queen mother's leavings now that the king her husband was dead, found she had no condiments to make *To*[1] sauce for the chicken feet she had just cooked. Forgetting her rivalry with her co-wife, and perhaps to attempt a reconciliation, she went to Fatumata's hut and said:

'I've cooked some *To* for my children. But I have no baobab leaves to make the sauce with. Could you give me some, if you have any?'

1 *To*: chicken feet

'Why, of course!' Fatumata replied at once. '*My* son, for whom no great destiny was predicted, but who can walk, who can run and jump, brings me some every day, plenty of them! Whereas *yours*, supposed to be a superman, but who drags himself around in the dust like a chameleon, is not even capable, even at his age, of performing the least service for you! Here, take these baobab leaves, go and feed your good-for-nothing son, make him big and fat!'

And she held out to Sogolon a calabash full of *gnugnu*[1]. At the same time, her mouth split open in a horrible laugh, a laugh both horrible and insulting.

Sogolon did not take the calabash, nor did she make any reply: there are affronts whose cruelty freezes the heart and paralyses the tongue. The woman of Dô, on the brink of tears but controlling her emotions, turned back. As she entered her hut she said, wretchedly, as if talking to herself:

'It is better that the children and I should die of hunger than be helped out by Fatumata who is quite prepared to give us baobab leaves if we will accept her insults with them.'

She lay down quietly, and, as if to veil her eyes, took off her scarf and covered her face with it. Probably she did not want Diata to see the tears that were beginning to blur her vision. But her breast, heaving painfully, attracted the attention of her son who was busy licking out a calabash of millet – for Sogolon's son was a great eater and was passionately fond of his food. Noticing that his mother was tired, Diata, in a firm voice, suddenly said:

'Mother, I'm going to walk today!'

Sogolon was so surprised, she uncovered her face, then waited a moment before replying, with an almost grave serenity.

'Ah! Really?' she said.

With those words, she lifted her head and gazed a long while at Diata. Probably she was thinking what a disagreeable surprise it would have been for Fatumata if she had heard him speaking thus. Probably she was also wondering if her son would really succeed in walking. Then, suddenly, leaning on one elbow, she raised herself up and sat up in bed. Again she turned a passionate gaze upon him, and all at once she sighed:

1 *Gnugnu*: leaves.

129

'I'm frightened, I'm frightened, Diata – afraid you may not manage to walk! Yet I've tried everything, all the medicinal plants, I've never ceased making offerings to the divinities of Dô and invoking the memory of my ancestors so that they may give you the use of your legs. Can you walk, my son?'

'Mother!' Diata cried.

'Son . . .' she said in a faint voice.

As she spoke, he was observing the strong line of her mouth, her vigorous chin, the bushy tufts of her greying hair, the hump on her back that, as she grew older, seemed ever heavier, and his heart was wrung with pity for her.

'Mother! Today I shall walk . . .'

This time Diata had spoken with stubborn determination. Then, fixing his eyes upon her with infinite tenderness, he asked:

'What's the matter, Mother?'

'Nothing!' she replied.

No, there was nothing she could say – it was beyond words.

'Why don't you go on preparing the meal?' Diata continued.

'I don't know.'

'Get up!' he said.

'Yes,' she answered.

'The meal . . . An empty sack cannot stand upright,' he remarked sadly.

Why did he, too, now seem so thoughtful? Had he sensed his mother's confusion? He always sensed so strongly whatever was in his mother's mind. But a moment later the eyes of Diata were drawn back inevitably to the calabash of millet. And the image of Fatumata inflicting daily humiliations upon his family never left his mind: he frowned.

All at once, he called to Nan Bukari in the courtyard.

'Nan Bukari!' Diata cried.

'Namu, nkoro[1]!' he replied.

'Go and tell my griot Balla Fassali Kuyaté to ask Farakurun to forge me a stick, as heavy and strong as possible, and to bring it to me at once.'

Diata's plan to start walking suddenly appeared to Sogolon under a gloomy light, extremely gloomy. She was still sitting up

1 *Namu, nkoro*: my brother Namu, yes.

130

in her bed of beaten earth; she was facing the hearth, and probably it was just as well that she was seated, for if she had been standing, the emotion might have made her collapse. The words: 'Today I shall walk!' repeated so stubbornly had sounded so surprising, Sogolon could hardly believe her ears.

'Yes, you shall walk, Diata,' she said, brushing away the tears that blurred her eyes.

'Don't cry, Mother, don't cry!'

'I can't help it, Diata. It's too much! Too much for me!'

He was sitting down, with his usual tormented and anxious look, but his eyes kept returning to his calabash of millet that he had licked clean. Then he seemed to hear stifled sobs. He raised his head and looked towards the bed. Sogolon had started sobbing and was weeping as if her heart would break. Perhaps he should have tried to comfort her, but he did not know how she would welcome his attentions: perhaps she would not have been so very happy to hear words of comfort. Sogolon needed more than words to bring her consolation: what she needed was some deed, some great deed! Believing himself to be the cause of all his mother's woes, Diata turned his head away and once more cast his eyes upon the empty calabash. Then he said for the third time: 'Mother! Today I shall walk!'

Sogolon made no reply; by now, she was calmer, or at least she seemed to have gained control over herself. It now appeared as if his mother's apparent calm had really given his suffering a new direction. For he suddenly dragged himself to the veranda, and cried:

'Mother! Mother! Today I shall avenge the affront you received. Do you just want some leaves of the baobab?'

'No, my son! The leaves of the baobab are not enough. In order to wipe away the affront made to me by Fatumata Bérété you must bring me the baobab itself! I want the baobab, roots and all, here in front of my hut,' said Sogolon, drying her tears.

Balla Fassali Kuyaté, alerted by Nan Bukari, went to the royal workshops, where he found Farakurun surrounded by his three thousand workers: they were engaged in making all kinds of agricultural tools. In all the hearths, flames were leaping up around the metal. When the bits of metal became incandescent, the workers seized them with their long pincers and laid them on

131

the anvils. Others worked them with great hammer blows sending out sparks that showered painfully on the idlers squatting against the walls of the workshops.

The pieces of iron hammered thus became axe-heads, hoes, spades, rakes and all those modern utensils that the Manden-Ka peasants – thanks to Maka-Taga Djigui Dumbuya, who had imported the original implements on his famous voyage to Mecca! – were always to make use of.

When Balla Fassali asked Farakurun to forge a stick, the latter answered, smiling:

'So the great day has at last arrived?'

'Yes,' replied the griot. 'This is a day like no other. Today will see the 'Nankama' standing upright for the first time in ten years! Today will see the 'Nankama' awaken! Today is comparable only with that Monday on which he was born, when the whole of the Manden trembled with astonishment and terror!'

Farakurun was the son of Nunfaïriba and had succeeded him. He ordered six of his workmen to carry to Sogolon's hut the great bar of iron standing at the entrance to the workshops, for what purpose no one had ever known. But old Nunfaïriba, just before he passed away and returned to the village of God[1], had had it forged, saying: 'The one who is destined to bear this staff shall call for it when the hour is come!'

The men who carried the bar of iron dug a hole in front of Sogolon's hut and planted it firmly in the ground. The many people who had seen Balla Fassali followed by the six workmen with their heavy load had come out of curiosity to lean over the wall of the royal palace. And because any group of people in the Manden, and particularly in its capital Niani, had a tendency to increase; because, too, the passage of the workmen bearing the heavy staff had an almost irresistible attraction, all the inhabitants of Niani were seized with curiosity. They had all made their way to the palace and had literally invaded its outer wall, to which they were clinging like swarms of locusts!

Diata was still sitting on the veranda of his mother's hut, and he had now cast aside the calabash which he had finished licking. A moment later, he crawled on all fours towards the iron staff.

1 Return to the village of God: to die.

Then he lifted his head and gazed at the crowd. Among the crowd he noticed Fatumata Bérété. She had brought herself along, in her own disdainful manner, as if deliberately to provoke the crowd. It was as if she had come to mock someone. But whom could she mock? Was not Diata, whom she and her cronies had been in the habit of mocking, was he not, though issued from another woman, the son of Naré Maghan, her beloved husband? The rivalry that set her against Sogolon, who was the cause of her cruel hatred, compelled Fatumata to show herself off. And so, her mouth was split from ear to ear in wicked laughter.

'It's never too late, and better late than never!' she cried, ogling the crowd. 'But I'm afraid Sogolon's son will not be able to stand up on his own two legs!'

As no one answered, she pulled a face at the crowd, looking from one to the other for support. That grimace showed that she did not believe at all that Diata could stand up on his own two legs. And looking straight at her sister-in-law Kanko, she suddenly shouted:

'Do you really believe that this boy can stand up on his paralysed legs?'

She had shouted at the top of her voice, as if to make herself heard by the entire crowd.

'I believe he can!' Kanko answered stoutly.

Just at that moment, murmurings were heard coming from the crowd, which had now grown tense and very excited: *N'Koro! Idjidja! Hon! Hon!*: 'My brother, stir your stumps! Yes! Yes!' It was the voices of Nana Triban and Sogolon-Kanko speaking thus.

But what explanation could be given of all these contradictory behaviours? What explanation could be given of this duality in the attitude of Fatumata and her daughter? Why had Nana Triban become so attached to Diata? Was it because of patrilinear links? Perhaps. Perhaps, too, it was simply because of the sharp awareness she had – much more so than her brother Dankaran Tuman – of those links, and perhaps it was because of her unalterable faith in the destiny of the son of Sogolon.

Diata heard distinctly the war of words between Fatumata and these two girls. He gave a faint smile, as if in reply to the malevolence of his mother's co-wife. And without further ado, he

133

set one knee on the ground, keeping the other in the air. For the moment, he seemed to see everything in the best possible light, and his controlled breathing, the prelude to some supreme effort, could now be heard. Suddenly, he seized the iron bar with his right hand. He still did not utter a word. And perhaps this self-imposed silence was greater than usual, perhaps it meant that those guardian spirits that inhabited him, the buffalo and the panther of Dô and the lion of the Manden were already coming to full power within him? Perhaps . . .

His confidence in himself had visibly increased. It could be seen in his face. And because he was aware of the rows of inquisitive eyes upon him gazing from behind the wall, he concentrated hard, clinging to the bar with his right hand, whilst his left knee served as a support for the other hand, that soon joined the right . . .

Fatumata was no longer pulling faces. She now seemed very tense, and in her tension to be seeking – in the very depths of her being – a means of escape from that tragic tension. She found her release in a gigantic sneeze, a grotesque sneeze that unleashed a cascade of spit, to the indignation of all the crowd; but it had served to exorcize her fear.

Diata lowered his head as if examining his feet still trailing on the ground. When he lifted his head again, he saw nothing but the bar before him. The next moment, his muscles swelled, his biceps bulged. Now, embracing the bar, he boldly hauled himself up, his head completely thrown back, and his eyes half closed so that his view would not be obstructed by the sweat drenching his body. The faint smile that had played on his lips a moment before had completely vanished.

When he judged that he had climbed high enough, his knees, which for the first time he tried to brace, began trembling frantically, like a field of corn whipped by the harmattan. Suddenly, in a supreme effort, he gradually managed to stretch himself completely upright; then, releasing the bar, he found himself still upright, planted on his own two legs! But the great iron bar had become twisted and had taken on the form of a bow. Was it Diata's strength that had bent the bar? Perhaps. Perhaps, too, it had been done simply by the combined forces of the buffalo and panther of Dô and the lion of the Manden.

The son of Sogolon paused a moment, racked with fatigue, drenched with sweat, and panting, but satisfied with himself. When he stood upright there, really upright, and cautiously began to stretch his legs, Balla Fassali, Kanko, Nana Triban and Sogolon jumped for joy. For a while they were silent, so great was their astonishment. But soon their joy burst forth. They started singing, one after the other. Their songs mainly referred to the greatness of Diata and the wickedness of Fatumata Bérété. The Mandenka, who are accustomed to extravagant hyperbole, nevertheless laughed at the tops of their voices when they heard them. Balla Fassali Kuyaté was the first to raise his voice. On the spot, he created a new chant: it was the 'Niama', which even to this day our griots like to sing on the occasion of grand ceremonies:[1]

> *Niama, Niama, Niama,*
> *Fén Bè bi idon na Niama, lé kôrô*
> *Niama tè don fén kôrô!*

> Filth, filth, filth,
> Everything is covered by filth,
> But nothing can cover you, you filth!

Scarcely had he finished when Kanko, in her sunny contralto, carried on:

> *Bi wo, binyon tè*

> Today, today is a day without compare.

Now it was the turn of Sogolon to show that she, too, was in seventh heaven: she, too, intoned her own chant, making her way through the crowd to the centre of the circle:

1 With this chant we have one of the very first that Balla Fassali Kuyaté created for Sundiata: it expresses the idea that Diata was the rampart behind which Sogolon, insulted by Fatumata Bérété, had found refuge. This chant has remained celebrated to this very day. It is sung for men behind whom their peoples find refuge.

The Guardian of the Word

Sila da la da, doi ba brondo!
Doi ba kadila!

The sorrel by the roadside –
Some gather it, others tear off its leaves.

Then came the turn of Nana Triban to show her radiant happiness, and she, too, composed her own song, thus:

Nfa la bolon da, hérè bayé!

The door of my father's vestibule,
What great happiness!

When he had completely regained his breath, Diata walked. He had barely gone a few steps before the whole crowd leaning on the palace wall swarmed around him, complimenting him, covering him with praises, at the same time congratulating Sogolon who had given birth to such a hero. Kanko, deeply moved, began a new song:

Manden Kéba ni Manden Musso lu albo,
Naré Maghan Diata tamara!

Men of the Manden, Women of the Manden, come and see –
Naré Maghan Diata is walking!

Sogolon, as if to make a fitting reply to the affront offered her by Fatumata, and to bring the occasion to a close, intoned this final song:

Tora ro ii ikani igna mala bèrèkan ji ma,
Bèrè Kan ji gbè ni woua!

Water in a hole, do not compare yourself with
The water of the spring –
The water of the spring is limpid!

136

The crowd was amazed to hear pouring from the mouths of these four people, songs so full of images. No one at that moment could have given greater proof of their total delight than those four persons. Indeed, they participated directly, actually, in Diata's triumph. And the people who thronged round the son of Sogolon were also seized with transports of joy. Their attitude had completely changed, changed overnight. Just a few moments ago, Fatumata had been pulling faces at them! For years, the town gossips had paid Diata no attention, except to mock him. Now here he had become the object of universal admiration. And people did not just admire him, they were hailing him as a hero! The crowd was howling *Wassa Wassa* in praise of his triumph. Fatumata, seeing Diata on his feet and the crowd acclaiming him, felt shudders run all through her body. Indeed, she had no reason to feel at ease. And when the son of Sogolon had taken his first steps, which were giant steps, her one thought was to run, to run away and hide herself in her hut, with all her foolish shame!

Many of her sorceresses and her cronies, leaning on the wall, were also quaking with fear and trembling. The sorceresses of the clan of Sogolon, Sumusso Konkoba and Kéndakala Gnuma Damba, were exultant. But for Fatumata Bérété and all those who had supported her, though to a lesser extent, the awakening of the 'Nankama' was a signal defeat!

And as Diata walked round the iron bar, not for one second did he abandon the self-imposed silence in which he had seemingly immured himself. But perhaps this silence meant nothing, perhaps, too, the guardian spirits which had simply helped him to his feet were still within him, sealing his lips. And so long as they did not leave him, he would remain immured in this mutism which was the symbol of his own explosive force; and precisely because he could not utter a word, because his mouth now was as if shut by a heavy lock, he would not pause – as he ought to have done – to reply to each triumphal paean of praise; he would merely raise his arm in a gesture of triumph, and to thank the entire crowd at the same time.

Burning with impatience, Diata threw himself into the crowd in search of Nan Bukari. But the sorceresses of Fatumata Bérété, still leaning on the wall, could not take their eyes off the crowd howling with joy. In that gaze, there was something Sogolon found deeply displeasing, though she could not have said what. Doubtless it was some kind of sly trickery. Because, like everybody else, those sorceresses were transported with joy – or pretended to be. Were they truly transported with joy? Was it not a trick, some sly pretence, pure hypocrisy?

For years, these women who reigned in darkness – who possessed the secret of the dark itself! – had not ceased directing their enchantments against Diata, in order to rob him of life. And during all that time, they believed they had made their mark on him, made a slight mark on him. They believed their evil spells had been able to paralyse that boy, upright and honest – one only had to look in his eyes, those black eyes, direct and candid, to know that! – but now, they knew they could do nothing against the son of Sogolon, and that no human power on earth could do anything against him, and that nothing, absolutely nothing, could now come between him and his destiny. This was something they realized too late: but now, they could see clearly the workings of fate: the sound limbs of Diata, leading him surely to the throne of the Manden. Ever since the birth of the 'Nankama', they had never ceased to cast their evil spells of all kinds upon him: but from now on, they must be content with watching the wheels of destiny turning. And what could have been done to stop them turning? One could only watch them turning, watch the wheels of destiny turning: the destiny of Diata, thanks to his three ancestral totems, was to become a great man! And so in the event the sorceresses pretended no longer to attempt to thwart that destiny, and, like the rest of the crowd, they were jumping with joy! But when Kanko and Nan Triban looked them straight in the eye, these witches were as out of countenance as if a thunderbolt had fallen at their feet. As soon as they had recovered from their surprise, their own thought was to run away, so they, too, fled, just as Fatumata Bérété had done.

Indeed, their situation from now on did not look very rosy. For no one in the city of Niani had been unaware of their backbiting and their evil spells against Sogolon and her son.

Not far from the palace there was a baobab tree bearing on its summit a mysterious fruit that was very rarely seen. For some time now, the soothsayers had been predicting that whoever saw the fruit, gathered it and ate it would become the most powerful king of the savanna.

Diata, escorted by Nan Bukari, by his griot Balla Fassali Kuyaté and the crowd, was now marching towards that baobab tree. Who would have believed, who would have admitted that, a few moments ago, the son of Sogolon was dragging himself along the ground like a chameleon? No one, now, would have believed or admitted it!

When he reached the foot of the tree, he raised his eyes and gazed at the summit. There hung the fruit! But was it not extraordinary, was it not miraculous that the fruit of the baobab should have become visible? It was not always seen, and did not appear every day, except on this very day when Diata had walked for the first time! It was clearly visible on this day! For the son of Sogolon, this rare apparition came as no surprise. Was not the mysterious fruit hanging up there on the top of the baobab for him, for him alone? Had he not been waiting for it a long, long time, waiting always just for its appearance? And Diata's right arm grew enormous, grew long as a pole, and at the end of this pole his right hand, wide open, closed on the fruit and plucked it. At once that hand crushed the nut, and, at one gulp, he had swallowed its pulp! When he lowered his eyes and brought his arm back to normal size beside his body, the son of Sogolon beheld the baobab planted solidly in front of him. With one twist of the wrist he uprooted it, heaved it on his shoulder, and proceeded, followed by the crowd, back to his mother's hut. As he entered the main gate of the royal palace, he cried out:

'Mother! Mother! Mother!'

He bellowed these words at the top of his voice, as if wanting them to be heard by all the residents in the palace, and by Fatumata, his mother's rival.

But Sogolon did not respond: the recitation of incantations she was making as she sacrificed a chicken to the memory of her aunt Dô-Kamissa whose double she was – to thank her for having made her son sound of limb – prevented her from replying. And because his mother had not replied immediately to his call, Diata felt a lump rise in his throat. Or was it because he was still brooding over the affront of Fatumata Bérété? Was it because he

139

had just avenged his mother and wiped out that affront? Was it because a new sun had risen for him on the horizon, or because, finally, and as if miraculously, he had found the use of his legs? Perhaps. And since he had uprooted the baobab and heaved it on his shoulder, since he had borne it to the gate of the palace, he could do nothing but shout 'Mother!' But a strange discouragement had overcome him following the great joy he had felt in bearing the tree right in front of Sogolon's hut. Or could that instability be attributed to his recent physical mutation? For years, his legs had been paralysed. Now . . . Was he really cured, now? Was he really on his feet again? He was cured, he was a perfectly healthy adolescent now. No, he was no longer a paralytic. Now he could walk like everybody else. Now, he could run and jump better than Dankaran Tuman. He was in perfect health! It was the first time in his life he had felt such immense joy, and yet at the same time this strange feeling of dejection had overcome him.

'Mother! Mother!' he repeated.

Sogolon, who had finished making her offering, came out of the hut to meet him.

'Well, I'm waiting for you! Here I am, don't you see me, Diata?'

'Yes! I see you all right. But you can see me too. Here are some baobab leaves for you. From today on, it shall be in front of *your* hut that the women of Niani – including Fatumata! – shall come for their supplies.'

And he let fall the tree which fell with a heavy sound to the earth.

Manden Bori, who was playing in the hut, was surprised by the sound, and looking out of the door, stammered:

'N'koro, my brother, you have come back?'

And the little boy had smiled. Diata understood at once why he had smiled. While his elder brother had been gripping the iron bar, he had remained in the hut. And all that time, he had been more moved by the sight of the dense crowd clinging to the palace walls like swarms of locusts, than by Diata's destiny then at stake!

Although later his mother had told him that his brother could now walk, although he had seen his aunt Kanko, his mother,

140

his sisters Sogolon-Kanko, Nana Triban and all the crowd dancing with joy, he had not understood the real meaning of all the fuss. Perhaps he had been thinking of a tom-tom? Perhaps. *He* had not seen his brother gripping the iron bar, so what was there to prove that his mother had told him the truth? But now, he had seen Diata with his shoulders heavily laden with the baobab, now he had seen him standing upright on his own two legs, and though he was still just a little boy he had suddenly understood everything, he was truly happy, and he was smiling, laughing, showing all his little white teeth.

'N'Séwara Kossobé, N'koro – I am very happy, my brother!' he stammered.

And he rose, stood upright, made some uncertain steps towards Diata and his mother. When he was under their admiring eyes, and living to the full this great moment that a great triumph vividly illumined, Diata opened his arms, took him and pressed him to his breast. And as if to efface utterly the words with which Sogolon had left Fatumata Bérété that morning, Diata said, with infinite tenderness:

'Now are you satisfied, Mother?'

'Yes, my son, I am, completely!'

'Now, it is *our* sun that is shining!'

'No, son. Your sun has risen. But many years must pass before it can dazzle the whole of the Manden . . .'

EXILE

When Diata had got the use of his legs, his aunt Kanko and his uncles decided to reward him by having him enter the association of the non-initiates. This association, introduced into their customs by the fourth king of the Manden – Kalabi Bomba or Kalabi the Great – was in fact an association of all the uncircumcised adolescent boys in the kingdom. It was a kind of pre-initiation preparation for the great test of circumcision.

Diata, accompanied by several princes of the savanna invited for the occasion, heard 'Konden Diara'[1] roaring from beyond the shallows of the River Sankarani. But not until one year later did he know – after having danced like his ancestors the 'Coba'[2] after his circumcision – who 'Konden Diara' was. And he discovered, as his elders had before him, that the risks in that childish bugaboo ceremony were non-existent, but he was not allowed to know this until the time had come for it to be revealed.

After his circumcision, Diata was also initiated into the art of hunting. Often he would go off into the bush accompanied by his griot Balla Fassali Kuyaté and the comrades with whom he had undergone the rites of initiation.

One day however, when he was hunting in the bush, Mansa Dankaran Tuman had sent Balla Fassali to Sosso: he had named him ambassador at the court of the powerful king, Sumaoro.

The members of the embassy, whose designation had been approved by the Council of the Ancients, had left Niani the same day, in the company of the head of the mission.

What feelings and what political reasons could have motivated Mansa Dankaran Tuman to take Diata's griot away from him? Was it a lack of confidence in Diata's future, or a pretended ignorance of that destiny which already was beginning to irradiate the horizon? Perhaps. Perhaps, too, it was fear that the

1 Konden Diara: see *The African Child*.
2 Dance of the 'Coba': the Great Event introduced into their customs by Diata's great-grandfather Mansa Bélé, whose surname Mari-Diata he bore; see *The African Child*.

son of Sogolon guided by Balla Fassali, considered by the king to be the evil genius of his rival, might overthrow him and enthrone himself upon the royal lion skin, and thereupon carry out exploits that the king himself knew he was incapable of equalling. Perhaps it was simply out of a concern to preserve his prerogatives as king of the Manden against the meteoric rise of Sumaoro's power. Who could tell? Who could have put his finger on the source of the mystery and made the chord of truth vibrate? Who could have analysed this paradox, the paradox of a Manden-ka sovereign removing from his younger brother the griot who had been solemnly presented to him on the very day of his baptism? Who could have explained the taking of Balla from his young master, or his being sent to Sosso? Only Dankaran Tuman, but he would never tell!

Now, in that cruel solitude suffered by Diata and his family, a solitude resulting from the malevolence of the king urged on by the queen mother; in that terrible hatred which the reigning branch of his family directed against him – hatred that cut him to the quick – Diata, strangely enough, had found a true supporter in his griot. The loyal attitude of Balla of whom the king had just deprived him had, until then, helped Diata to face, with as little resentment as possible, the political quarrels born of family rivalry. The friendship his griot bore towards him did much to attenuate the anger of the son of Sogolon against all those within his own family who were hostile to him.

When Diata came back from hunting that evening, and his mother told him of Balla's departure to Sosso, he protested violently:

'No! No! Taking away my griot is not allowed! Dankaran Tuman must give me back my griot if he wants to live in peace!'

'My son, do not start any trouble. It is Dankaran Tuman who is mansa!' said Sogolon. ('Mansa' is of course Malinké for 'king').

'Dankaran Tuman is mansa of the Manden, but he is not mansa of my griot nor of me!' he replied scornfully.

Then, turning to Nan Bukari, he said to him:

'Follow me. We're going to see him!'

The two princes left their mother's hut. When they arrived in front of the dwelling of Mansa Dankaran Tuman, Diata had a lively tussle with the royal guards who wanted to stop him and his younger brother from seeing the sovereign. But they forced the barrier, and found themselves before him.

The son of Sogolon and the son of Namagbè glared at one another: they were boiling with rage. Suddenly, Diata seized the king by the collar and shook him vigorously three times; his anger was such that he could not bring himself to utter a single word! And it may well be said that he showed great temerity, for the guards, with drawn sabres, were ready to intervene. Any other twelve-year-old child would have lost countenance at this display of arms, but Diata kept calm. All the same, the flame in his eyes flashed fiercely; he looked the guards up and down in a contemptuous manner, then spat upon the ground.

Dankaran Tuman, looking from one brother to the other, exclaimed:

'What has got into the pair of you tonight?'

'It so happens that you have taken away Diata's griot,' replied Nan Bukari, 'and you have no right to do so! Why did you not send your own griot to Sosso?'

Diata had released his grip on the king's collar, and, ready to defend himself if need be, had retired to a corner of the hut to observe the dispute.

'Nan Bukari!' the king said brusquely. 'Can you witness to the fact that our father had presented the griot Balla Fassali to Diata?'

'Naturally, I cannot witness to that fact,' he retorted. 'The gift took place before I was born. But the entire population of Niani can testify to it!'

And he raised his right hand to add more weight to his declaration.

'Do not try to intimidate us,' Diata intervened. 'We are going far from here, as you do not wish to see us beside you, but sooner or later we shall return!'

'You are leaving, but you do not know if you will ever return,' Dankaran Tuman sententiously replied.

Diata was already preparing to leave when Nan Bukari, firmly restraining him, said to the king:

'Before it is too late, will you decide whether or not to give back Balla to his master?'

Dankaran Tuman, embarrassed, scratched his head, then replied firmly:

144

'You should know, my dear brethren, that the griots are in the service of the kingdom only: they are not the property of any prince, not even of the king!'

'Very well!' replied Diata, 'we shall speak of it no more. This day has been the day of Balla's departure, and for me, a day of mourning, so we shall retire. We now know what is to be done.'

They said no more. Besides, the royal guards were beginning to crowd into the sovereign's courtyard, intent, it seemed, on throwing out the two princes by brute force.

Diata, before retiring, looked the king sternly in the eye, then cried, in a threatening manner:

'You do not want us? Very well then, we shall depart far from here, but we shall return, do you hear me? We shall return!'

The tone of his voice was so authoritative and so categorical that the king took fright. He was so terribly frightened, he started trembling all over.

The two brothers, as they left the hut, slammed the door. The queen mother, informed of the incident, at once ran to her son: she found him almost fainting with terror.

'Mother,' he said. 'Nan Bukari and Diata are asking for their griot back! They are ordering me to give him back to them, otherwise they will leave the Manden! But why should they leave? I can recall Balla Fassali, and I can just as well name someone else as ambassador to Sosso!' he whimpered.

'Very well, recall Balla Fassali!' countered Fatumata, whose nerves seemed to be at breaking point, 'recall him, if you cannot live up to your responsibilities. Indeed!' she cried, 'you do not wear trousers, but the loincloth of a woman! Are you afraid of those good-for-nothing brats?'

And she turned her eyes upon heaven, and addressed it thus:

'And I thought I had a son! But instead of a son I have something that trembles before a couple of youngsters, like a young bride before her husband!'

Then she lowered her eyes, and again looked at Dankaran Tuman:

'Have you no shame?' she shouted. 'Then give up your royal lion skin to your sister! Certainly Nana Triban would be able to govern the Manden better than you!'

'Mother! Mother!' the king pleaded. 'Don't you realize they

145

are going to leave here?'

'Very well then,' she retorted, 'let them leave! If only the pair of them would take their hump-backed mother with them, we could live in peace in Niani!'

'Mother!' he began again.

But she broke in violently.

'I won't hear another word! You are a coward! And I, your mother, will have nothing to do with cowards. I shall leave here and go to my parents where I can die with dignity in my own village, instead of dying here, dying of humiliation, because I have a son who is afraid to rule!'

Fatumata Bérété made such a scene with her son that the latter suddenly found he had the soul of a tyrant. He declared he was the sole mansa of the Manden: he did not want anyone objecting to his orders, and no one in the kingdom had any right to dispute his decisions. By now, if he had happened to meet the two brothers, he was ready to stamp them out like a couple of black beetles.

Before the two princes reached Sogolon's hut, Diata told his brother:

'It is you who must announce our departure into exile to our mother.'

'No, we shall both tell her together. It will take both of us, I can tell you!' Nan Bukari answered.

Now they had reached the hut where Sogolon was giving Dia-Mori his last millet pap of the evening. Nan Bukari stood there a while watching Sogolon feed spoonfuls of pap to her last-born. The boy did not know where to begin; he knew that the decision they had reached would surprise Sogolon, and they both were heavy at heart. They stood there, watching Dia-Mori greedily swallowing his pap: Diata, standing somewhat apart, with an awkward expression, did not dare raise his eyes. But their mother did not take long to sense the news. She only had to look at her two sons, and realized that they had created a scene with the king.

'What do you want, children?' she asked.

And in the excited state of her fevered mind, she clutched tightly the handle of the spoon, as if she were trying, for want of anything better, to strangle the spoon. Then she put the spoonful of pap back in the calabash. Finally, she raised her head and gave them both a questioning look:

'What is it? Dankaran Tuman had words with you again?' she asked scornfully.

'Yes, Dankaran Tuman!' Nan Bukari replied, in a low aside.

'Even if you had not said so, everyone would know what had happened,' she went on with a changed tone of voice.

Then Diata approached her and said:

'Mother, as Dankaran Tuman and his mother are always picking quarrels with us, we have decided to depart from here, and to leave the Manden!'

'Son!' cried Sogolon.

'Mother!' cried Diata.

'If that is what you want, we shall leave here.'

'Yes, mother. We feel stifled in this palace; don't you feel so too?'

'Yes, it's true. However, before we shake the dust of Niani from our feet, I have some advice for you, my son!'

'What's that, Mother?'

'Like the princes of Dö, you must have four symbolic plaits in your hair!'

But she said this rather listlessly.

'Four symbolic plaits? What are they?' asked Diata.

'The first plait signifies: "Love your wife, but never tell her state secrets!" ' Sogolon hastened to reply.

'But why would one love one's wife and yet never tell her state secrets?' Diata asked, interested.

'Because a woman gives in much more easily. Oh! unconsciously, perhaps, but all the same no one has ever been able to capture a king, in our land, a powerful king, without the complicity of his wife. Consequently if one day you should come to take your seat on the lion skin of kingship, you must remember my advice. If you have to face, courageously, an army of ten thousand men, you have hopes of gaining a victory; but beware of women, son, because behind the rise of every great man there is the blind love of a woman, and behind the fall of every great man there is the terrible hatred of a woman! Therefore one woman alone seems more formidable than an army of ten thousand men!'

'I shall remember that, Mother! Now, tell me about the second

147

plait,' said Diata.

Sogolon was silent a moment, then went on:

'The second plait means "a king has no friend!" Indeed, the only reason guiding a king is reason of state, which is not necessarily that of ordinary people,' Sogolon said sententiously.

'That's true, Mother! Dankaran Tuman is my brother, but today, because he is king, he treats me as if he was not! Now I want to know the meaning of the third plait.'

'The third plait! It tells us that "the son of another is not your son! The land of another is not your land!" Dankaran Tuman cannot have with me the same manner as he has with his mother! On the other hand, we are going to leave the Manden because you want to. But whatever the rank you occupy abroad, you must one day cast off those honours, without fail, and come here, for you must never forget that the Manden is your homeland.'

'I shall remember that, too, Mother! Now, tell me the significance of the fourth plait.'

'The fourth plait!' Sogolon said, 'is this: "a kingdom cannot be run without the co-operation of the old!" Indeed, the ancients are the kings of the shadow. That is, sitting calmly in the shade, the old can see what the young – called the kings of the sun because they are always carrying out their activities in the sunlight! – perched at the top of a great tree fail to see! The young give the kingdom the power of their muscles, the old the fruit of their experience: they complement one another.'

Diata doubled up with laughter. When he had recovered, he asked his mother:

'When are we leaving?'

'Whatever day you choose, my son!'

'Don't let us stay any longer than necessary in this palace. Let's leave tomorrow, at dawn!'

'Very well!'

Indignation, and the sense of being the victim of great injustice, tormented Diata's soul. He suddenly shut himself away behind a wall of silence, just as the other members of his family had shut themselves away, all except Sogolon, who suddenly – as if her anger had gone to her head! – put Dia-Mori down from her lap. With one bound, she was standing upright, then slowly she advanced a few steps into the courtyard of the royal palace and turned her head in the direction of Fatumata's hut, shouting at the top of her voice:

'As we do not appear to be wanted in this palace, we shall leave it tomorrow morning, and we shall depart far from here! Ever since the death of my husband, my children and I have always been the victims of your bullying tricks. We have no peace, neither in this palace, nor in the city of Niani! Before, Diata was ridiculed because his legs were paralysed; today, now that he is perfectly healthy, just to provoke him and make him take a dislike to his father's house, his griot has been taken away from him. Tomorrow – who knows what you might do to us tomorrow? We really are having to live with people well-versed in cynicism. Not knowing what to do, we prefer to leave: we do not want to become mad. We shall vanish from this place at dawn! We leave this palace to the king and his mother. Yes, we shall leave them the city of Niani, we shall leave them the whole of the Manden!'

In a fever of resentment, Sogolon's voice carried far in the night. Its force impressed Fatumata Bérété and her son, who only too often had shown undue disdain for the woman of Dô and her family. At present, Fatumata could tell, from the tone of the shouts of her co-wife, that the latter would no longer let herself be bullied and insulted, and she was crestfallen.

Sogolon turned her eyes to the heavens, and addressed them thus:

'Ever since I was married, there have been thirteen winters during which there has been no end to my persecution!' she shouted. 'And now, it is my son's turn to suffer!'

Then she lowered her eyes, and again stared in the direction of the door to Fatumata's hut, crying:

'Who is it did all this to us? Who is riddled with jealousy like a crab[1] if not my rival, who hears well what I say!'

But Fatumata could hardly bring herself to put her head out of her hut to cast a furtive, fearful glance at Sogolon in all her anger: then she at once withdrew her head into her hut.

Later, Nan Bukari went up to Sogolon, speechless with anger, and drew her back to her dwelling place.

Thus was their exile decided upon. Thus it was that one day, at the second crying of the cock, the woman of Dô and her children

1 Malinké proverb illustrating excessive jealousy

left Niani, without bidding farewell to anyone, without saying goodbye to the old people of the clan – their hearts were too full for leave-takings! These aged ones were mostly the women who had taken part in Sogolon's marriage ceremonies, and seen the birth and baptism of Diata.

Would they ever see again those to whom they could not say farewell? Faced with this uncertainty, it was as if they were abruptly taking leave of their own past, of their life in the city of Niani – a life that would certainly have been pleasant if it had not been troubled by that stupid family rivalry.

Accompanied by her children, Sogolon made her way along a path winding between fields of wild grasses that swayed softly in the fresh air of the morning, and in which already there were a few bulls grazing quietly. They were escorted by a chorus of cicadas.

After two days' walk, as night was falling, they arrived, exhausted, at Badou Djéliba. They had only been walking for two days, but they felt as if it had been ten. Sogolon had been overcome by an inexplicable heaviness. In fact, she was holding Sogolon-Kanko by the hand, and carried – as well as her weighty hump! – Dia-Mori on her back. She felt an indescribable heaviness in her shoulders and back. The heaviness seemed to concentrate itself there.

Badou Djéliba was a city situated downstream on the River Niger. It was the capital of the sorcerer king Kansa Konkon, who greeted them pleasantly enough as far as words go, but whose welcome was in fact full of mistrust.

However, his somewhat distant tone did not discourage the travellers, who, it must be said, were so exhausted after their two days' march that they wanted at any cost to take some rest.

'But I'm forgetting!' said Sogolon. 'We have not yet introduced ourselves. Allow me to proceed with the introductions . . . I am Sogolon Condé, wife of the late Naré Maghan Kön Fatta, king of the Manden. And these are my children: Mari-Diata, Nan-Bukari, Sogolon-Kanko and Manden-Bori, who is still called Dia-Mori!'

As she named them, each one vigorously shook the hand that Mansa Konkon extended to them. He in his turn proceeded to introduce himself:

'I am Mansa Konkon in person!'

Then he added:

'Now that we know one another, would you, queen of the Manden, kindly make yourself at home here in my palace?'

Sogolon accepted the invitation, and the king took them to the right wing of his residence. On the way, he talked with enthusiasm about his kingdom.

'It's strange!' he said, bursting out laughing, 'I've never seen you here before. Is this the first time you have come to Badou Djéliba?'

'Yes. . . It is the first time I've come here,' replied Sogolon.

And she looked about her, trying to estimate the size of the palace she had just entered.

'You are so different from the people of these parts. You are dressed in the manner of the Manden-ka women!' said Mansa Konkon.

Sogolon made no reply. She was keeping an eye on her children who were following her in a noisy group. But Mansa Konkon wanted to keep up the conversation.

'I hope that you will not find it too tedious among us. Take a good rest tomorrow, and if you so wish, my 'change wife' will bring the meals to your room.'

Sogolon replied, somewhat embarrassed:

'Oh! I don't know if my two big sons, who are rather lively, will want to stay in bed. But I shall take a good rest myself tomorrow.'

'I can see that the children play a big part in your life. What do these two strapping lads do with their time in your country?' Mansa Konkon asked.

'Well! Diata and Nan Bukari go hunting. They are very fond of hunting. And it makes them forget their other worries, or so they say. In fact, they have lost their father, you know! The younger brother lost both father and mother. His mother, who was my co-wife, died some time ago.'

'Were you obliged to bring him with you?' Mansa Konkon asked.

'Not exactly, but . . .'

She stopped short just as she was about to say:

'I could not leave him in Niani.'

Why speak of the malice of Fatumata and her son tonight? It was better to face their first night of exile in a calm frame of mind.

At first, on leaving Niani, Sogolon and her children had felt it was rather pleasant to be relieved of the tyranny of Fatumata Bérété. But as Mansa Konkon did not give them any work to do, Diata and Nan Bukari spent their days hunting. That was certainly the best way to overcome any nostalgia for their country, because indeed now they were in Badou Djéliba, but they were not altogether in Badou Djéliba: they were still in Niani. Indeed, one's native earth, notwithstanding the hospitality one may find in other lands – the land you are going to knows nothing of rank or status! – one's native earth must always be more than just earth: it is the Whole Earth itself!

Yes, even though one cannot enjoy there, as was the case with Sogolon, the solidarity and understanding of all members of the family – and of everyone else in this world – one's native earth remains, despite everything, the only familiar horizon and the only way of life, which one carries away with one, but which one is never willing to compare with the reality! Diata and Nan Bukari were still in Niani, yet were no longer in Niani! They were here and they were there: they felt torn. Indeed, the two boys found exile very difficult to bear, but they did not say so, for their life in their own native land had in many respects been unendurable.

As for Sogolon, she seemed to have acquired a sort of balance. Life now lay before her like a beautiful river. She joined the king's wives and gladly helped to carry out domestic tasks from which Mansa Konkon had nevertheless excused her. Others perhaps, unlike Sogolon, might have been able to accustom themselves to the regimen of total repose her host tried to make her accept. But Sogolon could not. She became completely integrated into that royal family, and, in the palace, did her share of the work like all the other women; and probably it was in this constant activity that lay the secret of her good humour.

After the first few days, the daughter of the king and Nan Bukari began to take a liking to one another. Soon they became inseparable. When he was not accompanying her to her friends' huts, he would walk with her in the vast courtyard of the palace,

152

whose every corner was familiar to him now. Or else he would go and find Diata, and give him long accounts of how he had spent the day with the young girl. But Sogolon's son's replies were always brief and devoid of the imagination and day-dreaming that his brother enjoyed so much.

Hawa – that was the name of Mansa Konkon's daughter – would often go to Sogolon's hut to ask the Manden-ka prince to came and play with her.

'Well, now!' Nan Bukari told her one morning, 'you never told me that you were the only daughter of the king of Badou Djéliba!'

'You never asked me,' she retorted. 'I am his only daughter, but I have five brothers.'

'If Diata hadn't told me, I should never have known,' replied Nan Bukari.

One night of the full moon, the two sweethearts crouched in the dust to play shovelboard, but hardly had they begun than they jumped up to have a game of hide-and-seek!

'I shouldn't like your father to catch us at this,' the young Manden-ka prince said.

'Hum!' said Hawa.

'You know, he could be roaming around, as fathers always do when they have children?' Nan Bukari replied.

Then, changing the subject without warning, she suddenly came out with:

'Did you know? My father received two messengers this evening?'

'Two messengers, did you say?'

'Yes, and they came from the Manden. They gave plenty of gold to my father, sent by the queen mother!'

'Sent by the queen mother of the Manden?'

'Yes ... I was hidden behind a door – as usual – and I heard everything!'

'What did they talk about?'

'The messengers spoke about your brother! The queen mother of the Manden wants him done away with! But be sure never to repeat what I've told you to anyone: if my father knew, he'd kill me!'

She paused a while, as if to judge the effect of her words on

Nan Bukari, then went on:

'Tomorrow my father will surely call your brother out to the game of "Wori"!'

'The game of "Wori"?' asked Nan Bukari in bewilderment.

'Yes! My father is a great sorcerer, and his power resides in the game of "Wori" which was revealed to him by the guardian spirits!'

'My brother is a great sorcerer, too!' Nan Bukari said proudly.

'Your brother may well be a great sorcerer, but he could never beat my father!' Hawa retorted.

At that moment, Diata appeared at the gate of the royal palace and called to Nan Bukari to come to bed, as it was getting late, and as he walked towards him, his elder brother started teasing him:

'I somehow get the feeling that you are sweet on the daughter of Mansa Konkon!'

'Yes! N'koro, if you want to tame the lion, you must be on good terms with the lion cub.'

'That's so. You'll tame the lion as long as he isn't angry, but if he is, he'll tear you to pieces like an old rag!' Diata replied, laughing.

They went back to their dwelling, making fun of one another all the way.

Next morning, Diata had no sooner finished breakfast than Mansa Konkon sent one of his guards to fetch him. As he was finishing his millet porridge, Sogolon's son looked at the sky. The sun was still not very high.

The king of Badou Djéliba lived in a palace of seventy doors. This palace was a vast building with thick walls, spacious rooms that were fairly comfortable, but dimly lit by oil lamps of various colours. Indeed, the palace was a veritable labyrinth.

The guard entered the royal residence fearfully, walking in front of Diata whose calm gaze slowly took in every piece of furniture, every object of this multi-coloured interior.

When his eyes had grown accustomed to the dimness, the son of Sogolon saw the king waiting for him, sitting on the skin of a bull. But, with his eyes closed, he appeared to be plunged in deep meditation. Was he thinking of the trick he was hoping to play on Diata? Was he thinking of the gold he had received from the queen mother of the Manden? Now that his eyes were closed and the satanic little flame in them was hidden, his face had become quite good-natured. When he heard footsteps, he awoke with a start and asked:

'Is that the guard with the boy?'

'Yes, it is,' the guard replied.

Like an automaton, the king made several gestures with the back of his hand, as if to brush away some bits of food that might have fallen on his boubou; but they were grains neither of rice nor of fonio he was brushing away: he was just making gestures of a conventional kind, as if to give himself countenance before Diata who, pretending not to notice, exclaimed, as he gazed up at the fine weapons hanging on the wall:

'What magnificent weapons you have, Mansa Konkon!'

And he took down from the wall a sabre – the most beautiful one! – which he drew from its scabbard, and began skirmishing with an imaginary opponent.

When the king raised his head, he saw Diata, sabre in hand. For a moment he gazed in astonishment at the wonderfully gifted boy, and then made as if to snatch the weapon from his hands, but he controlled himself . . . In fact, it was the first time anyone had been able to draw that sabre from its sheath. Moreover, Mansa Konkon had expressly forbidden his arms to be touched by anyone, but the son of Sogolon, who was a stranger, doubtless did not know of this interdiction.

'Where did you get that sabre?' the king finally asked

'Where?' replied Diata. 'It was hanging on the wall there, to your right.'

The king gazed fixedly at the boy for a moment, then cried:

'If I ever catch you playing with my arms!' he threatened.

'Me?' queried Diata. 'I'm not playing with your arms. I like this sabre very much.'

'Hang it back in its place!' Mansa Konkon ordered in a loud voice.

He thought that shouting would frighten the lad. And he was seeking some pretext, with the sabre. But he saw at once that his loud voice had no effect on the son of Sogolon, who calmly answered:

'You called me, Mansa Konkon? Here I am.'

155

And he hung the sabre back in its place.

'Yes! Sit down beside me. I called you here to play "Wori" with me,' said Mansa Konkon. 'It's my habit to play "Wori" with my guests,' he added.

Then he asked solemnly:

'If I win – and I *shall* be the winner! – what will you give me?'

'Anything you want: I mean, everything you ask me.'

'If I win, I shall kill you!'

'You are very sure of yourself, Mansa Konkon!' said Diata. 'And what if I am the winner?'

'If you are the winner, I'll give you anything you ask of me,' the king replied. 'But *I* shall be the winner, because I am unbeatable at this game.'

'If *I* am the winner, all I ask for is that sabre,' said Diata.

And he pointed with his finger at the sabre hanging on the wall.

'Done!' agreed Mansa Konkon.

And the king approached the 'Wori' game. It was a section of a tree trunk made cubical by the adze of a clever craftsman who had also carefully hollowed out the holes of the 'Wori' block.

Then, he put four pebbles in each hole, and began redistributing them in various holes, chanting:

> *Idoon Kussu la! Idoon Mama la!*
> *Kokoji Kokoji N'né ni jina bè ala tuma min*
> *Mô tè n'fè yé!*
> *Koni N'Dén kè nin n'séri la, m'bi fàl*

Here's to him who offers the least! Here's to him who offers the most!
Kokoji Kokoji I was alone with the guardian spirit!
But my son, if I win, I shall kill you!

And Diata, taking the pebbles from one of the holes, went on with the chant:

> *Idoon Kussu la! Idoon Mama la!*
> *Kokoji Kokoji Karifa Ko ra kélà gné*
> *N'né lé fôlô ka n'karifa ima!*
> *N'né fôlô lé kora kélà gnél*

Here's to him who offers the least! Here's to him who offers the
 most!
Kokoji Kokoji the guest comes before the order condemning him
 to death!
I am the first to entrust myself to you!
I have forestalled the order you gave for my condemnation!

'I've been cheated!' howled the king. 'Someone has betrayed
me – who?'
'Who would betray you?' Diata answered.
'I expect you would have some idea who it was!'
'Mansa Konkon, I have now been living in your abode already
these three months, and you never invited me to play "Wori" with
you before! But today, suddenly, you call me for a game. When
you see a chicken's intestine stiff and straight, it's because there's
a stick in it . . .'
Looking very embarrassed, the king replied:
'Very well, then! You are the winner, but I refuse to give you
the sabre I promised. And to put paid to your machinations, I
order you to leave my capital, at once, son of the devil!'
'Very well!' said Diata. 'Thank you for these three months'
hospitality. I'm leaving! But feet beat the earth, the serpent sways
on the earth, and the two shall not fail to meet!'
So, early in the morning, Diata and his family once more trod
the path of exile as if they had only just begun, with high hearts!
It was cool, but it was a deceptive coolness; it soon passed, and
now their bodies were drenched in sweat, for the heat was becoming oppressive, the air was heavy. Sogolon-Kanko trotted
along behind their little procession.
After a while, they halted their march to take a little rest in the
shade of a citron tree. Diata, his face haggard, raised his head.
What was he looking at? The road? Perhaps. Perhaps at the
mountains, far away, and the city of Tabon, not far from those
mountains. And perhaps not. Perhaps Diata's eyes were register-
ing nothing. Perhaps it was because they were looking at nothing
visible that they had become so distant and so absent. After the
travellers had walked on again, they found themselves in the
palace of the serpent-man, Sadi So-oro, the father of Fran
Camara, their friend.

Sadi So-oro reigned over the kingdom inhabited by the 'dalikimbon' Camara[1], and by the Djallonké. The old king of Tabon had long been a trusted ally of the court in Niani. He was a descendant of Abdul Wakass who, like Bilali-Ibumana, the ancestor of Diata, was a freed slave. He had settled in Tabon and married there. His son was Fayala whose son was Fakémoko. Fakémoko had as son Saran Laye whose son was Nunféré, who had as son Mamadigbé, who had as son Sadi So-oro, whose son was Fran.

Not without a certain pride, Fran took them on a visit of the city of Tabon, and his Manden-ka friends marvelled at the fortresses of his capital and the arsenals of the king. To make their pleasure complete, the prince of Tabon offered his guests from the Manden a hunting trip. Once they were out in the bush, the three princes of the savanna swore an oath:

'When you are king of the Manden,' Fran Camara began, 'what will you give me?'

'If I become king of the Manden, I shall name you viceroy. But you'll have your own inherited titles, because then you will be king of Tabon, your father being so old now!' Diata said.

'Yes! The entire Tabon army will be mine. The blacksmiths of the dalikimbon Camara and the Djallonké are invincible warriors!'

'We'll be stronger than you are!' Nan Bukari boasted.

On their return to the royal palace, Fran found there a messenger from Sibi, despatched urgently by his cousin Famandian Camara – a 'sininkimbon' prince[2] – commanding him to send Diata on his way as soon as possible, as he was being sought by Sumaoro.

Sadi So-oro, who was already very old, and fearful of seeing his kingdom invaded and destroyed by the army of Sumaoro, immediately sent off Sogolon and her children on the road to N'Gumbu, capital of Wahadu, (formerly Ghaha); he gave them warm introductions to Sumaba Cissé, the king of that land!

Sadi So-oro had given them mounts, and had entrusted them to the protection of a caravan.

Diata having left Tabon so abruptly, he had to put a rein on

1 Dalikimbon: a blacksmith prince of Tabon.
2 Sininkimbon: a Camara prince of Sibi, non-blacksmith.

his imagination, in order to think no more about his friend Fran Camara, with whom he had felt so at ease, particularly during the hunting party and the exchange of oaths.

Indeed, he felt no affinity whatsoever with these caravaneers, who were for the most part Arabs. When they talked to him about the power of the great king of the times, Sumaoro, and especially of his cruelty, he would listen to them, pretending interest, but thinking of his sad expatriate destiny, or of his faithful griot Balla Fassali Kuyaté kept from him in Sosso!

The caravaneers passed one night at Bérédugu. Next morning they set off for N'Gumbu. As they approached that city, Diata observed the form of the Wahadu buildings; they were very different from what he was accustomed to see in the Manden: seen from afar, at first sight these constructions looked like cubical mounds. As he drew nearer, he was astonished by their huge size. Moreover, the whole city of N'Gumbu was of a scrupulous cleanliness. So much order and cleanliness rejoiced his soul, after the desolation he had felt during the long journey on camel-back across immense and monotonous seas of sand.

Diata felt inspiritated and refreshed by the sight. What he was a little concerned about was the lack of water in the region of Wahadu. But there were numerous mosques, because the Sarakholés were devout Muslims, whereas at Niani there was only one mosque.

When Sogolon and her children entered the magnificent palace of Sumaba Cisse, he happened to be at his devotions. They were greeted by his brother.

The king, when he returned from the mosque, received the strangers. King Sarakholé was slender, thin as an ascetic, and friendly; he seemed very glad when he saw Sogolon and her children. When he had pressed their hands in greeting, his brother, acting as interpreter, introduced him to the Manden-ka.

'I extend a warm welcome to all strangers who come to N'Gumbu!' he said.

'We salute the king, his family and his entourage!' Sogolon replied.

'You come in peace to N'Gumbu, and may peace be with you in our capital!'

'Thank you!'

'The king gives leave for the strangers to speak!'

'We are from Niani,' Sogolon began. 'The father of my children was Naré Maghan Kön Fatta, king of the Manden. My husband is dead. His eldest son, who succeeded him, and his mother, my co-wife, have been persecuting us everywhere we go. We are weary with travelling: today I have come to beg for asylum from Sumaba Cissé, king of Wahadu!'

As Sogolon was speaking, the king did not take his eyes off young Diata, who was gazing ecstatically, but quietly, at the magnificent decorations in the reception chamber of Sumaba Cissé. The king went on observing him for a long while out of the corner of his eye: he seemed moved by the story of Sogolon and her family. And possibly he was thinking about that family broken by the forces of destiny. Possibly he was also thinking of the centuries-old friendship linking his kingdom with that of the Manden. Then he suddenly made a decision.

And strangely enough, to the great astonishment of Sogolon and her children, Sumaba Cissé began speaking the language of the Manden. Indeed, he spoke it better than some Manden-ka.

'Queen of the Manden!' he began. 'I knew your husband personally: he was my friend. Consider my court as your court. My palace as your palace. The friendship linking Wahadu to the Manden was not born yesterday. Everyone knows that!'

Then, turning to speak in a friendly way to Diata, he said:

'Come closer, cousin. What is your name?'

'I am called Mari-Diata. I am also called Naré Maghan Diata. But everybody calls me Sogolon-Diata. My brothers? My younger brother is called Nan Bukari and the last-born is Manden-Bori: he is also called Dia-Mori. My sister is called Sogolon-Kanko.'

'You will make a great king, for you forget no one!' Sumaba said in a great burst of laughter.

After this initial interview, seeing that his guests were tired, Sumaba Cissé ordered his brother to see that they were royally installed and treated at the court of N'Gumbu.

For one long year Sogolon and her children remained with the royal family of N'Gumbu, and became a part of it. Diata, his brothers and his sister Sogolon-Kanko found themselves on an equal footing with the princes of Wahadu, and were even treated with greater indulgence than the sons of Sumaba-Cissé.

Yet among the Sarakholés, so hospitable and friendly, Sogolon was unable to find lasting peace. In fact, the air of the city of N'Gumbu – not situated on the river – hardly seemed to agree with her, and the king, despite all the esteem he felt for this distressed family, decided, regretfully, to send Sogolon and her children to the court at Méma, to his cousin Mussa Tunkara. Méma, not far from Timbuctoo, was a big city. Moreover, it was the capital of a powerful kingdom, and besides, it was situated on the banks of the River Niger. Nothing could suit Sogolon better, for she had so long been accustomed in Niani to the breezes from the River Sankarani.

So Sumaba sent them on their way to Méma, after putting them in the care of caravaneers well known to him.

When their caravan arrived the king, Mussa Tunkara, was absent from his capital. But his sister Nansira Tunkara, forewarned by a messenger from Sumaba Cissé, received them royally. In fact, practically the entire population of the capital went to the city gates to greet the strangers. And as soon as they saw the new guests advancing across the savanna, the whole crowd began clapping their hands and uttering shouts of joyous welcome! It was as if Mussa Tunkara in person was making his entry into the city. Nansira, very friendly, lodged her guests in one wing of the palace; she confided to Sogolon that her brother had no children. At the court of Méma the only children were those of the vassals, whom Diata, showing early powers of leadership, held sway over from the moment of his arrival in the city.

After the dry season, the king, who had set out on an expedition against brigands on the right bank of the river who periodically invaded and sacked his country, made a triumphal return to his capital. Yes, the victories of Mussa Tunkara during that campaign had been many and brilliant.

To celebrate his return, the women of Méma stood in long rows along the palisades to raise paeans to his glory. To the sound of drums, the king passed by on horseback, making his steed dance and perform graceful steps as it rhythmically swayed its head adorned with magnificent reins. Then the king gravely saluted the crowd and advanced triumphantly in good order towards the royal residence. Other cavalrymen and footsoldiers formed an impressive escort, while the prisoners of war, their

161

hands tied behind their backs, their heads hanging very low, were driven on in front of them, booed by the delirious crowd.

When the king made his entry into his residence, his sister Nansira Tunkara handed him a letter from Sumaba Cissé, recommending Sogolon and her family, whom she thereupon introduced to her brother.

Mussa Tunkara, very amiably said, quite simply:

'In the letter I have just read my cousin Sumaba Cissé tells me of the reason for your departure from the Manden. This letter is enough for me! I wish you to know that by coming from N'Gumbu to Méma you have merely changed houses. Be welcome here, and consider yourselves at home in my capital!'

So Diata and Nañ Bukari made their first campaign at Méma. Whenever Mussa Tunkara – who was a great warrior! – set out on an expedition, the son of Sogolon, now fifteen years of age, was always at his side. From the very start, the Manden-ka prince had won the admiration of all the *sofas*[1], for already he showed himself to be as agile as a panther, noble as a lion, and impetuous in attack as a buffalo. Yes, already he seemed to symbolize his three ancestral totems!

One day, in the course of a skirmish against mountain robbers, the army of the king of Méma met with stiff resistance and several of his warriors fell in battle. The others retreated, surprised on the one hand by the enemy's ardour, and on the other by the hail of lances. At that moment, Mussa Tunkara made the gesture which usually drove to a frenzy those of his warriors whose personal pride was at stake: he threw his assegai into the midst of the mountain band! But his warriors, hotly pursued by the enemy, still went on retreating in disarray. Only Diata, wildly excited, sabre in hand and uttering loud war-cries, rushed so impetuously upon the advancing foe that the king, delighted but with his heart in his mouth, watched him with admiring though dubious eyes.

The son of Sogolon struck out wildly in all directions: his sabre split from top to toe all the bandits he encountered, it slashed their mounts to pieces with such force it embedded itself in the earth as in a ripe papaya! His steed, as full of mettle as himself, overthrew those of the mountain men who tried to stop

1 *sofas:* warriors, soldiers.

162

his headlong dash! The brigands, panic-stricken, took to their heels.

And now that he was within reach of the royal assegai, shining like a sun on the ground, Diata made his horse rear, and, with a single movement, leaning down over its flank, seized the spear; then, regaining his seat on his galloping steed, rode hard to rejoin Mussa Tunkara.

The warriors, dumbfounded at the sight, exclaimed:

'No force can resist the son of Sogolon! What a great king he will make!'

When he drew rein beside the king, the latter said to him, beaming with enthusiasm:

'God has sent you to me at a time when I have no son and so no inheritor for the throne of Méma. I shall make a great king of you!'

From that day onwards, Mussa Tunkan began to pay particular attention to Diata: he no longer had eyes for the vassal princes of his kingdom. All the talk was of the heroism of the son of Sogolon in the army. Such was his popularity that finally it spread beyond the walls of the camp and into the city of Méma, like a lighted trail of powder. His fame spread even beyond the mighty River Niger. The mountain bandits, more and more fearful of his reputation, were less and less willing to invade the fields of Méma!

Diata was growing. He had now passed eighteen winters. His short warrior's jacket, of a reddish-brown colour, and his narrow pantaloons of the same shade, gave him the air of a real warrior; garbed thus, he appeared at least ten years older.

Mussa Tunkara, more and more proud of him, named him viceroy. Whenever the sovereign was absent from Méma, it was he who took command. Both the army and the people approved Mussa's choice.

The son of Sogolon was now an adolescent shooting up into the sky like a young bombax tree. Six years had passed since his departure from Niani – six long years! And now life lay before him like a beautiful river. It seemed that his destiny was to be fulfilled in Méma. Was he not already viceroy there? Was he not admired and respected by all the people in that kingdom? Was he not going to succeed to Mussa Tunkara? And – what was even more wonderful – had there not already entered his life a Méma maiden, adorable Aïsha Aminu?

One evening, however, while Diata and his family were chatting on the veranda of their residence in Méma, Sogolon Condé, who had nurtured the child that all the world would know, and who knew that the end of her mission in life would coincide with the beginning of Sundiata's, said:

'Son, remember that, like all the princes of Dô, you have four symbolic plaits on your head! One of these plaits is called: "the son of another is not your son, the land of another is not your land!" Do not let yourself be deceived, Diata. Your destiny should be accomplished in the Manden: that is where we were humiliated by Fatumata Bérété and her son Dankaran Tuman. That is where we had to run away like thieves in the night, and that is where we must take up the challenge – for better death than shame! – Never forget that, son!'

'I shall never forget it, Mother, and today, more than ever, I am determined to take up the challenge, to wipe out the affront of Fatumata Bérété and her son Dankaran Tuman!' said Sundiata.

SUMAORO DIARRASSO,
THE POWERFUL KING OF SOSSO

Sundiata had been in voluntary exile already for six years, to escape the wiles of his brother Dankaran Tuman, who knew his brother was the predestined one. While he was spending his last year in Méma, the powerful king Sumaoro Diarrasso annexed the Manden. The same thing had happened to all the other kingdoms of the savanna, whose chiefs, trembling before the redoubtable fetishes of the sovereign of Sosso, and before his even more redoubtable army, hastened – fearing to be annihilated – to acknowledge his growing authority. Thus the embassies accredited to Sosso were suppressed, and the diplomats sent back to their respective countries. Alone, Balla Fassali Kuyaté, retained by Sumaoro for his own pleasure, had remained in Sosso.

On the other hand, nine of the kings who had ventured to oppose the annexation of their territories were executed, to set an example to the rest, by the powerful ruler, and the heads of these victims adorned, in the hall of idols, the sacrificial vessel on the fourth floor of the formidable tower he had had constructed, and which dominated his capital. As for their skins, they served as seats, and decorated the interior walls of his palace. Who was this Sumaoro?

Sosso, of which Sumaoro was the powerful king, was a kingdom founded three hundred years after the death of the Prophet Mohammed. Before this period, Sosso, an insignificant village, was – like the Manden – a dependancy of Wahadu.

The kingdom of Sosso – which grew at the expense of Wahadu – had as its founding king the blacksmith Diomaté Fodé Diarrasso. He was the first to discover fire by rubbing two stones against one another; the first, too, to bring fire to the Manden!

Diomaté Fodé Diarrasso had as son Kabiné Diarrasso, who had as son Kani Diarrasso, who had as son Burama Diarrasso, who, in his turn, had nine sons, none of whom sat on the royal skin. It was Diarra Diarrasso – the brother of Burama Diarrasso – who seized power. The powerful king Sumaoro Diarrasso, whom the Manden-ka called (and continue to call to this day)

165

Sumaoro Kanté, or Sumanguru Kanté, was the son of old Diarra Diarrasso. He was also the son of Kaya Touré, Daby Touré, Sansun Touré, the three wives of old Diarra Diarrasso.

But perhaps in the womb of his three mothers the foetus Sumaoro Diarrasso was already a wizard of the highest abilities and an exceptionally gifted magician? Perhaps . . .

For in fact these three mothers took it in turn to give birth to the future tyrant of Sosso: Kaya Touré was the first to become pregnant with Sumaoro who, three months later, transferred to the womb of Daby Touré. During the last three months it was the turn of Sansun Touré to carry him in her womb. It was Sansun Touré who gave birth to Sumaoro Diarrasso. But in fact, all three wives of Diarra Diarrasso felt the same violent birth pangs at the same time!

When Sumaoro Diarrasso became king of Sosso he had the notion of reclaiming his heritage of Wahadu. However his father Diarra Diarrasso who enjoyed a reign of fifteen peaceful years, and his predecessors, had never attempted anything of that kind.

To accomplish his ends, the king of Sosso resorted to a reign of terror and cruelty.

The new king of the Manden, Dankaran Tuman, frightened and intrigued by this growing hegemony, hastened to give his younger sister Nana Triban in marriage to the sovereign of Sosso. By doing so, perhaps he thought to be spared by the latter!

Nana Triban, not long a widow – her first husband had died tragically in a hunting accident – was escorted to Sosso and offered as wife by Balla Fassali Kuyaté to His Majesty the King blacksmith Sumaoro Diarrasso, as a sign of courteous allegiance.

But just like her brother Dankaran Tuman, Nana Triban reacted strongly to the agonies and sufferings of the Manden-ka people. And as she knew that Sumaoro was invulnerable to arrows – did he not possess sixty-three totems? – she resolved to accomplish her mission as princess of the Manden with her terrible husband, in whom, moreover, she at once inspired, thanks to her legendary beauty and charm, the liveliest of passions. Her task was to uncover the secret of those sixty-three totems, the secret of her husband's invulnerability.

So she refused to submit to him for a whole week. Yes, she refused categorically to give herself to the man she had just married. One by one she brought out her feminine wiles – charm, dissimulation, lies. But perhaps in order to succeed at such encounters, it is necessary to be more than just one woman, and she managed to play many parts. Soon she began to move around easily in her web of lies, as at home in guile as a fish in water, so much so that at the end of a week she caught out Sumaoro at his own game! This is how she did it:

At the end of the week, she had them prepare hydromel for the sovereign of Sosso, whom she had left in hopes of a long, sweet night of love. . .

So when night fell, as soon as the king had entered his dwelling, she covered his feet with kisses, all the while stammering confessions of love that she seemed to have been repressing a long time.

'You know,' she said, 'you must have confidence in me. I came to Sosso of my own free will! I admired and loved you as only we women know how – silently, year after year, and with what anguish! Sundiata, whom you seem to be wary of, has left the Manden for ever. Before leaving us, he and his family did not get along with either my mother or my brother Dankaran Tuman. Your spies surely informed you of all this!'

'Yes, that is so,' replied Sumaoro.

'Come, sit beside me, and put your trust in me, for the basis of love and of everything, everything in life is trust! Now here is some delicious hydromel I have had prepared for you!'

'I am going to rest, after having had a good time with you first,' said Sumaoro. 'After this night spent in your company I have a long journey to make: I have to make a tour of the states under my control.'

'I shall not keep you any longer than you wish,' said Nana Triban. 'Do me the honour of tasting my hydromel and tell me what you think of it!'

She held out to him a full goblet, then disappeared for a moment to bring fire to light her husband's pipe. Already she seemed very satisfied with herself.

Sumaoro began to drink deep: he was drinking more than was good for him. And Nana Triban, in order to ensorcel him, appeared before him as Hawa!

'Not bad at all!' he said, smacking his lips as he looked her over. 'You are better built and certainly more seductive than any of the three hundred wives in my harem. And your hydromel is excellent!'

Nana Triban, in her Hawa shape, went closer to him and poured a little more hydromel into her husband's goblet.

'Drink it down quickly now,' she said. 'It's good! There is plenty of honey in it,' she added, in her most loving tones.

'Yes!' he replied. 'But if I don't stop drinking, I'll soon be making a fool of myself!'

For a whole week he had been expecting this scene. Now that it was actually taking place, he hardly knew whether it was real or whether she was some figment of his imagination – an image he had had in his mind one whole week, and that his eyes finally saw as something divorced from all reality.

No, the scene was real enough . . . Above the rim of his goblet, he observed his young wife whose dark bronze skin and per-fectly-sculptured form recalled the superb physique of both Naré Maghan Kön Fatta and that of Fatumata Bérété – and gave promise of immediate bliss. Thus, seated on his bed, a low couch lit by the faint glow of the lamp (oil lamps provide flickering flames that seem only reluctantly to spread a little light) every-thing that passed over the face of Sumaoro Diarrasso could be clearly seen. Nana Triban saw a lustful look, saw his nostrils flaring, saw his eyes gleaming voluptuously in the light that illumined her husband's face, a light that now spread all over it, devouring it with a lustful radiance, for meanwhile she had lain down on the couch in an attitude that was irresistible.

As Sumaoro drank ever more deeply, the hydromel began rising to his head in an alarming way; but he knew that, despite his intoxicated state, his desire that night was not far from being realized. After having placed his goblet on a bench, he rose with difficulty from his seat, then, tottering somewhat, moved towards Nana Triban, who, pretending great passion, opened her arms to him!

'Oh, how beautiful you are!' he said, lying on his back next to Nana Triban, very close to her. 'I've been longing for this moment ever since your arrival in Sosso,' he added.

And he began to laugh a crazy laugh, because by now the hydromel had well and truly gone to his head.

'Come to me!' he said. 'I want you, want you so much!'

Now that his first words of love had been spoken, he was ready, without realizing it, to continue his discourse for hours. But with a sudden movement, Nana Triban, so slender and agile, swivelled round and sat astride him!

Then, having taken her husband in this attitude, her hips, supple as cotton, went into action. The young woman went on jiggling for a long time. All this time, her softly-exploring hands were caressing Sumaoro's massive torso; faking orgasm, she was sighing and groaning.

As for her husband, his eyes with their burning intensity never left Nana Triban's breasts, swinging right in front of his face; breasts not yet slackened, still firm – the breasts of a woman who has not yet had a child – breasts as round and warm as ripe oranges. And Nana Triban was redoubling her jiggling movements. But perhaps there was some purpose behind them: perhaps those jigglings were just too much, and because they were performed with scientific precision, and because they were becoming just too much to bear, Sumaoro, despite the hydromel vapours that had gone to his head, and despite the fact that he was lying under her in a passive attitude, was beginning to writhe convulsively, twitching his toes that kept stretching and closing insensibly. Perhaps he and his wife had already climbed the tree of pleasure, and perhaps they had succeeded in hauling themselves up to the summit of glittering leaves? Perhaps! For already Nana Triban's panting breaths were gradually getting longer until finally there poured from her throat sounds like distant, plaintive yowlings coming from deep in the virgin forest, and a tremendous love-rattle, the gasping rattle of dizzying ascension, made Sumaoro's massive chest vibrate. It rose higher and higher, until the room seemed torn apart by it. Sumaoro would have liked to suppress it, to conceal this passing weakness, but could not stop: that love-rattle soon rose to a deafening clamour, that went on and on until there descended upon him the floating peace of exhausted submission. Yes, the old king was suddenly the great tyrant love-rattling as the newly-wed he had become in the arms of his young wife of twenty winters; for the tyrant he had always been, that tyrant whom all other kings named with trembling lips, no longer existed in the nuptial chamber. Now that so-called tyrant was nothing but an old man of sixty who was trembling before the deviltries of Nana Triban.

When they had both come down together from the tree of their pleasure, the young princess of the Manden, stretching out beside Sumaoro, asked him:

'Do you find me good and sweet?'

'Yes, sweet as a ripe papaya with tender, juicy flesh and pulp, that stills thirst and assuages hunger. From today, you are my favourite.'

As if in a gesture of gratitude, she clung close to him, caressed his chest, and showed him a face apparently overwhelmed by passion. Sumaoro in return gave her a triumphantly tender look.

'Don't look into my eyes,' she said, 'for no woman on earth is able to bear the brilliance of your gaze. What woman in your harem would not have been mad with ecstasy during those marvellous moments I have just experienced with the most powerful king in the world, for that is what you are? But tell me, Sumaoro, tell your Nana Triban who for many, many moons admired and desired you even before meeting you – tell me, are you a man, or are you some supernatural genius? Your arms have the strength of ten men's! Tell me what is the guardian spirit that protects you and makes you so powerful, so that, in order to be protected as you are, I may adore it in my turn?'

Sumaoro's male pride was flattered, so he replied at once:

'I haven't just one guardian spirit, Nana Triban. I have sixty-three! I can take the form of sixty-three different things.'

'So that is why the kings shake and tremble when they pronounce your name! Oh, how right I was to marry a king as powerful as you are!' she said

'Yes!' Sumaoro boasted. 'If the kings shake and tremble when they pronounce my name, it is thanks to my sixty-three ancestral totems . . .'

'Your multiple totems make you the most powerful of kings, and those who are jealous of your power shall be punished,' she agreed sententiously.

And she shivered with admiration. But perhaps that was just a sham shiver? Perhaps . . . She crushed herself even closer to Sumaoro's chest, but suddenly her memory began to stray over her past life: she rejoined in thought her young friends of the Manden,

170

her parents, the River Sankarani – and that was enough for her: she no longer felt she was an instrument of pleasure in the hands of Sumaoro Diarrasso. It seemed to her as if her mother Fatumata Bérété, her uncles, her aunt Kano were alive beside her. It seemed to her as if she were once more living in their warmth – her heart was filled with warmth! And beside her there was no longer the old tyrant stretched full length, it was not against the chest of Sumaoro Diarrasso she was pressed, but against her young husband, accidentally killed, who rose up before her eyes – it was *his* chest she was pressing herself against, and it was he she was clasping so tightly in her arms!

She closed her eyes. But that only helped her to see better the body of her former husband, and she managed, without too much difficulty, to erase from her mind the tyrant of Sosso and to superimpose the image of her first husband upon that of Sumaoro Diarrasso.

A moment later, she opened her eyes; she tried to fix them on something, anything to occupy them so that they would be spared the spectacle of what lay beside her, the old man of sixty with his dubious virility, but whom she was forced to accept in marriage in order to consolidate the shaky throne of the Manden, and to spare her brother Dankaran Tuman the fury of the tyrant of Sosso.

Nana Triban's hands kept moving, moving. So many memories kept flooding back, memories of the Manden, and so all at once her hands stopped caressing the body of Sumaoro, who was trembling with bewilderment, because all her memories of Niani were there before her. And it so happened that her hands stopped exploring because her mother and her brother Dankaran Tuman were standing there, before her, because suddenly she saw them as they were when she had taken leave of them, forced by them to go and live with the sovereign of Sosso.

And she had to loosen her embrace: her eyes were bathed in tears, and she was sobbing as if her heart would break.

'Why! you're crying, Nana Triban . . . what's wrong?' asked Sumaoro.

'I'm crying because I'm afraid you'll abandon me one day! I love you and I can't live without you, but you will abandon me one day, Sumaoro!' she cried.

171

The old king, to console her, put his arm round her neck and drew her against him. He clasped her to him, and she submitted.

Thus, conscious on the one hand of their perfectly adjusted common sensuality, and on the other hand of the fact that excessive sexual indulgence has the virtue of encouraging a man to bring into the open the secrets of his innermost heart, Nana Triban brought her ardour to an even higher pitch; she gave herself up to Sumaoro in a way only a woman knows when she truly loves a man or when she is pretending to love him, and at the same time she started to question him again, in her most soft and most caressing voice, about one thing and another, about everything that came into her mind. In so doing, she was only acting as any other woman might have done. But in the bed of the old king she was doing this to hide what was really occupying her attention – the moment when the love-rattle would begin to shudder out of Sumaoro's powerful chest, which was when she would ask, as if it were nothing special, the question she had so much at heart. And soon, seeing that he had been overcome by the dizzying ascent into the heights of sensual bliss, she abruptly stopped her lascivious jigglings, keeping her husband gasping for more, and said:

'Sumaoro, tell me if there is anything I should not do in case it might diminish the powers of your sixty-three totems.'

She spoke these words tenderly, crooning them like the most voluptuous of women.

Sumaoro, eager to continue his vertiginous mounting to the sparkling summit of the tree of pleasure, and in order to persuade Nana Triban to go on with the blissful motions that alone would conduct him to the top, released the phrase that was the key to the secret of his power:

'I can be killed only by the spur of a white cock.'

'I'll take good care of that, believe me, N'Yarabi[1], I'll take good care of it!' said Nana Triban.

And in order to bring complete satisfaction to the delayed desires of her panting spouse, Nana Triban recommenced her jigglings with devilish agility. It was a sweet night for the king of Sosso. As for the princess of the Manden, it can be said that her mission, which was to penetrate the secret of Sumaoro's power,

1 N'Yarabi: my indispensable one.

had been accomplished. It only remained for her now to keep up her pretence until a suitable day arrived for her to escape from Sosso, accompanied by Balla Fassali Kuyaté.

Anyhow, from now on there was no longer question between them of the powerful king of Sosso's sixty-three ancestral totems. The love climax had passed – but how true it is that the most beautiful woman in one's life is the one with whom one has not spent just one night! – and the vapours of the hydromel had cleared from his brain.

But from that day on, as soon as a chicken was being killed in the palace courtyard, Nana Triban would run to watch with avid curiosity. She would look at the plumage of the fowl being slaughtered. Generally it was always one of the three queen mothers who cut its throat, and it was always a black or a red bird, for the three old widows of Diarra Diarrasso were also in the secret of their son's *tana*[1]. Indeed, Nana Triban had found out everything, had noticed everything that went on in the palace of Sosso, and she had understood everything she saw there: she saw that in her husband's domains no white chicken was ever killed! That had thrown her mind into inextricable confusion, but it proved to her that what Sumaoro had told her was true. He had not lied to her.

Moreover, as the days went by, sweet-talking Nana Triban enjoyed the total confidence of her husband, who had her come and live in his magnificent seven-storey tower. He may even have entrusted her with the keys of all the rooms in it.

For one day Sumaoro was absent from the capital. The young woman from the Manden opened the door of her husband's secret chamber for Balla Fassali Kuyaté: this room was on the fourth floor of the tower that dominated the entire city of Sosso.

When the griot had entered the chamber, he was stunned by what he saw: the walls were covered with human skins of various sizes. The largest one was spread out in the middle of the room: this was the one Sumaoro prayed on. In one corner, death's heads formed a circle round a sacrificial vase. It looked as if the

1 *Tana*: interdiction formulated by an ancestor possessing one or several totems and which his descendants must respect. In the present case, the Diarrasso of the dynasty of Sosso destroyed their own magic powers if they ate the flesh of a white cock.

heads had been placed there as an offering to the idols and in order to honour them. Strangely enough, the heads resembled those of the nine kings who were executed by Sumaoro as a warning example to the sovereigns of the savanna, to all those sovereigns of the savanna who might be tempted to revolt.

As he drew nearer, the water in the sacrificial vase suddenly trembled, and all at once a monstrous serpent, luxuriantly spotted with yellow and white, lifted its head towards Balla Fassali: it lifted its head almost insensibly, with a quick undulatory movement, and when it finally reached the brim of the vase, it rested its head there to gaze fixedly at the griot. In the eyes of this reptile there was no spark of friendship: on the contrary there was a bitter animosity for the intruder who, by entering the chamber, had disturbed its repose.

Balli Fassali, who was also deeply versed in the arts of sorcery, recited magical incantations, and the serpent at once slid back into the vase!

But when he raised his eyes to the ceiling, Balla saw, seated on a perch, two black owls: the avian sorcerers were tilting their heads curiously at him, and ululating softly!

Strange-shaped knives, covered with coagulated blood, that had been used to execute the disloyal kings, lay scattered everywhere. Perhaps it would have been a profanation of the sacrificial vase to pour in it the blood of those who accepted without protest the hegemony of Sosso? Perhaps . . .

These evidences of orgies of blood that had taken place in this macabre room had horrified and completely upset Balla Fassali. He wanted to run away, to escape from this chamber full of idols, to flee all those death's heads and those human skins stretched on the walls, and which gave off a nauseating stench. He wanted to dash out of the place at once. He tried to scream, but no sound came from his throat: anguish gripped his throat so tightly. He was shaking from head to foot, shaking so much, he could not lift his feet! In despair, he began to intone magical formulas and his terror suddenly vanished . . .

It was at this moment that he discovered, behind the door of the room, a balafon[1] bigger than any he had ever seen in the

1 balafon: a kind of xylophone.

Manden: this was the balafon which the blacksmith and powerful sorcerer king Sumaoro Diarrasso played to sing his own praises after each of his victories.

Balla could not help feeling a surge of happiness, for now joy had overcome his fear. He sat down and played a few notes on the balafon – which was his favourite musical instrument – using little mallets which had one end covered with rubber. The bars produced an extraordinarily harmonious and melodious sound at the slightest touch of the mallets.

Then, as if intoxicated by this soft music, he unconsciously began to strike the bars harder – how true it is that the only things one strikes harder when they produce good words are the balafon and the tom-tom! – and the death's heads began to come to life again. Yes, all those heads began to show a sudden animation, began to flutter their eyelids and lift their lips in smiles, as if they had all at once become living heads.

Sumaoro, absent from the court of Sosso, but in constant rapport with his magical xylophone, knew then that someone had entered his secret chamber.

Furious with rage, he dashed back to his palace, quickly ran up the steps of the high tower. When he reached the fourth floor, he rushed, sabre in hand, into the hall of the idols, shouting:

'Guardian spirit or man?'

The flame in his eyes was brighter than ever before.

'It is I, Balla Fassali!' the griot calmly replied.

Then, in a melodic variation, he began to improvise music in honour of the sovereign of Sosso, and his tenor voice rang out:

> *Sosso kémo dén Sumaoro!*
> *Musso Saba dén Sumaoro!*
> *Kaya Touré dén Sumaoro!*
> *Daby Touré dén Sumaoro!*
> *Sansun Touré dén Sumaoro!*
> *Mbé Sonko li là!*
> *Mô gbolo Duruki ilé min kana!*
> *Mô gbolo sii fén ilé min bolo!*

I salute thee Sumaoro the ancient of Sosso!
Sumaoro of the three wives!

175

Sumaoro of Kaya Touré!
Sumaoro of Daby Touré!
Sumaoro of Sansun Touré!
I salute thee, O thou that wearest a boubou of human skin!
I salute thee, O thou that dost take thy seat upon human skin!

The sovereign of Sosso, flattered by this chant and by the melody accompanying it – was he not a man and did he not share the weaknesses of all men? – declared joyfully, for now his anger was giving way to joy:

'I shall never touch this balafon again. From now on you shall be my griot, and it shall be your duty to play on this instrument after each of my victories.'

But probably he did not know that by keeping Balla Fassali in Sosso and making him his personal griot, he was only increasing Sundiata's fury.

THE RETURN

Sumaoro undoubtedly thought only of himself and of his own pleasure. He who already was husband to three hundred wives – not counting Nana Triban, his new confidante and favourite! – had gone and fallen for the only wife of his nephew, Fakoli Koroma, Fakoli Dâ bâ (Fakoli of the big head, Fakoli of the big mouth), the general-in-chief of his armies. Moreover, he made no secret of it: he had openly carried her off and locked her up in his palace – he had had no qualms about that! Therefore, in the eyes of his nephew, he had become a veritable wild beast that had to be killed . . .

But why did he have to choose Kéléya Kanko[1], the wife of his devoted nephew Fakoli, to commit incest with her, when practically all the women in his kingdom could be said to belong to him? No one could explain it. Probably he who is condemned to death by destiny cannot have any ears!

Was this not a grave offence against Fakoli, and against his father and mother, Makata Djigui Koroma de Nora Sobâ, and Kassia Diarrasso, Sumaoro's own sister? But perhaps it would have been sufficient if his uncle had given him back Kéléya Kanko for normal family relationships to be resumed? No, there are insults and injuries which cannot be effaced, that nothing can redeem. All the water in the River Djóliba would not suffice to wipe out the offence just done to Fakoli. But perhaps, by making him pile up error upon error, God wished Sumaoro to be the instrument of his own downfall? Perhaps . . .

After resigning the powers his uncle had entrusted him with, he returned to his uncle's house in a rage and told him:

'As you are not ashamed to commit incest with the wife of the nephew I was, I want you to know, Sumaoro, that I am no longer any relative of yours! From now on, I shall make war against you!'

Fakoli left the generalship of the army he was in charge of,

1 Kéléya Kanko, wife of Fakoli Koroma, head of Sumaoro's armies, was a great sorceress: all on her own she could cook a meal quicker than the three hundred wives of Sumaoro all together, enough to feed the entire army of Sosso.

and took to the bush with warriors loyal to him. This was the drop of water that makes the cup run over. At that time, he himself did not know that all the inhabitants of the savanna were waiting only for such an action in order to rise in rebellion.

Dankaran Tuman, the phantom king, for his part used the opportunity to enter the battle arena. But at once he was so badly harried by the army of Sosso that he had to retreat with his men into the forest. By doing so, he rejoined one of the branches of his family that had been settled there ever since the shining sun of his great grandfather Mansa Bélé – a branch which had at that time called the region 'Faramaya'. Dankaran Tuman added to it the name of Kissidugu – land of salvation! – an afforested zone which henceforward was to bear the double name of 'Faramaya-Kissi'.

The city of Niani was wiped out by Sumaoro. Therefore the Manden, without a king and in full rebellion, was seeking out its new destiny. The kingdom's soothsayers were unanimous in saying that only the prince with the triple baptismal name and the triple totem could bring the country out of chaos, restore its dignity and even extend its frontiers. . .

The old people remembered. The prince with the threefold baptismal name was Mari Diata, Naré Maghan Diata, Sogolon Diata. His totems were the lion, inherited from his father, Naré Maghan, and the buffalo and the panther of his mother Sogolon.

They quickly formed an embassy which was sent in the direction indicated by the soothsayers, that is, downstream on the River Djéliba. The members of this secret mission were the five marabouts of the court at Niani: Tomono Mandian Bérété, Siriman Kanda Touré, Saidou Koman, Sengben Mara Cissé, Sadi Maghan Diané, and one woman griot, Tuntun Manian.

These persons were to visit all the royal towns along the River Djéliba. They took with them condiments from the Manden: baobab leaves and dried gombo, sumbara and so on. The women who would ask for them could be only Manden-ka women, as no one in the savanna lands except the Manden-ka used such condiments. In this way several royal cities were explored, to no avail.

But during this time Diata, at Méma, was receiving very bad news from the Manden, and this saddened him. He learnt that

Sumaoro had invaded his native land, and that Dankaran Tuman, instead of putting up a resistance like the other kings of the savanna, had taken flight. He learnt also that Fakoli Koroma, having risen in revolt against his uncle who had ravished his wife, had taken to the bush.

On the other hand, the kingdom of Méma which had no expansionist aims and which moreover was a province of Wahadu, was relatively calm that year. The mountain brigands no longer invaded the country for fear of Diata at the head of the army. The viceroy was conducting no campaigns, so he had plenty of leisure.

But despite this relative peace, Sundiata was unhappy, because for one thing his native land was in peril and for another his old mother whom he dearly loved was now ill most of the time. It was now his young sister, of an age to be married, who looked after the domestic tasks and went to market.

One morning, Sogolon-Kanko had left Kome at dawn, but did not return until the sun was already high in the sky.

'What's going on at the market today? Sogolon-Kanko hasn't come back to start the dinner,' Sogolon wanted to ask. But at the same time a loud clamour arose from the market and roused her from her reflections. The market women were roaring with surprise to see the sister of the viceroy tuck up her loincloth and set off running home at top speed.

That clamour had been followed almost at once by shouts of joy from Sogolon-Kanko who suddenly rushed into the palace. She was returning with condiments from the Manden which she had bought from some foreigners: baobab leaves, gombo, sumbara, pimento and so on.

'Mother, look what I've brought back from the market!' she cried.

And she handed the condiments from the Manden to Sogolon.

'But these are baobab leaves, gombo, sumbara – all the things I used to grow in my kitchen garden at Niani. How did you get all this?'

'In the market: some foreigners sold them to me. They are selling them in the market and want to see you!'

'Go and bring them here, my daughter,' she answered.

When Sogolon-Kanko had gone, her mother started turning

over and over the rare condiments, wide-eyed with astonishment.

Meanwhile, Diata and Nan Bukari, coming home from the hunt, could be heard calling:

'Mother, we're back!' Nan Bukari cried.

'Yes, we had good hunting. We've brought you some game,' added Diata, entering the room.

Sogolon's only reply was to show them the condiments from the Manden.

'But these are baobab leaves!' exclaimed Diata.

'And there's dried gombo too! Where did you find all these?' Nan Bukari asked excitedly. 'They don't grow here at all!'

'Sit down, my sons, and you'll see the answer in a moment.'

Soon Sogolon-Kanko appeared, accompanied by a group of people. These were the notables from the court at Niani. Sogolon had known them in the days when her husband was still alive. Greetings, prolonged and courteous, were exchanged.

'Let me introduce my children to you: it's a long time since Dankaran Tuman chased us out of the Manden! They've grown up!'

Tomono Mandian Bérété humbly began to speak:

'I am ashamed of the earth, I am ashamed of the sky, to see you now, Diata. Forgive the foolish deeds of Fatumata Bérété, I beg of you!'

With the tip of his index finger he wiped away a tear from the corner of an eye, for he was in tears.

'Well, now, that's something I'll gladly do!' said Diata. 'Your frankness has won me over, and I agree. I pardon Fatumata Bérété for all her faults.'

'Ah! you forgive us!' said Tomono Mandian Bérété. 'You're giving us back something more precious than life itself, and I shall never forget that.'

'Let's speak no more of the past,' said Diata. 'It's forgotten. What happened to me was destined. Now, give us some news of the Manden.'

'Allah is great, most great, and very merciful, for today we are here with Sogolon and her children. We have been searching for you for two months, visiting all the royal cities along the river, selling condiments from the Manden. In all the places we visited, no one would buy them. Here at Méma, the one who showed interest in the condiments, miraculously enough, was your sister, Sogolon-Kanko!'

All this time, Diata kept strict silence, and listened attentively. But he was looking at the messengers from the Manden with friendly eyes.

'The Manden was devastated by Sumaoro Diarrasso,' went on Tomono Mandian. 'The people there are outraged! Dankaran Tuman, instead of giving his life for his country, preferred to run away. The Manden is without a master . . .'

Diata, thinking of Dankaran Tuman's cowardly behaviour in taking away his griot and naming him ambassador to Sosso, not, certainly, because Balla Fassali Kuyaté could play any significant part there, but simply to humiliate him, Diata, for the pure pleasure of humiliating him, protested vigorously:

'A man does not run away before another man,' he said sagely.

'Don't worry, Diata, the men have taken to the bush and are fighting courageously and without respite. Fakoli-Koroma, general-in-chief of the armies of Sosso, is waging an all-out war against his uncle, who ravished his wife. When we consulted the guardian spirits they informed us that only the prince with the threefold baptismal name and the threefold totem could save the Manden: our kingdom is already saved, because here you are before us!' declared Tomono Mandian Bérété, who went on: 'I salute thee, Naré Maghan-Diata, son of Naré Maghan! I salute thee, Sogolon-Diata, son of Sogolon! I salute thee, Mari-Diata, lion of the faithful. You inherited the lion of your father, the buffalo and the panther of your mother. I now salute thee, Sundiata, king of the Manden, for lo! thy sun has risen, the throne of thy fathers awaits thee, the weeping mothers await thee, thy humiliated people pray only for thy name. All the kings of the savanna have gathered and await thee: thy name alone inspires them with confidence. The words of the soothsayers shall be fulfilled! Thou art the cyclone that shall sweep forever from the lands of the savanna the tyrant Sumaoro.'

Diata promised to avenge the outrage without further delay. After the messengers had revealed the aim of their journey, he suddenly said:

'Hum! This is no time for words, and we have no choice – we cannot stay on here. I am going to ask the king for leave, and we shall depart immediately.'

And he began thinking of Sumaoro Diarrasso! The tyrant every day humiliated more and more the peoples of the savanna. 'We have no more time to lose: we must leave immediately if we do not want to abandon a moment longer our poor compatriots to the hands of a great criminal like Sumaoro . . . We must depart right away,' he thought.

'Nan Bukari, see that the messengers from the Manden are royally treated,' he said. 'As soon as the king is returned, at dawn, we shall be gone!'

When Diata stood up, the messengers from the Manden did the same. Already he was the sovereign of their country!

When night fell, Mussa Tunkara, who had been away not far from his capital, returned to his palace at Méma. The viceroy, busy settling his compatriots comfortably, was not there to greet his return. But later during the night Diata was able to get away from his obligations to them, and for a while sat by his mother's bedside before retiring himself. His mother, still feverish despite the great fire of logs warming her room, was shivering under her bedclothes. But with a great effort she managed to say a few words to her son:

'Diata,' she said, 'remember that Nan Bukari is your brother. Nothing must come between you! Now go to bed, you're very sleepy.'

'Good night, Mother!' said Diata.

'Good night, Diata!' replied Sogolon.

When he got to his room, Aïsha Aminu, his sweetheart, was waiting for him. Perhaps, knowing he was worried, she did not want to leave him alone; perhaps she wanted to spend the night by his side, for between the two young people there existed a marvellous tenderness, a tenderness not yet troubled by desire.

When he was in bed, before speaking to Aïsha Aminu, Diata first addressed himself to God in these terms:

'Allah, Most High, I am about to depart for the Manden conquered by Sumaoro. My intention is to re-establish my legal authority there. I beseech thee, give me thy support and aid! If I should succeed in my enterprise, may I return to bury my mother here.'

Then he turned to Aïsha Aminu.

In the morning Sogolon, the buffalo-panther woman, was no more! And all the city of Méma bewailed the decease of the viceroy's mother. As soon as he awoke, Diata received the condolences of Mussa Tunkara.

Diata told him:

'I do not know how to thank you for your warm and generous hospitality. Thanks to you, Mussa Tunkara, I have become a warrior. But on the one hand, my mother has just died, and on the other my country is in peril and I must hurry to its aid. I resign the powers of viceroy with which you invested me, and before I set off, allow me to bury my mother in the blessed earth of Méma.'

'But what do you want to go to the Manden for? roared Mussa Tunkara. 'Are you not happy with me here in Méma? It's quite true – "the son of another is not one's own son!"' he concluded.

Then he went on:

'As you want to leave me, go away with the body of your mother, or, if you want to bury her in Méma, you must pay me for the ground in which she will lie,' he declared solemnly.

'I shall pay you on my return from the Manden! Now I must depart, because my country is in peril!' replied Diata.

'You must pay me at once, or she shall not be buried in my kingdom!'

At that, the fire in Diata's eyes burned more fiercely, and he went out. When he returned, he was carrying a broken old basket filled with guinea-fowl feathers, battered calabashes, old rags and rubbish of all sorts, which he laid at the feet of the king, saying:

'Here is the payment for the land!'

The fire in his eyes now seemed to flare up into incandescence.

'Diata, don't try to make a fool of me! This old basket full of trash is no payment for my land!' cried Mussa Tunkara.

The courts of Wahadu and its provinces were at that time full of technical consultants from Arabia. After the son of Sogolon had left, one of these consultants said to Mussa Tunkara:

'Give him the ground and help him to bury his mother with all honours. What he has brought you here – this old basket full of all sorts of trash – is filled with significance. If you do not give

183

him what he asks, he will make war on you! The broken basket full of guinea-fowl feathers, straw and battered calabashes signifies that he will destroy the city of Méma, that he will raze it to the ground and that only this rubbish of all kinds will be left to show where it once stood, and the wild birds shall come and bathe in its dust. Make a good friend of him by leaving him with a pleasant memory. Thus, he will become your best ally.'

The king saw the wisdom of his Arab counsellor's words, and the final honours were paid to Sogolon Condé, the buffalo-panther woman, with the participation of the entire population of Méma.

The next day, they departed. As soon as the sun had risen, Diata and his family were up and about. The son of Sogolon was then eighteen years old, Sogolon-Kanko was fifteen, Manden-Bori or Dia-Mori was twelve, whilst Nan Bukari, son of Namagbè Camara, was sixteen.

Lovely Aïsha Aminu saddled Diata's white horse for him. She held the stirrup while her friend mounted his courser. And when he was mounted, her loving hands caressed his boots, and from her lips came tender words which she had probably often murmured to him.

'Do not forget me, Diata!' she said.

'I shall never forget you, Aïsha, never! When the war is over, I shall have you brought to Niani.'

Then he seized her arms, lifted her and pressed her close to his heart before releasing her.

When the procession started, the eyes of the crowd of curious bystanders were all for the vigour of the steeds, and only after that did they notice the riders. The inhabitants of Méma had come in such great numbers to see them off that they literally blocked their path.

A horseman shouted:

'Come, clear the way! Make way! Don't you see we are in a hurry?'

But these words were no sooner spoken by the horseman than they were lost in the noise and tumult of the crowd. But then the people parted to allow Diata and his entourage to pass: they were brave warriors with quivers full of arrows slung on their broad backs, their lances whirling and sparkling in the sun, and all were dressed as master hunters. Their garments were called *sérébu*, very tight-fitting, of a brownish tone, and on their heads they wore a skull cap called *bamba dâ*[1] similar to the hats of young circumcised boys, worn after their recovery from the operation.

Diata was recognizable by the white turban of the Muslim kings he wore: he rode at the centre of his troops, followed by Nan Bukari, Sogolon-Kanko and Manden-Bori. The horsemen were divided into four groups: the warriors of Méma, whose chief was Bandiu Tunkara, formed the advance guard, and those of Wahadu the rearguard. These two groups of warriors had been given to Diata by Mussa Tunkara! The messengers from the Manden formed the flanks.

He who had just emerged from the crowd and who, ever since his meeting with the messengers from the Manden, had already in his breast the flame of vengeance, was Sundiata. He was to transmit this fire to everyone in the savanna lands, and in order to do this he first wanted to make for Tabon to request the help of his friend Fran Camara.

In fact, the son of Sogolon was not motivated by the desire for personal advantage, because already, before leaving Méma, he knew that after the death of old Mussa Tunkara, he could have become king of that country. No, rather he was obeying the demands of his sacred mission which was to liberate all the savanna from the yoke of the despot Sumaoro. Indeed, the inhabitants of all the lands adjoining the River Niger seemed to be up in arms. Was this because of their hatred of Sumaoro and his inhuman suppression of the vain individual attempts at revenge? Perhaps. Perhaps too their resistance was born of common resentment caused by the cruelties, the violences and the affronts perpetrated daily by the king of Sosso, and perhaps the destiny of Sundiata was to incarnate the collective consciousness of the outraged peoples of the savanna and create an incandescent brazier of rebellion against the tyrant who was Sumaoro Diarrasso.

Nan Bukari, running from one horseman to the next, managed to reach his brother's side, and cried:

'You look so happy, and we have just lost our mother! Do you

1 *bamba dâ:* alligator's jaws.

really believe you can conquer Sumaoro with this small army?'
'Yes!' Diata firmly replied.

And he angrily drew his sabre from its sheath, then declared:
'Because Diata means lion, synonym of war, and because
reason is on our side and God is on the side of reason!'

And he put his sabre back in its sheath.

The column of mounted troops, which had left the city of
Méma accompanied by the good wishes of the entire population,
was now making its way along the winding paths beside the
river, across the immense plain of the Niger. By doing so, they
skirted the kingdom of Sosso and were going in the direction of
Tabon. They were all soaking with sweat, fuming with sweat and
rage, and the horses were panting from having galloped so far.
At nightfall, the horsemen stopped in some village or other. But
they did not unsaddle their mounts: they took a short rest, then
in the morning they resumed their wild gallop. They met with
nothing to impede their course, no beast crossed the paths they
rode along. Where could the wild beasts be? Had they taken refuge
in the bushes? Perhaps. Probably the mounted warriors had
frightened them away, and they had sought safety elsewhere.

And the silence, in that vast plain of the Niger, preserved its
pristine purity. Sometimes, around the river bank, a beefeater
bird, hovering low, would tilt its head curiously to observe the
passing horsemen: perhaps it was astonished by the way their
galloping hooves broke the customary silence.

Nevertheless, Sumaoro Diarrasso, who was a blacksmith king,
therefore a great soothsayer, was aware that Diata was on his
way to the Manden. He decided that to halt his progress he must
be attacked immediately.

He sent his son Balla Diarrasso with part of the army to bar
the entry of Diata to Tabon. Like the son of Sogolon, Balla
Diarrasso was a youth of eighteen winters.

Arriving in the evening on the outskirts of Tabon, Diata gazed
with an ironical smile from the top of a slope at the thousands of
Sosso warriors spread across the plain, some in ambush on the
side of the slope, others among the tall grasses that covered the
immensities of the plain.

Nan Bukari, drawing near him, said:
'Don't laugh at me, brother, but you see that we cannot pass,

186

as the army of Sumaoro is barring our route!'

'And what ideas have you in mind, Nan Bukari, other than fighting your way through them?' Diata retorted.

'Other ideas?' said Nan Bukari. 'What makes you think I might have other ideas?'

'I don't know, of course. But you seem to be in a state of perpetual agitation before a few miserable warriors trying to bar our way to the Manden!'

Diata rose in his saddle and, speaking in a cutting voice, galvanized the energies of his cavalry who thought the battle would not take place until dawn. Yes, the son of Sogolon had suddenly forgotten his weariness and had recovered his habitual audacity. He was now fully primed with that audacity. And because he had completely recovered all his audacity, he was no longer the boy who had fled from family rivalries: he had become a bold young man capable of dying in order to see his ideals through to a triumphal conclusion. So all at once he spurred his horse to a gallop, shrieking his war cry and waving his unsheathed sabre above his head. His cavalry followed close behind. If the Sossos had been struck by lightning they could not have been taken more by surprise. Sabres, wielded with fury, slashed off their heads, assegais plunged through their bodies, and death had a festival.

Diata wanted to match himself against Balla Diarrasso. Seeing him in the midst of the Sosso cavalry, he uttered another shrill war cry and, like a cyclone, bore down upon him, sabre raised: as the sabre was swishing down, a Sosso warrior dashed between the two chiefs: Diata's sabre sliced him in two from top to toe like a ripe papaya! Balla, impressed by such strength, made off to seek refuge among his warriors, who, seeing him turn tail, were soon retreating in confusion . . .

Of the magnificent dash that had spurred the Sosso warriors to prevent Diata's entry into Tabon, nothing was left. And whilst Balla and his troops were routed in all directions, night fell with that dramatic suddenness it has in the savanna, which, in contrast to the dazzling brilliance preceding it, makes it appear all the more black and dense. Pursued by Diata and his cavalry, the son of Sumaoro and his warriors rapidly spread out across the plain. But several of them were captured and taken prisoner.

When Tabon Wana[1] Fran Camara and his archers reached the battlefield that very evening, alerted by the numerous wild beasts invading their capital in a panic-stricken rush – precursor of the presence of a cyclone in the region – victory had already been accorded to the son of Sogolon. The army of Fran, king of the country since the death of his father Sadi So-oro, was composed of blacksmiths and Djallonkés, but never mind! What mattered at the moment was not the origin of the archers, but their availability and their extraordinary fervour and willingness to accompany their king and his friend Diata on a grand adventure, for already, before dawn whitened the vastnesses of space, the news of Diata's victory over Balla Diarrasso had spread far and wide across the savanna, into all the villages of the savanna.

Fran provided plenty of food for his friend's army and all night long the tom-toms roared to celebrate this first victory over the Sossos: the reunion of the two great friends Diata and Fran was deeply moving to them both. By dawn, the victors, acclaimed by the population, made their triumphal entry into the city of Tabon.

As if carried on the winds, the news of the battle outside the walls of Tabon and the victory of the Sundiata army over Balla Diarrasso spread like a trail of wildfire through all the savanna. The various tribes of the Manden became more and more confident of their destiny which beyond all doubt would not be long in changing and making a complete turn-around, like night to day.

As for Sumaoro, he knew now that Diata was someone he had to reckon with. As he was a great sorcerer and perfectly familiar with the prophecies of the Manden, perhaps he already knew that the violent cyclone that was Diata would one day sweep the savanna clean? Perhaps . . . Because no one had ever dared attempt what the son of Sogolon had just brought off. Moreover, 'when a young man comes of age and sees his *paterfamilias* lying beside his mother, he realizes that his father is a man of mettle, an incomparable man!' In the eyes of Sumaoro, Sundiata was now that *paterfamilias* against whom he had done everything – notably during the boy's exile – to put an end to his

1 Wana: dread one.

188

life, but in vain. The son of Sogolon, at Tabon, had been warned by Famandian Camara, and he had then fled to N'Gumbu, then to Méma. All the time he had been fighting against Diata, he had unknowingly been assisting the son of Sogolon's development, far from the Manden, yet not knowing exactly where he was! Sumaoro's destiny now was to find himself fighting over the Manden, a land he thought he had subjugated, against its true master, Mari-Diata.

When Balla Diarrasso came back from Tabon, exhausted, with the remains of the army – for he had lost many men – he told his father:

'Father, Diata is not a human being, he is a genius: a supernatural genius! No one can resist him!'

'Shut your mouth, you little coward,' the king angrily broke in, 'Diata is only eighteen, the same age as yourself, and you shiver and shake before him!'

Nevertheless Balla Diarrasso's words made a great impression on Sumaoro, who made the decision to attack Tabon himself with all his might.

Sogolon-Diata, who was a reticent person and above all a man of action, had already completely mulled over his plans and decided on a course of action: to beat Sumaoro, destroy Sosso and return in triumph to Niani, his capital. And he quietly gained for his cause the support of all the rebellious kings who rushed to his side, and all of whom he placed in the service of his ideal. Each of them had a substantial army, and each was prepared to give everything he had to hasten the annihilation of Sosso and its powerful king Sumaoro, who drew up his forces against Diata in the Bouré, the Tinkisso River plain.

The gathering of forces of both sides was something extraordinary: in the neighbourhood of Naguéboria the son of Sogolon, taken aback, asked: 'What is that cloud over in the east?' He was told: 'It is the army of Sumaoro!' The latter, very uneasy, asked: 'What is that mountain of rocks in the west?' He was told: 'It is the army of Sundiata!'

When they had reached Naguéboria, the two opposing armies could not make out anything for a long time except an enormous cloud of red dust raised by the horses' hooves, a cloud that rose high in the sky and that they had already perceived from afar. Those horses, spurred to a gallop, were reined to a sudden rearing stop.

Sumaoro would have liked to give battle in the great plain of Naguéboria, but Diata, a born strategist, did not want it so. Taking the lead, he suddenly started his war tom-toms drumming, after having disposed his army in what seemed to him the most appropriate manner: he had arranged them in a square that could either contract or extend itself into a rectangle, according to the demands of the moment: each side of the square or rectangle consisted of a strong attacking group. In this way, he could harry the enemy by shoving him to the centre of the formation, taking him in his nets and strangling him to death. But in case of resistance from the enemy side, the square would become a rectangle. The archers formed fresh support troops who were to accelerate the triumph of the whole group.

Forced to give battle, Sumaoro placed his men in a straight line on account of the narrowness of the Naguéboria valley, while his wings were set out on the slopes.

The battle began: it was a fierce encounter indeed. On all sides, sabres sliced through shoulders, slashed off heads. Sundiata and Tabon Wana Fran Camara battled a glorious path through the Sossos.

When Balla Diarrasso saw the son of Sogolon bearing down upon him, sabre swinging, he took refuge among his men and the insurgent camp gave great shouts of triumph. All this time, the king of the Sossos, as if indifferent to the course of the battle, was perched on top of a hill: he was tall, very tall! Diata saw him there, wearing a black cloak that made his black skin look even more absolutely black. He was perched on a horse whose caparisons trailed on the ground – caparisons of black velvet cloth. Sumaoro was also recognizable by his helmet adorned with antelope horns.

He in his turn saw Diata, who was distinguished by his white djellaba and a turban on his head. Raising his hand, Sumaoro went almost up to the chief of the rebels and asked him to halt the battle. When all was still, he asked:

'Are you the rebel chief?'

'Yes, I am!' replied Diata.

'The land you are fighting over is mine by right of conquest. And anyhow, when two warrior chiefs meet, they should first fight together in front of everybody,' said Sumaoro.

'That is true,' Diata agreed.

'You can have first shot! I await your arrows!' cried Sumaoro.

Furious, Sundiata took an arrow out of his quiver; he bent the bow and the arrow sped whistling, but with a single movement Sumaoro caught it in flight, and, showing it to Diata, said:

'If I were vulnerable to arrows, do you really believe I could have become the incontestable master of the Manden? Now it's my turn!'

Sumaoro made his horse rear and his arrow whistled through the air. Diata, with a swift reflex movement, bent his head and just managed to avoid Sumaoro's arrow.

'You see, young man!' Sumaoro shouted, 'we are not in the same class at all! You avoided my arrow by ducking your head! Now it's your turn with the sabre!'

Beside himself with rage, Diata wrenched his sabre out of its sheath, and, lowering his forehead, uttered a blood-curdling war cry, then swooped like lightning upon Sumaoro. But, as he was raising the sabre to split him in two, he realized that the sovereign of Sosso had suddenly vanished. Where had he gone? He could not tell . . .

Then, the son of Sogolon gradually raised his head and searched the hillside with his eyes: Sumaoro was seated on his charger whose caparisons like the warrior's mantle now shone like robes of the sun. Diata shook his head vigorously, and realized he was not dreaming . . . there was the horseman at the top of the hill, and he could not mistake him – it was Sumaoro all right.

Suddenly, his desire to ride up to Sumaoro overcame his sense of disquiet. It would seem that hesitation – the hill was so high and steep! – played no small part in this decision. Yet it was that same hesitation, a hesitation that told him discretion is the better part of valour, that stopped Diata from carrying out his first plan.

His head felt heavy. As he went back to his army, dusk was falling. The sovereign of Sosso and his warriors gave ground: before disappearing into the distance, into the far reaches of the immense vastnesses of the plain, Diata went up the hill on foot and collected a little of the dust trampled by Sumaoro's horse. When he returned to his army, the dense opacity of night seemed to have removed the Sossos from his sight.

The son of Sogolon set up his camp. He felt sad and remained so all night despite the joyous throngs of people from Nagué-boria who came to do honour to their liberator, and at the same time, to present great platters of rice to the army. In the middle of the night, Diata retired alone, all alone to his sorcerer-king's tent, and thought sadly about his encounter with Sumaoro: 'How did he get away from me? Certainly he is invulnerable to arrows and metals, but with a single swipe of my sabre I could have broken his back.' And he passed an agitated night. He felt worn out, and his eyes had a feverish flame in them while from the other end of the plain came the roarings of tom-toms diverting the warriors who were now strangely light-headed, almost dropping with fatigue, but whose minds were curiously full, also of the victory which they already believed to be theirs.

Those of the Sosso camp who fled from that terrible battle of Naguéboria settled in a village which they called Ballaboria, at the entrance to the town of Dabola, now in the Republic of Guinea.

The moon that night, while running through the sky, had lost her milky-white tint: that silvery radiance gave way to an immense shadow. And it seemed that this change in the weather was attributable to the moon, for she had now entirely disappeared. The very sky which, just a short while ago, had been a meadowful of stars, also seemed to have disappeared: at the very most, one could sense the distant presence of faint constellations only by looking very sharply at the chalky glimmer of the celestial vault.

At daybreak, striking camp, Diata sent his army on its way: the night before, scouts had told him that the army of Sumaoro had reached Kankigné, where it would bivouac for the night.

The son of Sogolon posted his men in an ambush at the gates of this village. At midnight, he launched his devastating offensive against the Sossos who had already gone to sleep, thinking the battle would take place the next day.

Suddenly the village of Kankigné was encircled by the warriors of Diata, who then gave the order to attack. They made their assault uttering wild war cries, and their flaming arrows tore through the dark like shooting stars, coming from all directions. Soon all the huts of the village were on fire and Sumaoro's warriors, abruptly wrenched from their slumbers, ran away, their bodies aflame!

The next day, Sundiata and his army followed the river, riding further and further downstream, and set up camp at Dayala, a suburb of Sibi, in the vast plain of the Niger. It was now Diata who was barring Sumaoro's way, cutting off his route towards the Manden from his overnight halt at Kirina.

All the kings of the Manden had gathered at Sibi, at the palace of Famandian Camara, sovereign of that country after the death of his father. The 'sininkimbon' king Famandian and the 'dali-kimbon' king Fran had been the companions of Diata at the initiation ceremonies in Niani.

Yes, all the kings were assembled there. Among them were notably: Siriman Keita, king of Konkon Dugu whose capital was N'déku.

Sira Kuman Konaté, king of Toron, at the head of his brave warriors.

Séni Gnankan Traoré, king of Magnakadu Kankran, surrounded by his valiant soldiers.

Amadu Sonko, king of Kagnaka, in the midst of his men.

Fa Woni Condé, warrior chief of Dô, land of Diata's mother. His warriors with their twofold totems were all present.

Famandian Camara, the host-king and his forces!

There were the unbeatable Bobos archers.

The Sénufos, born warriors, had lent their support to Diata.

Fula Mansadian and the warriors of the Wassulun.

Fran Camara, requisitioned at Tabon when Diata passed through, was there with his Djallonkés and his blacksmiths with arms of steel.

Even more wonderful, Balla Fassali Kuyaté and Nana Triban had been able to escape from Sosso and reach Sibi. Diata, very eager to see them, went to where they were.

'Salute, my sister,' he said.

'Salute, my brother. I am pleased to see you again!'

'Salute, Balla Fassali Kuyaté!'

'Salute, Ndjeti! When I was told of your victory at Tabon I

knew that the cyclone had begun to rush down upon the savanna.'

All this time, Nana Triban's eyes were bathed in tears, so great was her joy at seeing again the brother who had left her six years ago on account of family intrigues.

'Do not cry, Nana Triban,' said Diata. 'What happened was not your fault. And anyhow, it was good for me to spend some years in exile: exile inspires wisdom.'

'Calm yourself, Nana Triban,' said Balla Fassali. 'Rather you should tell your brother what you know about Sumaoro. Women, particularly favourites, always know their husbands' secrets,' he remarked sententiously.

'Yes,' Diata nodded, anxious to know something about Sumaoro who could appear and disappear at will on the field of battle.

Nana Triban, wiping away her tears, began her revelations.

'During my stay in Sosso,' she began, 'I succeeded in making Sumaoro fall madly in love with me. I pretended to be so nice to him that in the end he took me as his favourite. On our first encounter, I made him drink a lot of hydromel, and in that way I loosened his tongue: his *tana* is the white cock. You should make ready now an arrow of wood to which you must tie the spur of a white cock – for he is invulnerable to metal! As soon as this vegetable arrow, primed with the spur of a white cock, touches him, the power of his sixty-three totems will abandon him instantly!'

'I am infinitely grateful to you, Nana Triban. If I am victorious, it will be all on account of you!'

Glad to know the *tana* of his enemy – for everyone who had a totem has some forbidden thing – Diata and his griot went back to their camp where there was an extraordinary deployment of all the troops of the savanna.

Now that Balla Fassali Kuyaté was present, it was for him to reassure, through his words, the hearts of poltroons and to make the brave even braver.

He spoke first of all to Famandian.

'Famandian,' he said, 'where is our host? Where is this father of the "sininkimbon" Camara? What shall I say about your powerful ancestral totem? What exploit are you going to carry out tomorrow against Sumaoro and his despotic tyranny, which shall

194

be recited by the griots until the end of time?'

Hardly had Balla Fassali Kuyaté finished speaking than Famandian, sabre in hand, uttering a ferocious war cry, spurred his courser towards the mountain of Sibi. Barely had he reached it than a peal of thunder was heard, freezing their hearts and making the earth tremble beneath the warriors' feet. A dense whirlwind of dust plunged the plain into total darkness. Was it the end of the world? Perhaps. Perhaps, too, it was only a demonstration of the power of the 'sininkimbon' father's totem. When the whirlwind of dust had died away and the sun and Famandian reappeared, the mountain of Sibi, run right through with a single sabre thrust, disclosed a terrifying tunnel.

The entire army was open-mouthed in admiration as they watched the return of Famandian.

When he drew near to Diata, he said:

'Thus shall my archers, tomorrow at Kirina, run through those of Sosso. As long as I am in the land of the living, Diata, the Manden shall be free!'

Then Balla Fassali turned to Fran:

'It is to you now that I address myself, Tabon Wana Fran Camara. You did not vanquish Sumaoro but you stood up to him valiantly. The father of the "sininkimbon" in piercing right through the mountain of Sibi has shown his warriors what their behaviour should be like on the morrow in the plain of Kirina. What must I say of the father of the "dalikimbon" to future generations?'

Hardly had the griot finished speaking than Fran Camara, rising in his saddle and galloping at top speed, sabre in hand, uttering his savage war cry, dashed towards the centre of the plain and for a brief instant stopped in front of the enormous baobab growing there. He raised his sabre on high and when he brought it down the tree cracked as if struck by lightning.

When the men lifted their horrified eyes, they saw that the enormous baobab was lying flat on the ground.

At once the entire army, wide-eyed with astonishment, bellowed loud hurrahs of satisfaction.

When he came back to the army, Fran Camara said:

'Even so shall the blacksmiths and the Djallonkés of Tabon slice through the Sossos on the plain of Kirina. The Manden

195

shall be free, or all my warriors will be dead!'

Balla Fassali Kuyaté began asking each one of them – after having praised those kings present – to carry out the exploit which would inscribe his name in the savanna's rolls of history. But just as he was about to call upon another king, a messenger appeared telling Diata that Sumaoro was already prepared for battle. He was now at Kirina and that is where the sovereign of Sosso made his declaration of war to Diata – for one does not fight without explaining why! – who replied by asserting his rights to the Manden, the land of his ancestors, and of which he was the present legal king.

One of the owls that Balla Fassali Kuyaté had seen in the macabre hall of the tower dominating Sosso served as messenger. Here is the dialogue between the two redoubtable kings, as relayed by the sorcerer-bird:

'Diata! I am the red-hot ashes in which you shall leave the soles of your feet!'

'Sumaoro! I am the deluge of rain that shall extinguish that ash and wash it away into the River Djéliba!'

'Diata! Take care! I am the liana that strangles giant trees!'

'Sumaoro! Look out! I have in my army blacksmiths who can destroy that liana by cutting through its deepest roots!'

Then, turning his gaze upon the owl, he said:

'Diabolical little bird, go and tell your master that I wish no further speech with him: I am not a griot, I am a man of action. Tomorrow I shall wage war.'

The owl flew away, disappearing never to return.

Two men, two warrior chiefs, had spoken! It was now the turn of their armies to speak and to decide!

When Diata was going to start his army off for the great battle, another army, thousands of men strong, came across the vast plain.

As it approached, the son of Sogolon recognized one man: it was a warrior chief waving his *bandari*[1], expressing thus a desire to parley:

'I am Fakoli Koroma, ex-general-in-chief of the armies of Sosso!' he said. 'Sumaoro is the brother of my mother Kassi Diarrasso, but he was not ashamed to commit incest with my

1 *bandari*: means flag.

wife. Neither my mother nor my father Makata Djigui are happy about it: we are all outraged. Sumaoro does not merit my loyalty. You have come to re-establish your legal authority in your own land. I am here to put myself at your disposition.'

Balli Fassali interrupted to say:

'Swear that you will not betray us!'

'I swear by Sani and Kontron that my heart is as pure as the gold of the Bouré.'

'Then come and join us. Diata will avenge the offence committed against you.'

Diata nodded his agreement.

Fakoli made a sign, and his army came to swell the ranks of Diata's camp . . .

KIRINA

Sundiata left his family at Sibi: it was composed of Nana Triban, Sogolon-Kanko and Manden Bori. The messengers from the Manden – Tomono Mandian Bérété, Siriman Kanda Touré, Saidu Koman, Sengben Mara Cissé, Sadi Manghan Diané and the woman griot Tuntun Manian all were to wait there too.

However, as he struck camp, he insisted that his younger brother, Nan Bukari, should accompany him to the decisive battle of Kirina.

Before Diata's departure, Nana Triban approached him and asked him, in a worried tone:

'Brother, have you done what I asked you to do?'

'Yes,' he replied. 'Don't worry. Look!'

He drew from his quiver the arrow of wood primed with the spur of a white cock, showed it to his sister, then put it back.

It was this very ordinary-looking weapon alone that would be able to destroy the extraordinary magical powers of Sumaoro.

When the son of Sogolon had left Dayala, he set up camp for his great army at a respectable distance from the city of Kirina.

All the rebel kings whom he was leading in this insurrection had an average age of eighteen. Yes, eighteen years of age, a time when a human being flares into life like the most brilliant of meteors – impetuosity, audacity, enthusiasm! – a meteor that loses its dazzling radiance with age.

Moreover, the entire armed force, both for territorial defence and for the hunting down of lawbreakers, depended upon their leadership. Was this because the kings were subject to orders from above? Perhaps. Perhaps, too, the defence of their kingdoms was the natural duty of free and noble men, and perhaps the concept of honour at that period compelled those in high positions in the kingdoms to guarantee the liberty and reputation of the territories that they controlled.

The establishment of armed forces here was an accepted activity for the nobility and for high dignitaries of the order of free men.

When Sundiata had set up camp for his great army, he sacrificed innumerable bulls, and, to please his men, he gave orders for the organization of a grand ceremonial tom-tom feast. But were his men happy with this abundance? They enjoyed it, though not without reservations: the battle on the morrow in the plain of Kirina would be a terrible battle indeed, and the prospect was not one to sharpen the appetite. The thought of that decisive battle to come plunged them into apprehension. It needed the warm encouragement of Balla Fassali Kuyaté's voice to galvanize their hearts and to fill with the joyful rumbling of tom-toms the entire plateau.

When the griot had finished admonishing the warriors, on this battle eve and in the midst of those grand public sacrifices, he apostrophized the son of Sogolon:

'It is to thee I do address myself this night,' he proclaimed. 'I speak to thee, Naré Maghan Diata, Mari Diata, Sogolon Diata, king of the Manden! Thou hope of tearful mothers, thou avenger of the kings degraded into vassaldom by Sumaoro! Thou art the deed; I, thy griot, am the word! Thou shalt make this decisive moment in the history of the Manden take on immortal stature!

'Long ago, the princes of Wahadu, the Cissé, were the masters of the Manden. Today, it is the powerful king Sumaoro who oppresses the savanna: yea, the kings tremble at his name! But shall Sumaoro dominate us eternally? Shall it be my fate, as a griot of the Manden, to tell of our humiliation to future generations? I do not think so; for, if Dankaran Tuman preferred to run away, thou hast chosen to confront the storm. But when the hurricane that thou art begins to blow, the storm will be swept away!

'Thou, Naré Maghan Diata, thou art the Manden: thou hast had a difficult childhood, I know! But the Manden had an even more difficult childhood!

'Now, Sundiata, I shall tell thee what I never ceased repeating before Dankaran Tuman separated me from you and sent me to Sosso:

'Thine ancestor, the Chad warrior Bilali Ibn Ka Mâma, whom the Manden-ka called Bilali Ibunama, captured in the Cameroons by Bubacar Sidiki, was to serve faithfully, for many years, the Prophet Mohammed (may the peace of God be with him). Latal Kalabi, one of his sons, left Mecca and came and settled in a

199

territory which he named "Manden", a territory situated between the Rivers Djéliba and Sankarani. Latal Kalabi had as son Damel Kalabi who made great conquests and expanded his territory. Damel Kalabi had as son Lahilatul Kalabi who was a great pilgrim. He had two sons: Kalabi Bomba (or Kalabi the Great) and Kalabi Dôman (or Kalabi the Small); but it was Kalabi Bomba who took his seat upon the royal skin. He introduced the rite of "Konden Diara"[1] into the customs to prepare the children of the Manden for the painful rite of passage that is circumcision . . . Kalabi Bomba had as son Mamadi Kani, the powerful king who introduced the brotherhood of hunters into the customs of the Manden. When he did so, he invented the hunter's whistle "simbon" and the costume of the hunter "sèrèbu". He conquered many lands and so it became easy for his fourth son, Simbon Bamari Tagnoko Kélén, by making use of these new institutions, to enlarge the Manden. Simbon Bamari Tagnoko Kélén had as son M'Bali Néné who brought peace to the Manden. M'Bali Néné had as son Mansa Bélé whose surname was Mari-Diata. Mansa Bélé was your great-grandfather; he introduced the dance of the "Coba"[1] or "great event" into the ceremonies of circumcision for children. He had five sons: Missa, Barry, Namandian, Konokoro Semba and Bélébakön. However, it was the third son, Namandian, who took his seat upon the royal skin. He was a great warrior. After the reign of Namandian, power came into the hands of descendants of the fifth son of Mansa Bélé. This fifth son was Bélébakön and his son was Naré Maghan Kön Fatta, Maghan Kégni or Maghan the Beautiful, who brought you into the world.

'From a tiny village between the Rivers Djéliba and Sankarani, ten sovereigns made of the Manden a kingdom of nine provinces.

'Dankaran Tuman has fled, preferring dishonour to death. thou, Naré Maghan Diata, Sogolon Diata, that art the twelfth king of the Manden. Thou art the son of the lion, ancestral totem of thy native land, but thou art also the son of Sogolon, princess from the great land of Dô; consequently thou art the son of the buffalo and the panther: thou art a king possessing three ancestral totems. It is this extraordinary power that thou must demonstrate tomorrow in the plain of Kirina, for men fear power:

1 See *The African Child.*

the power of muscles or of the mind! Those who do not fear it respect it. Now, in order that thy peers show thee their unanimous confidence in their destiny, thou shouldst continue to be the buckler behind which they may take refuge! Be thou their buckler tomorrow, in the plain of Kirina, by carrying out exploits that shall impose the supremacy of thy power – exploits that shall make future generations regret that they were not born under the sun of Sundiata.

'I shall cite the names, in passing, of the griots who have served the kings of the Manden, since the rising of the sun of your ancestor Latal Kalabi. They are: Sorakata Kuyaté, Mundalf Kuyaté, Faruku Kuyaté, Farkan Kuyaté, Kukuba Kuyaté, Batamba Kuyaté, Niéni-Niéni Kuyaté, Kanbassia Kuyaté, Haryni Kuyaté, Dikisso Kuyaté, Dantuman Kuyaté, Kaléani Kuyaté, Gnankuman Kuyaté, Dua Kuyaté who brought me into the world and was the griot of thy father.

'All these griots served kings with only one totem; I, Balla Fassali Kuyaté, I have the privilege to be the griot of a king possessing three totems – the lion, the buffalo and the panther! – no other prince of the Manden ever had such power: thou art the first to have such power.

'I must breathe life through the Word into the deeds of the exceptional king thou art. It is for thee, Naré Maghan Diata, to provide the deeds!'

It was the eve of the decisive battle that was to pit Sundiata against Sumaoro in the plain of Kirina.

After the griot's discourse, the son of Sogolon and his peers returned to their tents: they sat talking about one thing and another, without any worries about the outcome of tomorrow's battle. Through the Word, Balla Fassali Kuyaté had driven fear out of their hearts: his words had galvanized their very souls. Therefore, their talk betrayed no trace of anxiety.

When, late at night, they decided to lie down and get a little rest, the cock had cried for the second time. It was a moment in which each of the chiefs was deeply plunged in thought: but this short meditation was suddenly interrupted. In fact, they first heard, coming from far off in the plain, a long and fearful bellowing, then a mewing, then a roaring! The king of the Manden could not but assume that this was the means used by

his three ancestral totems to express their approval of his aveng-
ing campaign and to assure him of their indispensable support.

Meanwhile, the eagle, guardian spirit of Fakoli Koroma, flew
by uttering shrill cries. As for the ancestral totem of Balla
Fassali Kuyaté, the hawk, he stooped outside the tent of his
possessor; when he tilted his head, there seemed to be great
friendliness in the bird's gaze. Far off, the lion of Fula Mansa
Djan was heard roaring.

The black serpent, ancestral totem of Tabon Wana Fran
Camara, entered the tent and came creeping under his couch,
where it coiled up. In short, all the warrior chiefs, before dawn
whitened the vastnesses of space, had received or heard their
guardian spirits.

But was it not extraordinary, was it not miraculous that in those
circumstances all those ancestral totems should have manifested
themselves one after the other? They did not often show themselves. But at critical times, their apparition was a warning, an
effective warning they gave for their possessors' enterprises.

At daybreak, Famandian, king of Sibi, came to announce to
Sundiata that Sumaoro was engaged in deploying his troops in
the plain of Kirina. When he left his tent, the son of Sogolon
had donned his hunter-king's garb. His plan of battle had
already been minutely prepared: the Méma squadron of which
he was the chief would form the forehead of his army, the *kélé
tin*; Bandiu Tunkara with the squadron from Wahadu was to be
at its head, the *kélé kun*; Famandian Camara would be the
breastplate of the army, *kélé dissi*; Tabon Wana Fran Camara
with his blacksmiths and his Djallonkés the right arm, *kélé
boloba*, while Fakoli Koroma and his men would be the left arm,
kélé bolo numan. The rest of the men and their chiefs were to be
at the rear to reinforce the army's advance.

Orders had been strictly formulated: Sundiata and his squadron
were to open a glorious passage through the enemy lines which
Bandiu Tunkara and his men from Wahadu were entrusted with
enlarging to create a wide avenue, while Famandian, co-ordinating
his efforts with Fran and Fakoli, was to press on relentlessly to
Sumaoro's camp. As for the rearguard, it was composed of
archers whose mission it was to sustain the advance of the main
army.

The morning was cloudless, although the season was the beginning of winter, and already Diata, according to plan, had deployed his men in the immense plain, confronting the Sossos.

Sumaoro, visible from far away, was seated, as at Naguéboria, on his charger, and easily recognizable by his black mantle and his tall helmet adorned with antelope horns. Unlike the son of Sogolon, he had deployed all his forces; the Sossos were strung out all across the plain.

Suddenly, in the space between the two armies, three cyclones began to rage: they joined forces to become a hurricane. The scraggy thornbushes covering the immense plain shivered for a while. But perhaps this hurricane was not blowing for nothing . . . perhaps it was the union of the three guardian spirits that caused it; and because the hurricane was not blowing for nothing, because in the eyes of Sundiata it symbolized the latent presence in the plain of Kirina of the lion of the Manden and of the buffalo and panther of Dô, the son of Sogolon realized that this was the moment to make his attack. And, rising in his saddle, proudly defiant in face of the enemy, he raised his arm and cried loudly: *Angnéwa!*[1]

From the immense plain rose resounding echoes of the war drums. Then the Méma cavalry, in a decisive charge, began its assault; its ardour was communicated to the Wahadu cavalry, and soon the battle was in full swing.

Sabres were bared in Diata's army as well as in Sumaoro's, the blades lopped off shoulders and chopped off heads.

To the rhythm of the war tom-toms the drummers pounded frenziedly, the horses of Méma and Wahadu whinnied and reared above the dying groups of Sossos.

Diata's army was advancing, the clash of sabres was heard in the impetuous charges, and from height to height the tom-toms of war thundered their rhythms in time to the hoofbeats of galloping horses and the furious advance of Diata who, battling with the bravery of a lion, the ardour of a buffalo and the agility of a panther, brought carnage, massacre and slaughter to the ranks of the Sossos. His blade provided a feast for death. Now that he had cleft a glorious passage through the Sossos, his lieutenants, Famandian, Fran and Fakoli and the archers in

1 *Angnéwa!*: Charge!

the rearguard supported him and drove him on. But Fakoli was soon harried by Sumaoro, who was obviously punishing his nephew for having abandoned the generalship of his armies: in the end, all the Sosso forces were concentrated upon Fakoli, whose men seemed about to be overwhelmed.

Diata, warned of this just in time, reined his courser which reared up, then galloped off in the direction of the left wing of the battle, though the squadrons of Méma and Wahadu stood in his way. The son of Sogolon saw Sumaoro striking down the soldiers of Fakolo. Burning with rage, he cried:

Ilô, Sumaoro! Nimina! 'Halt, Sumaoro! Take that!'

The king of Sosso quickly moved out of the way, as if the words of Diata had burned him.

Diata's bow twanged, the missile whistled! Sumaoro saw speeding towards him the fateful arrow shot by Sundiata. Yet he did not attempt to catch it in flight this time. Was this because his magical powers had already deserted him, his totems finding themselves neutralized the very instant Sundiata took aim? Was it because he had realized, on discovering the absence of Nana Triban from his enormous tower, that the secret of his strength had been found out? Perhaps . . .

The arrow had simply grazed him. But its effect was instantaneous: Sumaoro shook, shook from head to foot. Had his magical powers vanished? Probably. He uttered a piercing cry and cast imploring eyes up to the sky: there he saw hovering about his head a big black bird – it was the bird of misfortune.

'The bird of Kirina!' he growled.

His mind, clouded by terror, was nevertheless alert. So, turning his head away from that omen of disaster, he spurred his mount, making it rear, and then galloped off at full speed! His son Balla Diarrasso called Sosso Balla followed after him . . .

The two were now driven only by fear, wanting only to escape, while there was still time, the hands of Sundiata and Fakoli who would chop off their heads.

With their flight ended the hegemony of Sosso over the savanna.

It was some time before the son of Sogolon and Fakoli realized what had happened. When they had recovered from their surprise, they turned their steeds and began pursuing the two great losers whose army was now routed . . .

The sun over the plain was in mid-course, blazing down in perfect splendour. This was the rise of the Sun of Sundiata.

When evening began to fall, the son of Sogolon and Fakoli had galloped far off into the bush. Night fell, pitch black: lianas and thornbushes impeded their path.

They found no trace of the fugitives who, knowing the region well, had changed horses at Bakumana.

But Fakoli, who also knew the country perfectly, said to Diata:

'They will have to take the high road so as not to be seen by the village populations. We shall take the short cut, a difficult road, but we shall have reached the destination before they do.'

They took the road through the bush and went on riding all through the night. When they reached Bakumana, they learnt that Sumaoro and his son had changed mounts there and galloped off towards Kulikoro.

'We're on the right track.'

'That's fine,' Diata said simply.

It would be difficult to say which of the two pursuers wanted the head of Sumaoro: one of them wanted to avenge his ravaged native land, while the other was up in arms against Sumaoro because he had ravished his wife Kéléa Kanko.

They rode on with difficulty all through the night, for their steeds, though they had had some feed, were obviously worn out.

At dawn, Fakoli said to Diata:

'We are not far from Kulikoro now!'

As they ascended the mountain, they caught sight of the fugitives not far away. '*Ilô, Sumaoro!* Halt, Sumaoro!' shouted Fakoli.

He did not want to kill his uncle: neither did Diata! The two pursuers wanted to take the king of Sosso alive and drag him through those lands that had sung his praises, so that their inhabitants might see that Sumaoro's power no longer existed.

Fakoli threw himself upon him, but the old king jumped on his courser, just escaping his hands. So Fakoli fell upon Sosso Balla, seized him by the neck and bound his hands behind his back!

Meanwhile, Sundiata was pursuing Sumaoro: throwing his lance, he made the latter's horse fall. The old king picked himself up. And then a wild chase began on the mountain. Twice the king of Sosso escaped the clutches of Diata. Perhaps he was still

205

fairly vigorous, for he could run well. The chase went on and on.

Before him appeared the gaping cave in the mountain of Kuli-koro. Terror had made the king completely lose his head. So not for one instant could he turn his head away from the cavern that seemed to be drawing him in against his own will. Diata's footsteps were sounding behind him.

He entered the cave! But he suddenly found himself trapped between two perils: the one represented by his pursuer at the main entrance to the cavern, the other by the broad, deep river with its bellowing waters across the secondary entrance. Was this something new, or had he only just noticed it? He would have been hard pressed to say. All he could have said was that the spectacle did not please him at all, was plunging him into the most awful terror, as Diata's presence, at the entry to the cave, loomed ever more menacingly behind him.

Meanwhile Fakoli Koroma, followed by Sosso Balla with his hands tied behind his back, caught up with Diata.

'He entered this pitch-black cavern!' said Diata.

'But this cave communicates with the other side of the river!' replied Fakoli.

Meanwhile, Bandiu Tunkara, accompanied by the griot Balla Fassali Kuyaté, came along also.

The king of Sosso had the impression that his nephew was casting him a sideways look through the entrance to the cave. The sight struck him to the quick, he felt his heart was breaking, and he swallowed nervously.

'My dear uncle,' were the words he heard. 'Did you not say that if I were at the head of your army or if I were not, it would still be victorious?'

Although the consciousness of the cruelties he had committed should have caused Sumaoro to keep quiet and well hidden in the darkness of the cave, the great loser nevertheless replied:

'N'Kan-te!'

Which means 'I did not say so!'

His voice rent the silence of the cavern, seeming to fill the whole place with its echoes. Again he heard his name called and heard the menacing voice of Diata calling:

'If you do not come out of the cave, I shall smoke you out with green leaves.'

The great loser then tried to run further into the cave, but in the darkness he fell face downwards into a clinging mud that filled his nose and mouth until he could hardly breathe. He tried to get up! But his efforts seemed only to plunge him ever deeper into the muddy, glucy floor of the cave. A cry forced itself from his chest: it sounded high and harrowing like the death-rattle of a dying man in a locked hut. Sumaoro would have liked to keep back that cry, but he could not help it. But perhaps he did not try very hard to do so, either, for that cry of despair that both terrified and exhausted him – he had eaten nothing since the night before – was nevertheless the last living thing within him. For one last moment he thought he heard his name being called again; he was not mistaken: Balla Fassali Kuyaté, standing at the entrance to the cave, shouted, ironically:

'Sumaoro 'Kanté, bô!'

'Simaoro *not-say-so*, come out!'

From that day forward the traditionalist and instrumentalist who was the griot Balla Fassali Kuyaté spread this new name, 'Sumaoro Kanté', throughout the new Manden. Later, after his death, his three sons shared the role of griot: Missa Kuyaté, the eldest son, inherited his father's balafon and guitar, and so became an instrumentalist griot. Missa Maghan Kuyaté, the second son and an old pupil of the Koranic School, kept the tarikh and became a traditionalist. Batru Mori, the third son, inherited the drum, and became, like his elder brother, an instrumentalist griot.

'Sumaoro, come out of the cave, or else I shall set fire to it!' Diata shouted again.

But the sovereign of Sosso no longer replied.

And it was not just the loss of his magical powers, it was not the fear of supreme punishment alone that prevented Sumaoro from speaking or leaving the cavern: it was something quite other – it was shame, shame as much as the fear of Diata and Fakoli, and also perhaps the fact that he had sunk into the mud!

And he was overcome with the sense that he had lost all. But had he not already lost everything from the moment when, in order to keep himself in power, he started terrorizing the savanna lands and cutting off heads? Diata could keep on threatening, and he would never come out of the cavern: he had brought his punishment upon his own head. He would remain forever enslaved to those human lives he had destroyed, enslaved to his idolatry, enslaved to those respectable old men whom he had publicly whipped: enslaved to those girls he had seized by force from their families, and who made up his seraglio of three hundred women who had to submit to him; enslaved to everything he had so thoughtlessly abandoned himself to. Ah! If he could have wiped out the past! But can one go back on one's own steps? If he could begin his reign again, he would be loyal to the peoples of the savanna and to himself. He would adore God whom he had always profaned; he would recognize that Allah is the One and Supreme, that it was not those idols he should have exalted, for now they could be of no help to him; that it was not even the Prophet Mohammed he should have exalted, but the message that the Prophet brought, and of which he was the messenger; that it was not Issa, the son of Mariama, either, that he should have exalted, nor confused with Allah, for Issa is a Word of Allah and Allah is a dictionary composed of millions of words – no, more than that! – Allah is an infinity of Words! When he knocks at our door – but has he ever ceased to be present in our hut? – he puts our punily-reasoning rationalism in its place, which is very little. He takes his own place again, a sovereign place, he who, with the help of a burning torch, warms and illuminates the entire universe at once, and with a love freely-given. He alone is power.

Sumaoro in his cavern remained buried in his heavy and eternal solitude: Diata, before leaving, set guards at the entrances.

The great loser now thought bitterly of the immense illusion he had lived through, all his vain activities while he had been king of Sosso.

And his conscience, imperturbable, showered him with reproaches.

'Sumaoro,' it told him, 'you see now that the world upon which you cast such a distracted gaze is not just what you saw and you believed!

'Life is not everything, Sumaoro!

'Death, too, is nothing!

'What lies beyond the life you have just lived is the wrath of Allah!

'For your death, in this cavern, is by no means a liberation for you!

'For death does not end everything, it is not the end of everything! It is the passage from life here below to Eternal Life.'

And so Sumaoro ended in that cavern, as all the tyrants of this earth end their days, abandoned and hated by everyone . . .

The son of Sogolon, his griot and his companions rejoined their great army and, at daybreak, they laid low Sosso-the-Proud, despite the savage resistance of the remnants of Sumaoro's army led by Frikama and Numunkéba.

In one brief morning, that arrogant city was destroyed to its very foundations and reduced to dust by the army of Sundiata. Frikama ran away and went to Fassia, whilst Numnukéba was taken prisoner. But how true it is that a serpent whose head is cut off is no more than a piece of old rope! The sun of the powerful king of Sosso had declined and fallen, all his allies were defeated or quickly subjugated by the new sun which shone in the heavens with an unendurable brilliance – the sun of Sundiata . . .

KURU-KE-FUA: THE PLACE OF
FESTIVALS

Sundiata, soon having had his fill of conquests – Kita had fallen
under his authority, for he had gained the help, through numerous sacrifices of bulls, of the guardian spirits inhabiting the Moya
Dji[1] on the mountain overlooking that city! – went back to Sibi
to get his family.

Famandian, the king of the country, had preceded him; the
victors of Kirina were to reassemble there for a grand celebration
and to name their supreme chief. At the entrance to Kabala, a
broad clearing that the king had had cleared of bush was chosen
as the site for this great assembly. A platform, mounted on
forked pickets, had been hastily constructed there, to receive
Sundiata and his companions: in another part of the clearing, a
makeshift village of temporary huts had been put up to accommo-
date the crowds.

On the appointed day, the son of Sogolon had sacrificed one
hundred bulls in thanks to Allah for having given him a resounding victory over Sumaoro.

For this occasion, the sovereign of the Manden had donned
his white djellaba, and on his head he wore an impressive turban.
He was escorted by his family and by his griot Balla Fassali
Kuyaté who, in the grand robes of master of ceremonies, chanted
his praises.

Everywhere in the clearing, tom-toms were thundering; they
were sending out their deep vibrations to all those men who had
come, it would seem, solely to perform war dances. They gave
themselves up with such frenzy to rapid and vigorous movements
– especially in the dance of the 'Dununba'[2] – movements so
agitated that they must have exhausted the dancers who nevertheless, on the contrary, seemed to find in them a new, ever-
greater ardour, as the tom-toms roared. And sweat, the sweat
of violent movement, was already staining their garments.

Suddenly, the griot called for silence; all those intrepid dancers

1 Moya Dji: water that develops a man's personality.
2 'Dununba': dance of the strong men.

soon stopped shaking and gesticulating, and grouped themselves behind their respective *bandari*[1].

When the place was quiet, Balla Fassali, carrying a long, shining lance, stood up and addressed the crowd in these terms:

'O ye peoples now reunited, we are now at peace after years of suffering, but we owe this peace to a man who, from afar, heard our lamentations. That man is Naré Maghan Diata. My dear friends, I bestow upon you all the salute of Sundiata. Peace has returned, and may God grant that it last a long time!'

'Amina!' the crowd responded with enthusiasm. Then the griot went on:

'Now I shall pass the word to Famandian, king of this country, for Kaba is a dependency of Sibi: we are the guests of the "sinin-kimbon" Camara! Salute Famandian, Naré Maghan Diata wishes me to pass the word to you!'

At once Famandian came down from the platform where all the kings were grouped round Diata; he mounted his steed and raised his right hand which he waved in a salute to the crowd. Before he began to speak, Balla Fassali Kuyaté, the master of ceremonies, had quickly come down from the platform and placed himself at his side so that he could transmit his words to the excitedly-stamping crowd in the clearing.

'I salute you all!' he cried. 'I shall begin by thanking all those who, like the Sénufo and the Bobos, were not directly concerned, but who flew to our help in order to rid us of the devil who was Sumaoro. I salute our neighbours of Méma with their valorous chief Bandiu Tunkara, I salute those of the Wahadu, those of Bélédugu and Kénédugu, not forgetting the blacksmiths and the Djallonkés of Tabon! I salute the warriors of the Manden, with the invincible Tira Maghan at their head, I salute the warriors of Dô, those of Fakoli Koroma, of Toron, of the Wassulun. I salute everybody. May all those I have not named forgive me, for my emotion is great as I stand before all these peoples reunited here today . . .

'Warriors, we have suffered, we have all suffered so much, but here in the savanna peace has returned: may God keep that peace for ever!'

1 *bandari:* flags.

'Amina!' howled the crowd.

He continued:

'Look to your left, and you will see there, bound and fettered, the Sossos before whom we were trembling, you were trembling yesterday!

'This peace we have regained is something we all owe to Sundiata. It is he who, from far-off Méma, heard our lamentations and began to do battle from Tabon onwards, and to fight with savage determination until the final victory. Which of us would have dared to face up to the king of Sosso? No one! If Sumaoro is no more, we owe, it all to Sundiata!

'From now on, Naré Maghan Diata, saviour of the men and women of the savanna, I recognize you as my supreme chief. You are my Mansa!'

The crowd, leaping up and down, howled with joy to show their welcome of this news:

'*Wassa wassa, Ayé!*'[1]

Famandian, leaning from his horse, firmly planted his assegai – symbol of royalty – in the earth in front of the platform, saying:

'Henceforward this assegai belongs to you, Sundiata!'

Then he got down from his horse and went up on the platform again.

'Now I pass the word to Tabon Wana Fran Camara!' cried the griot.

The king of Tabon came down from the platform, mounted his horse, and cried:

'Wassa, Wassa, Ayé!'

The crowd took up his phrase and responded:

'Wassa, Wassa, Ayé!'

The 'dalikimbon' king went on:

'The war is well over now. We chased Frikama to Fassia: we did not capture him, but Numunkéba is here, he is our prisoner, as is Sosso Balla whose father died in the cavern at Kulikoro. I agree with and will uphold all the opinions of my cousin Famandian. Sundiata, I recognize and acknowledge you as my supreme chief. Henceforward, Tabon will be a dependency of Niani.'

And he firmly planted his assegai in the earth, then got down

1 Malinké expression of satisfaction.

from his horse and climbed back on the platform to sit beside Diata.

Twelve chiefs of the savanna in turn came down from the platform and planted their assegais in front of Sundiata. With this symbolical gesture, twelve kings acknowledged the son of Sogolon, twelfth king of the Manden, as their supreme chief.

Two captives then seized the Tabala which soon was sending out an urgent announcement to the world that the savanna had just named its first Emperor. When the drum was silent, Balla Fassali Kuyaté intoned the 'Niama', the song he had created on the day when Diata, paralysed, had gained the use of his legs in Niani:

> *Niama, Niama, Niama*
> *Fén bè bi idon Niama lé Kôrô*
> *Niama tè don na fén fén Kôrô!*

> Filth, filth, filth,
> Everything is covered by filth,
> But nothing can cover you, you filth![1]

Before the festival started again, there was the procession of the prisoners. The Sossos captured during the destruction of Sumaoro's capital by Diata's great army passed in front of the platform, their hands tied behind their backs, their heads shaved and their eyes lowered. The crowd mocked and insulted them.

Then came the procession of the kings who had remained faithful to Sumaoro; they were on horseback, so that the crowd might distinguish them from the ordinary prisoners, but just like the latter the kings had shaven heads and hands tied behind their backs as they passed, eyes lowered, in front of the platform, booed by the crowd.

Right at the end of the procession of kings came Numun Kéba, he who, at the head of the remnants of Sumaoro's army, had undertaken the defence of Sosso-the-Proud after the disappearance of the sorcerer-king. He had been captured, and in the days

1 Here, this song expresses the idea that Sundiata has been the rampart behind which the peoples of the savanna, harried by Sumaoro, have taken refuge.

to come was to pay dearly for his crime. His accomplice Frikama had run away, and so had saved his life. Now Numun Kéba on horseback, head shaven, hands tied behind his back, eyes lowered, passed before the platform.

At the very end, it was the turn of Sosso Balla to pass before the platform. Like the others, he was on horseback, and like them he had his hands tied behind his back and his skull shaven. Asses laden with his father's idols followed him: the serpent-fetish in the sacrificial vase was dying ever since the sorcerer-king had been touched by the spur of the white cock, and the owls were languishing. All the inhabitants of the hall of idols in Sumaoro's tower now had a different look – they were dying! – and, on the backs of asses, they passed in front of the horrified crowd that heaped insults upon them.

Everyone recognized at once the heads of those kings who had been murdered by the king of Sosso.

Sosso Balla, closely escorted by royal guards, passed by. Were they afraid he might escape? Hardly. In fact, it would never have entered the heads of any of these prisoners of war to try to escape, even though they knew that after the Kuruké Fua celebrations they would be put to death. Not all of them! Exception would be made for some young bucks and a few young girls who would be kept in the village: these chosen persons are known as 'Gnuma-Si' – the best seeds! They would be spared the pains of death and their descendants would recall· the atrocities of the war of Sosso.

As soon as Sosso Balla had disappeared from the scene, the procession of prisoners of war came to an end. Balla Fassali Kuyaté, striding among the crowd, begged them to be silent. When the great clearing had become quiet, Diata suddenly stood up and walked calmly towards the edge of the platform: his spokesman and griot came back and placed himself at his side.

And now the son of Sogolon was making his first speech as 'Mansa' or king. But no one in the crowd was to hear his voice: in fact, it would have been incomprehensible that a king of the stature of Diata should raise his voice when speaking. The duties of a Mansa had exigencies which could not be avoided. His griot, Balla Fassali, took up his words and shouted them to the listening crowd:

'Alubé barika Kossobé bâra gnuma là!'

'Many thanks to everybody for the great work you have done!' he began.

'Peace has returned to our hearths! May God preserve that peace forever!'

'Amina!' the crowd responded.

'I now address myself to all of you assembled peoples: to the men of the Manden with Tira Maghan at their head, to those of Sibi, of Méma, of Wahadu, of Toron, of the Wassulun, of Kénédugu, of Bélédugu, to our Bobos and Sénufo friends, to everyone, without omission, I transmit the salutations of Sundiata.

'Our mothers, our wives, our children have once more found a reason for living. And I am also deeply touched by the welcome you have given me here. I am also embarrassed, extremely embarrassed, because I am not very sure that I am worthy of the honour you have shown me. That is why I would ask you to transfer this honour to the spirit that has guided our common action – the love of our respective native lands! Truly, it is to our love for our native lands that we owe our victory over Sumaoro. If consequently I accept with emotion my nomination by you to be the head of all our lands, I wish to give credit for this honour to our common patriotism.

'Therefore I have decided that all the kings who participated in this war should retain their own kingdoms; we shall be federated, and Niani will keep an eye on everything.

'To all those in this vast crowd who have lost a relative in this war, I would say that I ask their forgiveness: I only wanted to liberate our countries, but it is very difficult to take thorns out of your feet without drawing blood!'

And Sundiata wrenched an assegai out of the ground, saying:

'Famandian, I give you back your kingdom. Make the people of Sibi happy, as you have always done. I know you well ever since we were boys. We two were circumcised together. Famandian, you think straight, and you act straight in everything you undertake. From today onwards, the Camara of Sibi and the Keïta of the Manden are as one people. In all the Empire that has been entrusted to me, the Camara shall be as if in their own land!'

215

He gave back the assegai to Famandian who bowed to the ground on receiving it, in order to pay special tribute to the honour being done to him by his 'Mansa'.

Sundiata turned next to Tabon Wana Fran Camara.

'Fran Camara, my friend, here is your assegai, and with it your kingdom. From now on we are united. You welcomed me to your home when I was in difficulties. From today onwards, the Djallonkés shall be received in the Manden as if they were our relatives. And the princes Camara of Tabon shall grow up in Niani with the princes Keïta, and they shall be treated on an equal footing.'

In similar fashion, the twelve kings of the savanna received their kingdoms from the hands of the twelfth king of the Manden, named Emperor by them.

Then, turning to Nan Bukari, he said:

'Namagbé Bukari, you have always followed me everywhere like a man and his shadow: you are a true brother. So I give you the lands between Badu Djéliba and Kiriokun, near Kita. You and your descendants shall be kings there!'

He was silent for a moment, as if in meditation, then went on:

'You, my sister, Nana Triban, have always been faithful to me. You helped me to penetrate the secret of Sumaoro's powerful magic: it is to you I owe my victory. But you are a woman, and our customs do not allow a woman to govern. But your descendants may aspire to the throne of the Manden. I speak, naturally, of male descendants!'

Then he spoke more precisely on this point:

'Our Empire shall henceforward be called "Mali". The most powerful animal both in the water and on land appears to be the hippopotamus. We shall form a mosaic of peoples, as powerful as the hippopotamus.'

Last of all, Sundiata spoke to Sogolon Dia Mori, called Manden Bori:

'As for you, my brother,' he said, 'I give you the lands of the west.'

The villages of the west were founded later by Imuraba and by Démandjan, son and grandson of Manden Bori. Those villages were Balato, Korala, Kouroussa in the region of the Hamana.

So, Sundiata at the Kuruké Fua distributed the honours and

216

pronounced all the interdictions. He divided the world and gave each king his territory. Thanks to him, the peoples became brothers. The Emperor and his successors were to take their wives from among the Condé, who henceforward were to be the uncles of the Keïta of Niani, because of the successful marriage of Sogolon, originally from Dô, with Naré Maghan Kön Fatta.

The five marabouts of the court at Niani had their rights assured with the foundation of the empire.

Fakoli Koroma got back his wife, and also received from the hands of Sundiata the former kingdom of his uncle, Sosso.

The Wahadu and the Méma kept their kings who were considered to be the best allies of the new authority. They wisely did not wait long to declare themselves tributaries of Sundiata, to whom they had given shelter in the recent past.

The Konatés of Toron, the Sidibés, Diakités, Sangarés of the Ussulum were not forgotten.

As for the griot Fassali Kuyaté, the 'Mansa' said that he was the fifteenth griot of the Manden, but the first of the Empire! Consequently he had been accorded the right to make fun of all the tribes. The griot of the 'Mansa' of Mali would be chosen only from among the Kuyaté.

When the son of Sogolon had finished sharing out the territories, establishing the rights of each tribe and announcing the interdictions which, to this day, the peasants of the savanna observe, he returned to Sibi, where he sojourned for the rest of the winter season.

At the beginning of the dry season, escorted by his general staff, by his family and by his griot, he made his triumphal entry into the city of Niani, which he had left six and a half years before, and which had been destroyed during the reign of the powerful king Sumaoro.

He lovingly reconstructed it, and enlarged it. So the capital of the Empire became known as 'Niani-the-Great' or 'Niani-ba'.

After this preliminary work, Sundiata turned his attention to essential tasks: the organization of the Empire, the establishment of a solid social structure and the harmonization of customs, the development of agriculture, the setting-up of light industries, the formation and deployment of a permanent police force entrusted with the security of the goods and the people of the Empire, the

217

creation of a cowrie currency for merchants. He also supervised the formation of a permanent army with a roll call of two hundred thousand men placed in the outlying vassal kingdoms: these troops would be the first to react in the case of a surprise attack before the mobilization of the standing army. After a declaration of war made by the 'Mansa' himself, each kingdom was to arm its contingent recruited on its own territory.

In short, Sundiata gave the Empire its political and social framework, a religious life with the peaceful coexistence of Islam and Animism – a political framework that had been the one built up by his ancestors.

When Sundiata had finished putting these organizations in order, he carried out further warlike exploits, for *Kèlé lé ka Malilo* – it is war that made Mali! and *Kélè lé ka Malité* – it is war that ruined Mali!

The Mansa marched on Kumbi Saleh which he destroyed, then put under his subjection.

One of his best generals, Fira Maghan Traoré, subjugated the valley of the Gambia and the Djolof.

On the way home, feeling death approaching, that warrior and great sorcerer, before allowing himself to disappear in the waters of the River Gambia, charged his lieutenant to deliver the booty to the Mansa of Mali. Was his totem an amphibian? Perhaps.

Sundiata was the first great Mansa of Mali. With his arrival, carefree mothers gave birth to happy children, and desolation, the sign of Sumaoro's passage through the savanna, gave place to prosperity which burst forth everywhere.

Before his death, he gave orders that Sakura, an affranchised slave at the court in Niani, should take the succession! He also ordered that Sakura should go and set up his imperial capital at Takan (Manden).

After the death of Sundiata, Sakura became the Emperor of Mali, but forgot the recommendations of the son of Sogolon, and instead of installing the capital of his reign at Takan, installed it at Tékuré (Wahadu). He did not remain in power long. However, he extended the limits of the Empire by warfare. Under his reign, the Macina and the Tékrur became vassals of Mali. Sakura was a great pilgrim. Killed by bandits as he was returning from Mecca, his corpse was dried, transported to his country, and buried at Kôkan.

After Sakura, the eldest son of Sundiata, Kô-Mamadi, called Mansa Wulen Djurulenko, took power. He had three brothers: Mansa Wali, certain of whose descendants settled in Gambia, in the Cabu and at Tambacunda; Niani-Mamudu and Karifa did not move from Niani.

Mansa Wulen Djurulenko decentralized the Empire. He was a great Mansa. Three of his sons, Sérébori, Mansa Gbèrè, Séri-Banguru settled in the Djoma (Siguiri) and their descendants live there to this day.

After him, the son of Nana Triban, Abu Babari Fôlo[1] became Mansa at the age of fifteen. He brought a reign of peace to the Empire.

His successor was Abu Babari Filanan[2] who drowned at sea: he had been attempting to cross the sea with an expedition of hundreds of dug-out canoes, which were swallowed up by the ocean waves.

The successor to Abu Filanan was Gbonkô[3] Mussa, called Hidji Mussa, the magnificent pilgrim and the most illustrious of all the Mansa of Mali. Under his reign, the Empire reached its apogee, and a fame that spread throughout the whole world.

He had mosques constructed at Gao and Timbuctoo. It was he who created Sudanese architecture.

He placed the Mali on an international footing by inaugurating the era of embassies, and also by assuring the continuity of cultural exchanges between his empire and the Arab countries.

After Gbonkô Mussa, no emperor was ever so important! The decadence of the Empire, brought about by wars, was not long in coming.

Yes, everything that stands must fall down!

The Mansa once standing at all the crossroads of the Mali are laid low . . .

1 Abu Babari Fôlo: Abubakar I.
2 Abu Babari Filanan: Abuabakar II.
3 Gbonkô Mussa: Kanka Mussa, a name that the traditionalists do not seem to know. They added the name of Gbonkô to that of Mussa because Gbonkô was the mother of Mansa Mussa.

Everything that is seated lies down!

The palaces of Niani, once set securely on their foundations, now lie in dust!

How many glories engulfed by time!

How many dead civilizations, in that traditional Africa whose cultures, more rural than urban, once were the marvel of the world!

There remains eternally seated, author and witness of all these deeds, only Allah, forever the Superb, upon his throne!

May the example of Sundiata and his family illuminate us in our progress along the slow and difficult road of African evolution!

EPILOGUE IN RETROSPECT:
THE GREAT EVENT

Babu Condé, the celebrated traditionalist, claims that one festival day at Niani, capital of the Manden, the compound of Mansa Bélé – that is, the royal palace – was on the point of being invaded by a large band of brigands. Because they were taking part in the festivities, the warriors were absent and dispersed all over the place, so he saw that it was almost impossible to re-assemble them. So the king asked his two big sons Missa and Barry to go and face the brigands and throw them back. These two sons, more interested in the tom-toms, refused to carry out their father's orders. The old king wept with indignation, anger and helplessness.

But his third son, Namandian, an adolescent of barely eighteen winters, and still uncircumcised – children were circumcised very late at that period! – seeing his father in tears, took pity on him and went and opened the munitions chest. He took a bow and arrows of the deadliest kind after having donned his father's war tunic. Although still very young, he was brave enough to con-front the band of brigands who took fright, truly took fright at the sight of him: they thought he was a scout from Manoa Délé's army.

Namandian took advantage of the general consternation to kill the chief of the bandits: when one cuts off the head of the serpent the rest is just like old rope. His accomplices were pre-paring to flee, but Namandian, making enough noise for a hun-dred people in order to give the impression that he was at the head of many warriors, swiftly caught them and tied them up, then led them to his father.

What an agreeable surprise it was for the old king when he saw the bandits tied up and being led by his heroic son!

'Namandian!' he said. 'Today you have shown you can really take my place. So tomorrow, at dawn, you shall be circumcised, and after you recover I shall proclaim you king of the Manden. This evening no griot shall sing during the dance of the 'Soli' in honour of the happy circumcision. I myself shall sing in your

221

honour, a song that young Malinké boys, candidates for circumcision, shall always sing to recall this great event, to the end
of time'.

Mansa Bélé was a generous king, very generous; and so as to
act in a way befitting his legendary generosity, he invited the sons
of the poor to come and be circumcised at the same time as his
own son Namandian, called also Maghan Dian or Dubaro-
Maghan Dian, Dubaro being the name of his mother. They were
all made to wear the garments of those about to be circumcised,
and a tall conical cap was placed on each of their heads. Naturally,
the tom-toms were rolling and thundering in the most festive way.

As soon as Namandian and his companions had appeared on
the square of the giant bombax tree of Niani, the men ran to
meet them. The young boys were now advancing in single file
between two rows of men. Mansa Bélé, the old king, had placed
himself at their head. He wanted to show the adolescents how
the 'Coba' or 'Great Event' is sung and danced, for he himself
created it especially, in honour of his heroic son Namandian.

The latter was walking behind his father, whose permission he
had asked to place his hands on his shoulders; after which each
of the adolescents had placed his hands on the shoulders of the
boy in front. When their single file was thus firmly linked, the
tom-toms and the drums suddenly stopped, and everybody fell
silent: everything became mute and motionless on the square of
the giant bombax tree in Niani, for Mansa Bélé was present there
at the festival of adolescent boys, and it was the first time a king
would be seen singing and dancing.

He gazed imperiously at his people gathered all around him,
and, like a military command, he struck up in a high voice the
song which he dedicated to his heroic son:

'*Coba aye Coba Lama!*
Yiri ba Naré Maghan Dian Yiri ba Diarra Konkon
Adi diya O Naré Maghan Dian Dubaro Maghan Dian
Adi diya Adi gboa Naré Maghan Dian Dubaro Maghan Dian
Dji yé Folon Kôdô Fê Folon!
A Tami gbédé côdô don Folon!

222

The Great Event, bring back the Great Event
The great tree, Naré Maghan Dian the great tree, the lion of the
    bush
When it's good, it's Naré Maghan Dian, Dubaro Maghan Dian
When it's good, when it's bad: Naré Maghan Dian, Dubaro
    Maghan Dian
The water runs afloat in the torrent, afloat!
It is his eternal wake, his torrent!

At once the tom-toms started up again louder than ever, and
the adolescents and all the people had repeated the king's
phrases.

The adolescent boys were walking, like king Mansa Bélé, with
feet apart, as far apart as their boubou would allow, and naturally
with very slow steps. And as they repeated the six phrases one
after the other, they kept turning their heads, as the king did, to
the left, then to the right: and their tall conical caps prolonged in
a curious way this movement of the head.

Three times during that day Mansa Bélé appeared at the head
of the adolescents, under the giant bombax of Niani, to sing and
dance the 'Coba', then three times again at night, by torchlight.

And now for nearly a thousand years, every spring, the oldest
of the Keïta   he can exceptionally be replaced by a loyal old
griot – on the evening of the circumcision places himself at the
head of the adolescents as Mansa Bélé had done, to bring back
the Great Event!

CAMARA LAYE was born in Guinea in 1924. A
child of intellectual promise, he went first to
the technical college at Conakry, the capital
of Guinea, and later to France to study
engineering. In Paris he found a totally
different culture and, lonely and unhappy,
wrote his first book, *The African Child*.

This largely autobiographical work tells
the story of his childhood among the
Malinké tribe, surrounded by ritual magic
and superstition, and his emergence into
manhood and independence.

Twelve years later, having returned to his
native land, Camara Laye wrote *A Dream
of Africa*. In this sequel to *The African
Child*, the narrator – now influenced by his
experiences in Europe – sees an Africa on
the violent brink of independence.

He is also the author of *The Radiance of
the King*, a brilliant and highly-acclaimed
allegorical novel.

In poor health for many years, Camara
Laye died in 1980, in exile in Senegal.

In May 1979, *The Guardian of the Word*
was awarded a prize by the *Académie
Française*, France's foremost literary insti-
tution.